"For Nicole,

I hope that you will enjoy the history, mystery, and family secrets!

Debra A. Patrow

2011

ACRES OF BITTERNESS

by: Debra A. Patrow

Copyright© 2009 Debra A. Patrow

ISBN: 978-1-61584-289-6

Edited by The Liadva Group and Documation.

Printed by Documation, Eau Claire, WI

Printed in the United States of America.

This book contains a plethora of history and facts on the state of Idaho and the surrounding areas. Please bear with me while I share with you these things which I learned on my many visits to that part of the United States. While the topographical information is as accurate as possible, the time frames have been adjusted to fit the story line of the book. As a result some of the locations named quite possibly may not have been built in 1905 or 1935 which are the two primary years concerned, but were necessary inclusions to complete the story.

Please view the webpage at www.debrapatrownovels.com

ACRES OF BITTERNESS ACKNOWLEDGEMENTS:

No task is solely completed by any one individual; it is with the help of these persons that I was able to achieve my dream of being a published author.

TO: My husband Greg, who never objected to my writing jaunts across the U.S. and without whose support and occasional prompts of "how's that book coming?" kept me writing. He came to refer to it as the 'ten year book,' and in fact, it was completed over a span of eight years.

TO: My daughter Lisa and her husband Mike; my son Adam and his wife Tabetha; and my daughter Vanessa; whose enthusiasm and interest in hearing passages from time to time (and begging to hear it all) kept my excitement level flowing. They all gave me the encouragement to finish it in their lifetime!

TO: My grandchildren Ryan, Madison and Guyton Joe, whom I missed terribly on my numerous trips to Idaho. I hope to bring them with me in the near future to enjoy the beauty which I discovered there. And I hope that they can be proud of this book and their grandmother!

TO: GPD, SMP and MTF, who in the workplace recognized through the explanatory "sagas" that I would write to clients, that I had a potential that should not be overlooked.

TO: RAB and RES, who were fervent supporters all the way, and whose hospitality and pampering while living with them was superb. I always feel welcome with my Idaho family.

TO: JMF, whose recommendation of the City of Riggins and the Riggins Motel gave me the location for my book. The combination of the Salmon River and the mountains along the way hooked me instantly.

TO: AL, whose friendship and gentle pushes on the book kept me laughing and pecking away, especially when she would say, "I hope you crank the next books out faster than this one!"

TO: MRD and RGP, for coercing me out of retirement…again and back into the law office and making me realize a support system is necessary for any successful undertaking. And also to my good friend MRD, for the inspiration that I derived from friendship and childhood trials and tribulations.

TO: My cousins, MJW, RVW, and SMW for the enthusiasm of using family names for the characters and to LJB for the poem.

TO: The people of Riggins who have been friendly and helpful in my pursuit of knowledge of their town and the area. I have yet to catch a resident of Riggins on a bad day. And thank you to both Jan at Canyon Jan's and Sylvia at Riversong who are very accommodating to me each year when I visit Riggins.

TO: CEH and JRH, for the use of your studio, photographer and help in advertising book sales. The book could not have been put together without your great help.

I want to extend a very special thank you to all of my precious family, who were instrumental in seeing this project to its completion. And my efforts to truly make them feel a sense of pride in this book kept me striving for publication.

And for all of those family members who have sadly passed from my life, not to be forgotten but to live through me in this book. And that they feel a sense of pride for preserving family legacies and traditions which played a major role in my life and this literary work.

My thoughts go out to the descendants of the Nez Perce Native Americans who fought so hard to retain their rightful territories.

This Book is dedicated to the

Precious Memory

of

BRITTANY ANN SATHER.

CHARACTERS:

Josephine Anna LeClaire Curtis Liadva , Josie
Allen Liadva , Josie's husband

Josie and Allen's children:

Anna is married to Lee with one son, Michael
Allen, Jr. is married to Beth with one son, Joseph
Mae is married to Jack with one daughter, Madelyn

Isadora Blue Dove LeClaire Curtis, Josie's Mother
Frederick LeClaire Curtis, Josie's Father
Chief Ignatious Blue Dove, Josie's Grandfather
Annahah Blue Dove, Josie's Grandmother

Chief Alphonse Blue Dove, Ignatius's Brother - Papoose Cave
Chief Vincent Blue Dove, Ignatius's Brother – Canada
Chief Leopold Blue Dove, Ignatius's Brother - Oklahoma

Hubert Blue Dove, Isadora's Brother
Herman Blue Dove, Isadora's Brother
Luanne Blue Dove, Herman's Daughter
Roger Blue Dove, Herman's Son
Mary Jane Blue Dove, Herman's Daughter

Carl Blue Dove, Isadora's Brother
Shirley Blue Dove, Carl's Wife
Sharon Blue Dove, Carl's Daughter

Arnold Able , Josie's neighbor
Lucille Able, Arnold's Mother

Alfred Stellbisch, Motel owner
Doris Stellbisch, Alfred's Wife

Rose, Josie's Best Friend
Evelyn, The Ray Mon's maid
Alice, Evelyn's Granddaughter
George, Evelyn's husband
Edward, Widower
Paul & Mary, Edward's children

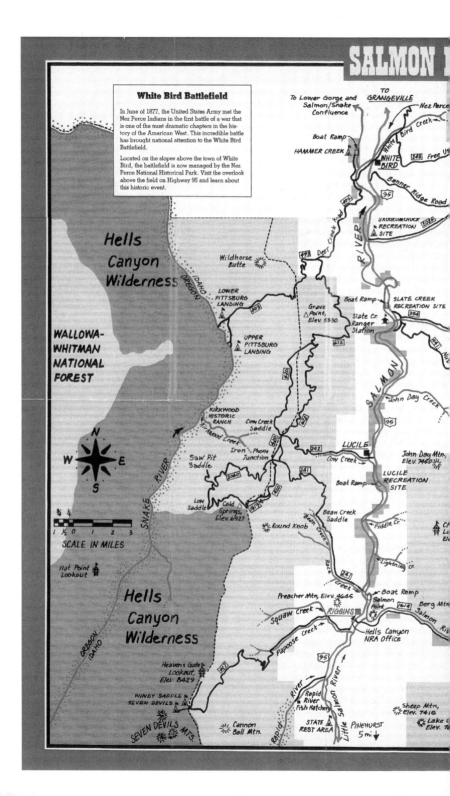

White Bird Battlefield

In June of 1877, the United States Army met the Nez Perce Indians in the first battle of a war that is one of the most dramatic chapters in the history of the American West. This incredible battle has brought national attention to the White Bird Battlefield.

Located on the slopes above the town of White Bird, the battlefield is now managed by the Nez Perce National Historical Park. Visit the overlook above the field on Highway 95 and learn about this historic event.

TO GRANGEVILLE

To Lower Gorge and Salmon/Snake Confluence

Nez Perce Creek

Boat Ramp

HAMMER CREEK

WHITE BIRD

243 Free U

Banner Ridge Road

SKOOKUMCHUCK RECREATION SITE

1012

Hells Canyon Wilderness

Wildhorse Butte

IDAHO OREGON

LOWER PITTSBURG LANDING

493 Deer Creek Road

RIVER

95

Grave Point, Elev. 5530

Boat Ramp

SLATE CREEK RECREATION SITE

Slate Cr. Ranger Station

354

WALLOWA-WHITMAN NATIONAL FOREST

UPPER PITTSBURG LANDING

672

341

Nav

SALMON

John Day Creek

KIRKWOOD HISTORIC RANCH

Kirkwood Creek

Cow Creek Saddle

95

N
W E
S

Saw Pit Saddle

Iron Phone Junction

242

LUCILE

Cow Creek

John Day Mtn, Elev. 7460

241

1040

LUCILE RECREATION SITE

Boat Ramp

½ ¼
½ 0 1 2 3
SCALE IN MILES

Low Saddle

1819

Cold Springs, Elev. 6927

Round Knob

Bean Creek Saddle

Fiddle Cr.

CH
Le
Ele

Bean Creek

Lightning Cr.

Hat Point Lookout

Hells Canyon Wilderness

Race Creek

341

Preacher Mtn, Elev. 4645

Squaw Creek

RIGGINS

Boat Ramp

Salmon Point

1614

Berg Mtn

Salmon Riv

Hells Canyon NRA Office

OREGON IDAHO

Papoose Creek

95

Heavens Gate Lookout, Elev. 8429

517

Rapid River Fish Hatchery

Little Salmon River

Rapid River

Sheep Mtn, Elev. 7415

Lake
Elev. 7

WINDY SADDLE SEVEN DEVILS

SEVEN DEVILS MTS.

Cannon Ball Mtn.

STATE REST AREA

PINEHURST
5 mi ↓

THE CHAPTERS

PROLOGUE:

Everyone has a certain curiosity about their heritage, and I have decided that the time has come for me to investigate mine. I believed it would be an enjoyable pursuit back into the archives of my genealogy; little did I know how far removed from the simple realm of things this adventure would be.

There has always been something missing, I have always felt, both in my heart and in my mind. Especially in my heart, I have had painful, pinching twinges that began almost to the hour that we left our beloved home on Allison Creek. And I would experience flashes of light and unfamiliar scenes quite often throughout my life, interrupting my normal thought processes and terrifying me in my slumber.

My birth name was Josephine Anna LeClaire. I am the daughter of a French-Canadian father and a Native American mother. My first name stems from a two-fold admiration; my father's to the Empress Josephine, wife to Napoleon Bonaparte and my mother's to Chief Joseph of the Nez Perce tribe, who was her uncle.

To begin tracing my mother's history appeared to be the logical point of origin. She was born in White Bird, Idaho, and was a member of the Nez Perce tribe. As for my father's origin, he was born in Alberta, Canada, in the wilderness area known as Gregoire Lake Provincial Park. The two met as young adults by mere happenstance and believed that they were fated to meet and fall in love. My mother's family had moved down to Riggins, just a short distance south of White Bird, and my father relocated there from British Columbia to work in the mill to be closer to her.

You are always taking a chance when you attempt to learn the complete story, that you may also be made aware of things that were not revealed for a reason. Which is why it is now, only after both of my parents are deceased, and all of my own children are grown and on their own that I am putting aside my present family life in search of my lineage. My father would always say, however, when my inquiring mind asked that, "You know all that you need to know, Josie."

My children, of course, met my decision with much skepticism and began strictly analyzing my motive and my need for closure in these matters. The general conception was that their mother and the grandmother to their children had "lost her mind." They thought I certainly must be mentally inept to even think of undertaking such a task. "But you could get hurt, or lost or worse yet, be killed." I responded by telling them that they were viewing it in the incorrect context; I will not be trudging through the mountains or careening down the river in a canoe searching for clues. Rather I am looking for the untold story. It has become my mission in life - my duty - to discover life lines to pass on to their children's children. Our history as it stands, based on the information I was given, is not complete and certainly not truthful. And now that I have reached this point in time, I have been presented with the opportunity to discover all of the pieces of the puzzle that are my life.

Part One

Chapter One   ≈

THE LETTER OF ENLIGHTENMENT

This letter which I hold in my hand could be most important piece of mail that I have ever received. It may contain precious answers I have longed for my entire adult life. My lingering ache that has spanned three decades could possibly be soothed within the lines of these pieces of paper. It was a moment that would change my life and that of all of my family as well. As I opened the letter that was postmarked on June 1, 1935, Riggins, Idaho, my heart pounded so loudly that I could hear nothing but the sound of waves crashing over rocks. I thought there was no one anywhere that knew what had become of us, let alone where we were. This was the golden opportunity I had been praying for, some indication that I could learn the secrets that my grandfather and parents had locked away forever. I may discover if there is any truth to the scattered thoughts and memories that I have been struggling with for most of my life. Is this the link to the genealogy of the generations of Blue Doves past, present, and even future? There are facts I need to discover, legacies to learn, and secrets to be revealed. My eyes are filled with tears, my hands are shaking and my ears are ringing to the point I think I shall faint. I wish someone was here to steady me, to catch me should I collapse. No, this is something I need to do alone, in absolute privacy to bask in the moment of any shred of truths that this letter may contain.

I have always carried with me the tragic sadness of having no relatives to bond with or talk over family history. Whether the facts were happy or sad ones, it would be wonderful to be able to pass on those legacies to my children. For them, they know only of tidbits of memories shared with them by myself, their mother, as best I could under the unfortunate circumstances. I could not properly educate them about all the members of the Blue Doves and LeClaires that once had been so prevalent in our lives. Our immediate family circle of five fled our beloved Idaho to Spring Brook, North Dakota in the late fall of 1905, and that became our past. But my father had kept a concise journal from the moment that we left home, so at least our history from state to state was documented with accuracy. My grandmother, Annahah, had passed away on the trip, so only my grandfather Ignatious made it to safety with my father, mother and I. My grandfather was only with us another few years; he passed away long before my little ones were born. However, my children were fortunate enough to have my parents in their lives and knew the love of grandparents until about the time that our youngest child started school. The fewer people in our lives, the less reminiscing there is done; therefore, there are so many details of lives left unspoken.

The ever present longing to truly know one's family's ancestry is an unfinished portion of many lives. I asked grandfather if he missed his brothers and wouldn't he like to go back and try to find them. He always said, "No, I'm better off thinking about the good luck they all could have found, and I do not wish to confirm that they did or if they all perished trying to escape." I told him, "But grandfather, that's impossible. They couldn't all be gone, there were too many of them, some would have gone back home after the Army allowed them to leave the reservation." I nagged at my mother too; didn't she want to see her brothers and their wives and her aunts and uncles and cousins? And my cousins and my friends; I missed them and I want to be reunited with them. But still no interest was sparked in returning to Idaho. That did not make sense to me; why wouldn't at least one of them want to go home again? They just plain ignored me most of the time. About the only answer I received was that we all have different lives now and we wouldn't even know them if we saw them. I believe this to be false, and an ignorant response. I would recognize members of my own lineag; family traits are undeniable and forever present on your physical person, and it hadn't been that long since we saw them last. I believe that was just a defensive response to a subject they didn't wish to address with me.

All these years have passed since childhood, and I still remember all of my grandfather's stories; some were pieces of his personal memories, and others tall tales. Some of them were told perhaps in the fashion that he wished their lives had been, but I can't know for sure. I was a small child sitting on his lap when he began his storytelling. I thought his word was golden, and I was mesmerized by every sentence spoken. Why would there be any question that anything that he had told me was fabricated or a falsehood? And then as a young adult of seventeen after we moved, I would feel sick sometimes while he was talking about the old days in our former homeland. I just knew that I had a story too, but it was never told; they just led me to believe I was just a child helping them with the farm, riding horse, and spending time with my best friend, Rose. My condition worsened as I got older. I was certain there were details omitted, and I was left feeling cheated more and more as the stories were told. I felt as if my mind was a piece of thread pulled apart into ten pieces twisting in all directions. There was something very personal and heart wrenching that had taken place, I just don't remember what it was, but my dreams have flashes of faces that I do not see here and do not know what they represent. But I was repeatedly lectured that nothing out of the ordinary had occurred, and it was the sickness that had plagued me and forced my mind into hysteria. My parents never offered any corrections, additions, or deletions to his stories to make me understand any better. I was constantly reminded that most people never recover from smallpox, and having done so made me a very fortunate individual even though there were large gaps in my memory.

I'm certain that my parents and grandparents felt that the decision that they had made to flee alone was the ultimate sacrifice that could be made for a child. And thereby, they would be protecting me from certain portions of the truth surrounding the turmoil that had occurred during the takeover of our town by the Army. It literally scattered everyone in different directions; no one could predict which family would succeed and which would fail. Not wanting to experience any risk of being found, my grandparents separated themselves from Ignatious' three brothers and their entire families. For the remainder of their years of living, due to such a cruel twist in the pleasant life that had been normal for them, no one would ever be reunited. So intent on retaining a totally remote hidden identity, our last name was changed to Curtis, and in no way did it resemble our former surname of LeClaire. Our tiny circle reduced to four would constitute our entire world, and the rest would be pushed deep into the black hole of my subconscious, only remembering what my mind wished to.

Of course, I was incredibly curious as to how the person who contacted me, in fact, found me. I had always been told that there had been two groups. Alphonse, whose family members had been hiding in plain sight during the entire ordeal, and Leopold and Vincent's families, who had chosen to allow their lives to forever be regulated by the government on reservation lands in Oklahoma. But since three decades had passed, some people had moved off the reservation and some had come out of hiding. Several history books have now been written on the Nez Perce war with the Army, so we have been able to confirm the journeys taken by Leopold and Vincent's branches of the Blue Doves. Shortly after the Army cleaned out our town and surrounding ones of the Nez Perce population and began herding them towards Oklahoma, there was an uprising. Vincent convinced his followers that the Army had lied to all of them; this was no paradise of freedom that they were heading for. They broke away from the Army and went straight north into Canada, where they were completely free from capture and prosecution. Leopold held his group to the blind belief that the reservation would be a wonderful place to live out their days and that the younger ones could create better lives there than in the wilderness of Canada, if they were lucky enough to make it there.

We learned from our reading that Leopold regretted his decision almost immediately after arriving at the designated area to be their new home. It was nothing more than a bunch of small, cheaply built cabins on a flat hunk of land and little else. They were promised a beautiful area with hills and valleys and streams, where each family would have their own house. No one was prepared for what they saw upon arrival, but it had been a long journey and they were too weary to think of a retreat at that time. So, they had settled in despite the facts that they might as well have pitched their teepees in the desert somewhere, this was certainly comparable to that. Nothing was ever mentioned concerning the fourth brother, my grandfather Ignatious, so presumably we were thought to be among Vincent's pack in Canada or dead. And never has a word been written about Alphonse's whereabouts ever having been discovered, so perfectly had his plan been executed. I'm sure that no accurate report would be written by the Army on the four brothers and their choices of refuge. That would mean they would have to admit to losing control of three of the four divisions of the Blue Dove Tribe.

I began to read the letter now, written in excellent penmanship. There would be no misinterpreting any of the words written therein. The writer said that he was an old friend of the family. Arnold Able, he said his name was. I did not know who he was, the name meant nothing to me. He wrote that his parents had been neighbors of my parents, so why would I not be able to remember his name? They may have lived there prior to my birth, but I am certain that they did not live there at the same time that I did. Arnold said that he was helping a carpentry crew a few years ago do some remodeling on an old house in Allison Creek, when he found something curious. The men had been putting a new floor in the kitchen of the house and found something wedged down under a piece of the linoleum that was loose. It was a photograph of a family of five people, and one of them was a young girl of about fifteen or sixteen years old. Even though it was black and white and badly discolored, he recognized the youngest person in the picture. He remembered that the thin girl with green eyes and medium reddish brown hair was always dressed in something that she had designed and created herself. Then he said that when he flipped the photo over, the name on the back of the photo was LeClaire, and he knew for certain that it was a picture of me, Josie LeClaire. Arnold had been astonished to come across such a precious momento in such an unlikely location, and it brought memories flooding back to him while holding it.

He discussed it with his wife, and they decided together that giving it to the museum would be the right thing to do, to fondly remember that our family had once been a part of their community. It was unknown exactly what had happened to five of the Blue Doves and LeClaires after they heart wrenchingly broke away from the rest of their relatives. But they were not forgotten about or dismissed as deceased; no one had ever allowed themselves to think that. The hope was that all was well with them wherever they might be and had been for the past thirty years. He also said that the devastating heartbreak their leaving had caused left permanent scars on their lives, and some of the people never got over losing them, "especially you Josie." That just further solidified my feelings of all these years, that there are indeed family secrets as I had suspected. So, here it is, in my hand, this piece of nondescript stationary that is the proof to decades of doubt. Doubt that my life or any of my family's lives were true or correct as the stories had been relayed to me all of these past years since settling in North Dakota.

Arnold said that finding that picture brought back to the surface memories and issues of the past when we were all just youngsters with dreams for our futures. And that he and his wife had a rough time with some of the memories. What could he be speaking about? This has to be my awaited-for link to what my nightmares and disturbing dreams could be representing. I have no memory of what happened for a long period of time before we fle;, that time was wiped out completely. Arnold said that he had come across our existence by random accident of geography and the reintroduction of me into their thoughts by the discovery of the photograph. He had simply been in our area traveling for his occupation of tool salesman. His company had given him a new territory to try and scout for customers, and that had led him to Spring Brook, North Dakota. He had stopped at our lumber mill and spoken with my son, giving him his usual sales pitch. Allen selected some of the items that Arnold had for sale; always a step up in business when you upgrade your equipment, no matter the size or definition. With a deal having been made, Arnold was on his way into the office to do the paperwork concerning the sale, when he stopped short and couldn't breathe. He saw my youngest daughter, Mae, who bears a strong resemblance to me- a girl named Josie, someone that he had known a long time ago. Someone that his wife and he had been thinking about recently and never dreamed they would have a chance of finding or seeing ever again. He knew his hunch was correct; he felt it deep in the pit of his stomach, with an undeniable stark twinge when he spoke with her. But he said no more, just concluded his sale and went on his way, anxious to get back home to Riggins and talk with his wife about his discovery.

I have often thought about conducting a search for family members, but did not pursue it as a possibility. It would not be proper for a woman of any age to travel the states alone trying to locate loved ones, but now that thought has been changed by the arrival of the letter. This will be an incredibly trying task to break this news to my family; I know that they will not approve of what I have decided to do. Even though my family is aware of how unnerving my life has been, convincing them and receiving their approval will be difficult if not impossible. But this was exactly the kind of circumstance that I could not let go unnoticed. I must purchase a ticket for a seat on the train and depart immediately. But I didn't really know where I was going. There wasn't a return address on the envelope, and the writer had explained that he didn't want to include it, should it be returned as undeliverable. Arnold thought that was better than stirring up any hopes, or that the Riggins Post Office would receive it back and start all sorts of rumors flying. If I indeed was the young girl that they remembered, many lives would be affected by the acknowledgement of my whereabouts today. He further said that both he and his wife both sincerely hoped that I would respond in the form of a visit to Riggins very soon. "There are many people to whom you were very special and were special to you also, and they have really missed living without you." There would be thirty years of important things to catch up on, "things that you desperately need to know Josie." And that they knew when I had left I was in a horrible physical and mental state. I had contracted smallpox, and as a result I had plunged from a wicked fever into a coma, and that was that last they knew of my condition or of my whereabouts.

I'm so very upset and bewildered. I do not know who is writing all of this, but it is obviously two people who knew me very well and are the key to regaining my lost youth. But who were they? This letter has revealed some astonishing details and the shock that I indeed had more relatives and possibly more personal history than even I had realized. My life has been a myriad of emotions, both jubilantly exciting and stressfully terror filled. It was wonderful to have married such a caring man and raised three upstanding children to adulthood with him at my side. If my husband, Allen, was still living, he would be the first to tell me to pack my suitcase and get started for Idaho. He knew how haunted my thoughts were both awake and while asleep, and would be happy that I am now being given the chance to straighten them out.

My children will be a little more apprehensive in letting their mother travel so far away and unaccompanied by anyone at all. But I have already made the decision that I am going no matter how vehemently opposed to this my children are. The idea of traveling this great distance has given me both a sense of excitement and longing, and yes, even a sense of fear. I would not dare to tell my children that, of course; that would be a strike against me in my argument to do this.

Chapter Two

<u>MY PRECIOUS FAMILY</u>

I grew up in a small town named Spring Brook, North Dakota.
It was really more of a burgh than a town, just northeast of
Williston, near the western border. We were fortunate that we
had moved where there was still exposure to Indian culture and
the experience of our new neighbors, the Canadians. We would
pack up and travel to Moose Jaw, Manitoba, in the summer
trading season, just to join in the festivities and observe some
tribal customs on special occasions. It was a one-hundred-and-
fifty-mile journey each way, but my parents, especially my
mother, wanted me to share in some of the joyful events
involved in being a Native American, so that I would never
forget my roots. We would dress up in the few items of our
native clothing we had brought with us and the rest we had
recreated since our relocation. My mother made deerskin shifts
for both of us; they were scoop necked with beads of turquoise
and pretty shells encompassing it. Our belts were made of fur
pelts using the entire animal stretched out the long way. Its
back feet were bound together to secure them in the back while
the upper and lower portions of the jaw had fasteners to hook
together in the front of our garments. Quite unique that idea
was; I was told that my mother and grandmother were the first
ones in our tribe to fashion such an idea for a clothing
accessory. The hemline of our skirts had the same trim work
along the bottom as did the neckline of the dress, but the skirts
were much bolder in their design. Mother had made designs of
animals and birds by sewing beads on one by one until the
picture was a complete colored work of art. She made our
moccasins from rabbit fur; very soft and fluffy, and I always felt

like I was stepping on a cloud when I wore them. They weren't very practical, but they weren't worn every day as footwear; rather they were reserved for special occasions. And to finish off our tribal attire, she made headbands from leather pounded soft with simple beading to not overshadow ones facial features. The clothing of my grandfather and my father was, similar to ours, but not as elaborately detailed and they refused to wear anything on their feet other than their sturdy everyday shoes.

We also enjoyed partaking of the original foods prepared in the primitive cooking methods used on the open range in my grandparents' era. And doing so gave me a strong sense of belonging somewhere or to something. I had wrestled constantly with issues relating to our move. It was difficult for me to be all alone with no siblings, cousins or my best friend Rose; no one from the first seventeen years of my life. I had repeatedly asked to return to Idaho to visit and was told that we might be recognized or captured and then all of this would have been for nothing. It was hard, but I did agree with them, this was our family here, no matter how small it was, and they had sacrificed and suffered along with me in the loss of our relatives back home. Our family always came first, and they made me recognize that family is the most important thing that you can do well. I would grow up to instill that in my children too.

I met my husband Allen Liadva when he came to work for my father's business, Curtis Timber, as a laborer. He was a muscular, strong man and worked many long hours, which were largely comprised of hard physical tasks. He had many years of experience working for a logging company during the summer months of his school years. Allen came from the town of Ambrose, North Dakota, just three miles south of the Canadian border. He had moved to Minot in early adulthood, desiring a change from small town life to a big city hubbub. But he soon discovered that he did not like the crowdedness or the confusion that came with areas of a larger population and moved to Williston and found the job at our business in Spring Brook.

I worked at the timber company and handled all of the bills of lading, and the payroll, so I met Allen the first day he came to work there. We struck up a friendship first, just eating lunch with the other employees and laughing and talking at work, but eventually that all changed. His handsome face held my interest when he spoke and I loved to listen to his slight Canadian accent and definite brogue so customarily heard up there. And we found that we were ready to be more than just friends and officially began to see each other socially. We started going to the Saturday night dances at the town hall and the barn dances whenever they were held. Allen and I spent every Sunday afternoon together after we had gone to church with my mother and father.

Allen and I married after six months of courtship and bought a modest, little white house on the edge of town. We needed to be fairly close to the lumber yard so that it wouldn't be a great distance to walk to work each day. So, we started our married life walking to work together with our lunch pails in hand. It was a chance to talk about what was coming up for the day, and on the way home we could discuss the events that had happened on that day. Later, when the children began to arrive, we moved into a large, two story home with lots of beautiful woodwork and a lot of character.

Allen and I were blessed with three children, Anna, Allen, Jr. and Mae. Allen knew how important my Nez Perce background was to me and was impressed that I wanted our children to truly be raised with a sense of Nez Perce and French Canadian cultures. We had decided before we started our family that we would begin exposing them to their heritage at birth and planned to give them a spiritual title as well as a name. Your title customarily depicts who you are to a certain degree and it is bestowed upon you by your looks, behavior and sometimes in hope for your future.

Our first born, Anna, was named so after my grandmother Annahah and Allen's grandmother Ann. It was undeniable that she was a descendant of not only me but of her grandmother Isadora and great-grandmother Annahah; the resemblance was so strong. She was a very pretty girl from birth, and we knew she would be a striking woman as an adult as well. She was every bit as petite as Annahah was and remained that way throughout her life, never growing as tall as Allen or I. It was a long difficult labor and birth, and Anna came into the world screaming and protesting all the way. We gave her the title of Radiant Fire because we thought that she would, like the flame, burn brighter and go out into the world a fighter; and that she did in everything that she attempted. She has dedicated and strong memorization skills that allow her to recite back to you almost word for word a book that she has recently read. As a small girl, she could do it simply from the repetition of what you read to her and seeing the pictures on the page again.

The women's place in the home and in the workplace is beginning to change drastically and it is natural for my girls to work outside of their home environment. They had grown up with me running the family business with their father part-time and keeping up with the household duties part-time. Women used to be employed as nurses, teachers, librarians and store clerks, but the world is opening its doors to women in almost

28

every category now. We knew that Anna would tackle more untraditional issues than women were usually categorized in when choosing a career for themselves. She loved to know what was going on around the world and couldn't wait for the weekly paper to come out to read the news. She had a great passion for knowledge, and she would read any book she could borrow or check out of the public library. She spent all of her free time there reading, completely oblivious to what was taking place around her in the room.

Allen and I were not surprised when she aspired towards an informational career that would provide her with links to what was happening around the world. She became a newspaper reporter who worked hard and eventually became the editor of the widely read weekly newspaper in McGregor, which is about halfway between Spring Brook and the Canadian Border.

She met her husband Lee while employed at the paper. He is owner of the Brook Valley Journal and also serves as the general manager. He also has a passion to get the information out to the readers and is so diligent he usually runs on five or six hours of sleep a night. He is constantly out in the crowds watching for reportable news, attending every town meeting, every school meeting, gathering details to print in the next edition of the newspaper. He takes very seriously his duties at the newspaper, wanting the public to know each and every detail of the area. He also spends countless hours at the presses, setting the type.

They have one child, Michael, who is a quiet boy, and likes to keep to himself or be with his family. He was the only grandchild for awhile and perhaps grew up faster because of it. He has been consistently interested in history and learning about what has happened in our country in the past. He has a passion for the wars that this country has been involved in and reads constantly as his mother did. He is working on a school project right now that has him poring over the history books and newspaper reports from World War I and the horrific tragedies that occurred. He will first create an outline of the events, and then he will write an essay to sum up what he has learned from his research, more from memory than from his notes. He spends many hours creating games with paper and crayons in great detail with difficult rules and setups, challenging even for adults to understand. Allen and I believe that perhaps he will be a historian or an inventor one day, something that requires details, facts and the meticulous organization skills that are easy for him.

On our next child, Allen Jr., we bestowed the title of Strong Fox. His large shoulders at birth would indicate an independent, strong willed person able to take on huge challenges and fear nothing. While also being tall and slender like the cattails in the marsh, we felt he would be able to move quickly and dodge perils easily. And he would also carry the Fox title down that was held by his great grandfather Quiet Fox. Allen proved to indeed be a stubborn one, always excelling towards the big picture in life and not giving up on something until he got it right. He held to a true course and he did not waste his time getting into any trouble along the way, or cause any as some young boys his age were doing.

Allen began going to work with his father, almost as soon as he could walk. He would throw a tantrum if he could not go and climb on the logs at the lumberyard. He followed him around everywhere he went, always anxious to figure out how everything worked and always taking things apart and putting them back together. By the time he was an early teenager he had analyzed every tool and piece of equipment in the lumber yard and had suggestions on how to improve the workplace. When he wasn't able to tag along with his father, he was out back building things of his own from scraps of lumber. He even excavated piles of dirt, laying out a town and giving it some character, with hills and roads and such. When he had completed his high school years, Allen Jr. went to work full time with his father, learning and contributing to the family enterprise. He brought to the company fresh and up to date ideas, allowing the business to flourish and move up from the small entity that it had been. He soon became indispensable to the company and to Allen Sr.; they were confident that Curtis Timber would grow stronger and continue on for generations.

Allen is married to a beautiful gal named Beth. They met in Columbus at a hotel where she was working at the front desk. He had travelled there to estimate how much lumber the hotel would need to construct a badly needed addition. He had taken a room there to finish conducting his business the next day with the owner of the hotel. Beth had been responsible for booking rooms, seeing to the guests' needs, planning menus, and ordering necessities for the hotel and restaurant. She was also charged with the everyday problems which arise in a situation that deals with the public and keeping them satisfied and happy. She aspires to one day own a hotel of her own, and I hope that will be a definite possibility in her future. I think she would be very successful running a business of that nature as she loves working with people and builds a very good rapport with them.

They have an infant son, Joseph, an ancestral name proudly being carried on in this family through him. The name being partially taken from his great-great uncle, Chief Joseph, who we are all proud to be related to, and using a portion of my first name of Josephine too. He is as handsome as his father and grandfather, looking exactly like them. He is a little young to predict his personality yet, but I would judge that he will not take no for an answer and will not let anyone get the best of him. He is strong willed like his mother and father and will push on until he achieves what he wants to, I believe.

Our last child Mae, was born in the springtime, when all the flowers are in bloom and perfuming the air around us. She was usually content and didn't raise a large fuss even when she was hungry or tired and was able to adapt to whatever surroundings she was presented with. We felt she would happily float around gently until finding just the right place to land and be as pretty as a spring flower. Allen and I dubbed her Lily in the Wind, and it fit her perfectly both in her beauty and in her disposition.

She resembles the maternal side of the family, as her sister does, and I wish that she could have met them all. Mae loves the arts as I do and would have enjoyed the opportunity to have my mother and grandmother pass their well-honed skills of the Native American ways onto her. She truly enjoyed listening to tales of my younger days as a member of the Blue Dove Nez Perce tribe and of the ways of life of her ancestors. She loved to play with her friends, taking care to include each one importantly, and when she was not taking care of them, she was happy to be at home with just me. She learned to do all of the domestic rituals such as gardening, canning and preparing for winter as well as the sewing and embroidering techniques passed on down to me. Mae was in line to take over my bookkeeping duties at the family timber business, but that was not to be. She wanted something more rewarding, and my job was pretty mundane. She was really interested in helping the abandoned and orphaned children she had met at Fort Berthold when they visited there, so she began by volunteering there. I like to think that all of these homemaking and nurturing skills prepared her for the job she chose taking care of less fortunate children and instructing them to care for themselves.

Mae married a man named Jack, who is a member of the Mandan Indian Tribe. He was raised in the little town of Mandree, North Dakota which is on the western border of the Fort Berthold Indian Reservation. It is home to the Three Affiliated Tribes comprised of Mandan, Hidalsa, and Arikara. Mae and Jack live near the location of the future Garrison Dam on the eastern side of the reservation, where Jack is employed as a construction engineer. He and a crew of other men have been doing work in preparation for the official construction of the massive earthen dam that has been designated for this site. It will control the flow of water more efficiently on this portion of the Missouri River. The official opening of the dam is almost twenty years into the future, from its conception to its completion, and Jack is dedicated to see it finished. When they open the dam, they plan to flood a portion of the reservation and create a lake which will be named Lake Sakakawea in honor of the revered Indian Scout Sakakawea.

Mae and Jack have one young daughter named Madelyn. She is a beautiful girl with dark, long curly hair. She has a sparkling personality and is very polite and conscious to leave no one out, to not offend anyone or hurt anyone's feelings. She seems to be quite a bit ahead of schedule in the learning areas; she knows so much for such a young mind. She has been intellectually stimulated very early, learning with the other children at the Fort who learn as a whole with all ages present. Madelyn is more than one half Native American and has such beautiful

33

features that she could possibly represent something in the public eye that requires beauty to be of importance as well.

The most precious gift that anyone can be bestowed with after children; are grandchildren. It's an honor to hold those precious little bundles of new life, about to witness their new surroundings for the very first moment. Babies are born with sweet innocent faces, tiny wandering eyes, sweet smiles and and clutched fists. They are small extensions of their parents and ourselves. They experience the immediate hunger and bewilderment of just being born into the world. Then there's the unconditional love received from them and returned to them tenfold upon seeing them enter the world and being placed into your arms. How fortunate Allen and I are to have been able to have the privilege of being grandparents to these three wonderful grandchildren. We watch in awe as they develop their yearning for knowledge and experience the wonderment of knowing.

Chapter Three ≈

<u>OBSESSIONS</u>

I know that it has been difficult for my family to understand my obsession to have knowledge of my history and that of my family to pass on to them and to their children. But ultimately, family is what you are made of, your mental capacities, your body chemistry, your emotional distresses, your health and soul all stems partially from your ancestry. They do not know the extent of the things that I hope to learn by my return trip to my homeland. I have kept them in the dark about that. I have never shared with them any of my inklings of a secret life, one that occurred before they were born and that I have held in my mind and in my heart for thirty years. A life that I do not even know for sure exists in the physical being or just in my mental being, one that I myself know nothing about. Except for flashes of faces and places and nightmares of the same, all I really have is heartache and feelings of something vastly significant that was lost to me.

My children are all things to me in life. They are my babies, my toddlers, my adolescents, my grownups, my sounding blocks, my advice seekers and my best friends. We deny fervently that we will do as our parents did; no, we will try harder and do better with our children. But even if we succeed partially, there will undeniably be portions of the things we swore not to do that will inevitably slip through. With my children I withheld the truths from them just as was done to me by those who had reared me. I needed to be strong for them, so Allen was the only other person privy to the haunting of my dreams and my agony of another life. I was exceedingly fortunate to have found a man with great compassion and patience; he rescued me from my ghosts and intruders in the night and was always there to comfort me.

While Allen would have wholeheartedly supported me in this quest, my children are vehemently opposed to my outlandish and dangerous idea that I should do this alone. My children have incredibly persistent personalities and will not accept things simply because someone has told them that is the way it is. They begged that at least one of them should accompany me. I said absolutely not. You will not disrupt your lives for my search for closure to my dreams, fears and possible fantasies. This is a dream come true for me, but it is my dream to embark on this search for the Blue Doves and for my personal past. And I told them that I am sure the facts that I uncover will contain things that will be both unexpected and astonishing. They argued that I did not even know the man who had written the letter to me telling me that I have things to find out and people waiting for me there.

They asked how I could even consider trusting that this is even real based on a letter and a stranger. "You taught us to live safe and conservative lives, not to take chances into what is unknown and unsure." I argued that because I have always known that there is more to the story of Josie and I would never be completely whole until I solved these issues that have plagued me since young adulthood. There is much more to our family than what has been handed down to me from my grandparents and my parents. I lost some of my memory when I contracted smallpox, but I know that I lost more than that. Based on what I have been able to piece together there is considerable time missing from all the stories that I have been told. And when hard pressed for information, they tightened up their faces and their bodies became rigid and refused to talk any further with me about any of it.

My husband Allen, bless him, was a patient and caring man. He helped me through all of the complex nightmares that transpired several times each week. He relayed to me after each episode that I was quite verbal, sometimes understandable and sometimes it was only mutterings and ramblings. He wished there was a way of recording not just my screams and chatters, but the actual dream sequence that my subconscious self experienced with each occurrence. The spine-tingling fear that begins to wake me from these horrific nightmares is a feeling of absolute terror coursing through each and every nerve of my body. I would slowly begin to awaken from my sleepy stupor with the sensation of not being able to move for fear of falling down or off, out or in. It feels absolutely certain that whichever direction I should fall, it will all without question result in my death. It continues on for what seems like an eternity, but in reality it is probably only a few seconds as dreamscapes go. I lay as frozen as a concrete statue, until my focus begins to return to consciousness and I can identify the outline of something familiar in my bedroom. I realize that I am alright, safe in my bed and safe from the horror I have just experienced.

I have bolted upright to scream at the man in my room to "get out, get out of my room." The man has a vague, very vague, shadowy face that I do not recognize and it is always the same face starring at me. All I can judge from it is that it is a young man, perhaps around eighteen to twenty years old, and that is all my vision allows me to register. I do not see the face of someone that I know, but I must know him somehow, because that same face visits me regularly and never changes. Allen is always there talking me back to the surface, and I recover enough to realize that nothing is threatening to lurch at me, and I return to sleep almost reluctantly. Allen and I spoke of it endlessly as to who it could be and what they are trying to tell me through these appearances and why I feel so terrified. If he was a friendly spirit, why would I tell him repeatedly to "get out?"

There have to be deeply imbedded reasons within me for these occurrences to have started around the time that my family moved here and have never, ever left me alone. Each night that they present themselves they are predictable; I will be horrified and left spent and sleepless from these demons of mine. I am dealing with something that is haunting my sleep, but yet I am readily willing to face slumber each evening without delay. We had decided that we would never tell the children anything other than that I have nightmares. Of course, Allen and I believed it to be a representation of something that actually happened to me at a point in my life which I cannot remember.

Allen took the truth of my dream secrets with him when he died that day while taking a nap. He died quite peacefully, sitting in his favorite chair in front of the large window in the living room with the afternoon sun shining upon him. He had been a great, caring man and we had the good fortune to have a happy life together with our three children and our prosperous lumber business. I fell in love with him at almost at first sight all those years ago; he was as charming as he was handsome, and his soft looking lips are what had me from the start. I could never have imagined the kind of loving traits which he possessed, especially after growing up with my emotionally guarded family who never gave away much affection.

My parents and grandparents were diligently patient teaching everyday living skills and passing on tradition and rituals which had held as legacy for generations. But when it came to emotions or any instructions of a personal nature; it almost a rigid duty for them to preach how life 'should' go, with no variations or alternatives. You are born, you grow up, you marry, have children and work hard to be a decent person in the world. What's so difficult about that; why would you need to be given any instructions on how to achieve these things? Not many explanations of life were given; physical and mental well being are all just concepts you were meant to figure out as you walked though life. Few words of advice, caution or explanation were given on what to expect from the different stages of life, it should just come naturally. What happened to them? They were this way even when I was a young child; they seem to have just frozen up when it comes to loving one another and to loving me. And it escalated with our departure from our homeland. I think it had a larger impact on all of them than they realized and certainly more than any of them would admit.

I was fairly unprepared for my wedding night; again, it should all just be a matter of instinct, no instructions or advice necessary. Allen and I were very confused on our wedding night. We each had few ideas of what to expect based on the experiences of friends. And of the events, one of them did not hold true and neither of us were ever able to identify the possible cause or explain it. But we were both upset by it and eventually Allen told me that he believed it related directly to the nightmare of the man in my room, and why he frightened me so severely. And neither of us ever spoke of it again after that evening, but it dwelled within me always.

After many days of arguing and discussing my trip, my children finally agreed to let me go alone and helped me to board my train for the western states. I had to promise to call them every third day as close to four o'clock in the afternoon as possible, provided the switchboard in Riggins was free. They would be waiting for the call to come in to hear my progress, if any, in locating my family and my tortured past. We were fortunate to have access to a private phone line downtown at the newspaper office, as we do not have any in our homes yet. My children needed to make sure that I was alright, and if they hadn't heard from me close to our scheduled time, they would be contacting the local authorities.

Chapter Four

MY CHERISHED ELDERS

Isadora Blue Dove was my mother, whose tribal name was Troubled Fawn. It suited her well. My grandmother had said that she had been born with a perplexed look on her face and was a small baby. Being an only daughter as she was, the burden of caring for her parents and having them live with her would fall only upon her. She grew into a beautiful young girl with a caring heart for everyone, and she possessed a natural talent for everything that she attempted. Her mother had schooled her well in the arts of basketry, beading and sewing techniques. By the time she was just a young teen she was the envy of the other girls in the tribe and even some of the older women of the tribe. Her cooking skills couldn't be matched either; again, a natural talent for whatever delectable food dish she tried to prepare. She was continually experimenting with the resources found in the woods, around and in the lakes, or growing out on the open prairie. She had a keen eye for herbs, flowers and roots that could be used to change the flavor of their staple foods. They ate a lot of venison, buffalo and other wild game daily, and she found that if she mixed in or sprinkled her natural seasonings on them, it could change the ordinary to the extraordinary. Camas root, also known as quawmash or Passhico root, is one of two staples that were available in abundance, the other being fish. The Nez Perce have been tending and harvesting these roots for generations and they are one of the healthiest parts of their diet. Comparable to a modern day potato, they were cooked and mashed or pounded and baked into loaves. The camas roots were usually set on the rock ledge around the fire to bake while the meat was roasting on a spit suspended above the fire. My grandmother would wait until the roots were almost cooked through and then cut a slit into them and stuff some of her spices in them. Even though she was only in her teens, she became an instructor in food preparation to all of the women in the tribe.

When I was a small child, I can remember seeing her looking very unhappy at times. She seemed to withdraw within herself so deeply that it was as if she was not there with me at all. I wondered if it had anything to do with me, I hoped she was happy that I was her daughter. Or was life just so hard on her that she didn't have a lot to smile about? I asked grandfather several times what was wrong with my mother; I had heard many stories of Indians that needed to go to the sweat lodge to cleanse their thoughts. I asked my grandfather if my mother needed to go there to clean out her thoughts because they were muddy like my hands always were. In a rare moment of affection, he would always grin widely and grab onto me and drag me up into his lap and squeeze me tight. Then he would always reply, "maybe so Josie, maybe so." But my mother never did go to the sweat lodge for a few days to clean up her muddy thoughts. Eventually, as I grew older I stopped asking and just accepted those moods as a part of my mother's personality.

My father, Frederick LeClaire, was Canadian-born in a remote area which covers both the borders of Alberta and Saskatchewan known as Gregoire Lake Provincial Park. His parents had died when he was five years old, and he and his brothers had been raised by various family members. Frederick, the youngest of the four brothers, was reared by his maternal grandparents, but the other brothers remained in the same town. While being placed with different families, they were still were afforded the luxury of knowing one another. I had been told that my grandmother's heart had given out and that my grandfather had died from something known as lockjaw. I understood, even as a little girl, that one's heart does all the work in keeping the body breathing and working properly. But lockjaw was a mystery to me until I was older and could comprehend what it was. My father told me that lockjaw was an infectious disease called tetanus caused by bacteria toxin which usually entered the body through an open wound. It causes the muscle of the jaw to contract tightly and eventually "lock" up as the infection increases. My father then taught me how to very carefully clean and disinfect a scratch or puncture to the skin to avoid it becoming infected or far worse.

My father's life had been filled with frustration, and he had a difficult time fitting into his own family. His grandfather, uncles, cousins and even his own three brothers were all about the same height, save a couple of inches. Each of them was in the range of five-foot-nine inches to six-foot-two inches and built as solid as one would imagine any lumberjack to appear. He was born the odd one, reaching adulthood at only five-foot four and one hundred fifty pounds; he was just not well suited for the lumberjack trade. So, he pursued a livelihood working for a guy who built and sold pirogues. Pirogues are fairly small, one man boats used to transport merchandise down river and are especially useful for shallow areas that another boat could not maneuver through. Based on their small distinction, it is necessary for the voyageur to be around five feet, five inches or slightly under to pilot one of these watercrafts. This canoe like vessel was carved whole from a cedar or oak tree, which resulted in the length limitations, as well as the strength of the tree itself. Frederick would travel down the South Fork of the Athabasca River to trade fur pelts, smoked meats and fish and other items for flour, sugar, coffee and numerous other supplies at Fort McKay and Fort McMurray.   There is only room for one man in these types of boats, and the cargo is packed in tightly around him.   Usually, the crafter had made previous arrangements for the boat to be sold at the fort, so my father would float with it downstream.   However, if for some reason the boat buyer didn't show up to take the boat, and he could not sell it to someone else, he would have to take it back to the craftsman.   That return trip upstream would be a tough one, carrying the pirogue on his shoulders as well as the goods which he had traded for.   And his small stature definitely presented a problem in getting back up to Gregoire Lake, taking almost four times the amount of time over land than it had taken him to float down the river.

Eventually, the individual craftsman hollowing out the pirogues in the remote areas of the high country came to an end. Factories were being built to mass produce all types of watercrafts and left the independent boat makers turning to new forms of employment.   My father had to make a change along with them, so this young man, now in his late teens, left his three brothers and their families behind in Gregoire Lake, not knowing if he would ever see any of them again.   He relocated down south to Castlegar in British Columbia on the Canadian border with the state of Washington directly south of it and the state of Idaho to the east.   He had heard of a lumber company there, and indeed after traveling down there he was offered a job.   It was located next to the Columbia River where the logs would be floated down and picked up at another lumber station. There was talk at that time that it was being proposed that a dam be built sometime into the future in approximately the middle of the eastern portion of the state of Washington. It would later become known as the Grand Coulee Dam.

My parents met one day after my mother tagged along with my grandfather to a traders day in the Castlegar area. It was one of the largest trading posts for hundreds of miles around. She had always begged to go along, but it was a rough excursion that took several days, and he wasn't sure that Isadora would be happy in the end that she had accompanied him this time. But he was proud of her; she was a good traveling companion and did not complain about the primitive camping or the long days in the horse and buggy. Grandfather was attempting to forge into a new era and set into motion a crop farming operation by planting corn and marketing it in advance. He intended to travel each spring to different sites to solicit for customers for the purchase of corn which would be ready for sale in the fall. No Nez Perce had tried anything of that magnitude before. If he was successful, it would open up huge opportunities for others to try crop farming also. New areas of obtaining profits needed to be put into place in the near future, but still most tribal chiefs refused to move on past the traditional trading of hides and horses.

Frederick was enjoying his day off of work and was down by the river skipping rocks with some other lads. Isadora was sitting on a huge rock, with her legs and feet still dripping wet from cooling them off in the water when he first saw her. His breath caught and he thought she looked like a beautiful mermaid sitting up there so stately and quiet, just looking out over the river. She had beautiful, shimmering black hair that was blowing loosely in the wind and her brown skirt with the turquoise beadwork was spread out on the rock as if someone had posed her there for a picture. He reluctantly turned back

45

away from her to pitch rocks again, trying to think of how to meet this lovely creature. Eventually, she saw the rocks landing in the water and became interested in the game they were playing and all of the teasing and shouting that was going on with a group of boys. Frederick was aware that she had been watching them and had looked her way several times and smiled at her. And after a few smiles, Isadora returned a smile to him. Before long he walked over to meet her, they exchanged names and told each other what they were doing here at Castlegar. She learned that Frederick was twenty years of age, just two years older than she was, and that he was working at the mill south of Castlegar. He told her how the lumber was sawed and then floated down the very river in which she was cooling off which was called the Columbia River in the state of Washington. He also told her the sad story of his family and how it was that he left home at such a young age.

Then it was Isadora's turn to talk about herself and she told him where she was from and that she had always wanted to come along on one of her father's trading trips. But she left out the part about Ignatious trying to initiate a new system to obtain money for the tribe by planting and harvesting crops for profit, it wasn't her place to talk about that. She told him about her love of cooking and craft work and that she had been doing those things since she was about eight years old. She told him that she spent some of her days helping others to learn cooking, basketry and beadwork and working with the tanned hides and designing of the teepees. She spoke of her duties as an only child, that helping her parents required a large portion of her time also as she was the only daughter. Even though she was eighteen now, the responsibility would be hers to care for them as they aged, and that day would eventually arrive. She bubbled over with excitement telling him about her few days free from those duties. She liked to wander around freely in the fields and streams searching for herbs and flowers to add to her cache of various items she had already gathered. That gave Frederick an idea for winning Isadora over; he would walk into the woods and pick some wildflowers for her.

Frederick asked Isadora if she was staying until the next day, when the annual trading festivities would end, in the sincere hope that he could find out more about her. She replied that yes, she and her father would be remaining there until tomorrow sometime, when he felt his business was concluded and it was time to start the long journey home to Riggins. He asked her if he could come by and visit them tonight where they had made preparations to sleep come nightfall and meet her father. She tipped her head downward shyly and told Frederick that she was very proud of Ignatious and would like it if she could introduce them. He was optimistic that he would be invited to accompany them to the festivities in the evening and be allowed to eat the evening meal with them. Isadora described the location where they had set up their makeshift teepee and said that she and her father had planned to meet there at sunset and that he should arrive around then too.

Isadora was sure that Ignatious would be apprehensive at first that she had invited a stranger to their camp and had spent the greater share of the afternoon talking with him alone. So, she was relieved when her father arrived first at the campsite so that she could prepare him for their visit from a young Canadian man. Not because he would object to the Canadian part, but every father hoped that his daughter would choose someone of the same background. Marrying another Native American would more likely ensure the continuation of the traditions in

47

their generation and of the ones to follow. Ignatious also hoped that she would not marry someone and move to his home village with him; he wanted her to always be within his reach to protect her. She told him about Frederick and all that she had learned about him that afternoon, and it was obvious to him that she was feeling happier than she had been in quite some time. He was surprised that she had broken out of her normally guarded personality and had taken such a bold step to extend an invitation to a person she had just met. Ignatious was satisfied with the easy acceptance of his proposal at the market today to plant, grow and harvest the corn to sell to those individuals who did not want to raise it themselves. So, his mood was light and cheerful, and his normal protective demeanor concerning his daughter was lifted. When Frederick came, her father was in very high spirits and received him graciously to Isadora's delight, and they were comfortable with each other immediately, and that began a new relationship both with his daughter and with Frederick. After conversing awhile, Ignatious welcomed him to join them around the giant fire to watch the dancing and rituals that evening. Isadora would be elated to try the special dishes prepared for the feast and find out how they were concocted before the fire. Ignatious couldn't put it into words, the feeling that he had about Frederick, but he sensed that this lad was of a trustworthy and honest sort. Part of the camaraderie of the trading days was visiting with the other chiefs that he seldom had the opportunity to see, and tonight he would be able to relax and know that Isadora was fine left alone with Frederick.

Frederick made several long trips down to see Isadora; hoping to be fortunate enough to be her husband someday fairly soon. It was a couple days journey to her town by horse, with taking only frequent rest breaks and a short night's sleep each time he stopped. He had to sacrifice a significant amount of pay to travel down there each time, so he inquired at the lumber mill in Riggins to see if he could seek employment there. He told the owner his history of working skills and the jobs that he had held and they hired him without delay, not wanting to pass over someone with his experience in the lumber trade. He went down to Allison Creek and told Isadora the good news. She was elated that he would be close by now and that there would no longer be a month between his trips to see her. And then he went to look for Ignatious to ask him the most pertinent question of his young life, of course, to ask his permission to marry Isadora. Ignatious was very fond of Frederick, so when he asked for the honor to wed his daughter, the answer was an exuberant yes. They married a few months after he had left Washington and transferred to the Riggins Mill, and they lived on Allison Creek with Ignatious and Annahah. Isadora knew she had chosen a truly caring and considerate man, and he told her that his heart was hers from the very first time he saw her.

My maternal grandparents were Grandfather Quiet Fox Blue Dove, and Grandmother Gentle Flower Blue Dove. They met just weeks before their prearranged marriage took place in her birth land of Lapwai, which was given its name by the large number of butterflies gathering by the millpond. "Laplap" is Nez Perce for butterfly and "wai" translates to water. In 1862, Fort Lapwai was established to prevent white interference upon the Nez Perce reservation and on the settlers. In 1866, it was inhabited by Army personnel and it was from this very fort that Captain David Perry with the First Calvary were ordered by President Abraham Lincoln to Mount Idaho and White Bird; beginning the first encounter between the Nez Perce and the

Army. In the years after she left, her peaceful little village became a mixture of Army personnel and Nez Perce that wasn't always so peaceful.

After the wedding, my grandmother traveled with my grandfather to live with his family and the Blue Dove tribe in White Bird, Idaho. Thankfully, their planned union was one of instant approval for both of them; neither of them had any objection towards the other one. They were a good match, and while it began as a marriage of convenience, they easily loved one another and sincerely were happy together.   A proposed arrangement such as theirs usually began with the fathers of the man and woman to be paired together. The father of the woman would approach the father of the man and ask him if his son would enter into a marriage contract with his daughter. My great grandfather felt that the Blue Dove extension of the Nez Perce in Idaho was a proper representation of their tribe, and it would be an honor to have such an association with them. And as was tradition, a dowry was expected from the bride's father, with the man's father on the receiving end at the marriage ceremony. And as in any contract, a good deal is usually beneficial to both parties, and is planned out carefully.   Gentle Flower's father wanted her to marry into the Blue Dove tribe and had chosen Quiet Fox to be the prospective groom, and he would be generous with the items promised to Quiet Fox's father. Some of the usual items could be horses, bows and arrows, or hide,; whatever one family may proudly possess would be given to the groom's father. In their territory, buffalo was in abundance, so Grandmother Annahah's father gave to Ignatious's father an appropriate amount of buffalo meat which had been dried and made into jerky strips. He made sure to give them enough to last him and his wife the winter season. Also, hide had been tanned and sewn together in preparation for use as a new tepee, which Annahah had tastefully decorated with skillful arrangements of beadwork and shells. She had painted scenes of a buffalo hunt, to be used as the focal point of the structure with the buffalo running and warriors in pursuit, arrows at the ready. And then the animal was downed with arrows protruding from the giant beast and the warriors gathered around it in triumph. In addition, the female relatives of the bride's family worked together to design a garment for the groom to wear for the nuptials, while the men in her family were gathering together the items agreed upon for the dowry. It is disrespectful to the groom's family for the bride to wear her ordinary clothing, so a complete set of new items were prepared for her also. Each article lovingly created with her own special ideas, and her mother, sisters and aunts helping her to sew it and decorate it along with the finery for her groom.

Parents of all generations want their children to marry well; both the bride and the groom should be skilled in some area to produce a fruitful life. My grandmother was quite proficient in the art of beading and created many tribal costumes and headdresses for the special events that took place from time to time. Beads were easy to acquire through the trading procedure of hides, corn, and horses, with each party obtaining something they did not possess in their homeland. Most of the beads came from Venice, and the favorite was turquoise, a welcome change to the costuming decoration that had mostly been shells. Her talent was so striking that she made the best of trades among the women in her village, and she was envied for the ease with which she created things. Annahah's Father had chosen Ignatious to ask to be partnered to his daughter because he was known as the new young warrior with ideas for planning new ways to live, grow crops and hunt with better and easier methods. He had introduced his tribe to better corn crops with working up the soil deeper and with placing horse droppings in with each seed planted to do what he referred to as "fertile them." He explained that he had observed that the wild grasses and flowers that grew out from beneath the area where the manure was piled was always bigger and better than anywhere else. And he proved that theory to be correct; his corn crops were the best in the region. Of course, his secret was not divulged to anyone but his own circle. But his reputation for those abundant ears of corn, his ideas for dwellings warmer than hide and to set more traps than plan long hunting excursions all raised his status, and thus he was a very desirable mate.

The generation of Native American peoples being known only by their spiritual titles eventually passed as did living in teepees. Once the white man became so heavily involved in their lives, they were forced to adopt names more suitable for acceptance into the white community. So, my Grandfather Quiet Fox became Ignatious and my Grandmother Gentle Flower became Annahah. But still, each of them refused to be completely drained of their heritage, so privately in their own domai they continued to address each other by their birth names. At the time they were born, the brave and squaw who created the child chose the name they would like to give to the baby. And then in a welcoming ceremony, the child was placed in the middle of a circle formed by the tribe and the parents declared that name now belonged to this child. They held these rituals in the highest regard and hoped that the child would always remain true to the tribal customs and religions that they had grown up respecting. Midwives brought them into the world whenever possible, and it was believed that these women possessed a gift of magic. At the ritual, the midwives were allowed to ask the gods to bring all good things to a child just born.

I was only privileged to have a grandmother in my life for what I would consider a short time. I loved her dearly, and she died before I could fully appreciate a grandmother's presence in a young girl's life. She was a woman of quiet, almost mysterious demeanor who sometimes retreated into her subconscious just like I had seen my mother do many, many times. Would I be subject to this condition also? Is this an unfortunate familiar trait passed down from generation to generation within our family unit? Or is there some immense underlying issue or tragedy placed upon them that altered them both so drastically that they needed to draw into themselves periodically? For me to grow up without my grandmother was a difficult ordeal for me, some things can only be shared with or learned from a grandmother.

I was truly blessed that my grandfather lived to be a very old chief, though long ago retired and my sole link to the heritage of the Nez Perce. He was the greatest influence in my life and taught me the value of family and tribal honor and tradition. He told me wonderful legends, some sentimental and enjoyable and others quite horrifying. But there was a trait that would always prevail, no matter what kind of tale he was telling to me. And that was a distinct hesitation every now and then that led me to believe that there was a specific, underlying reason for the pauses in his sentences. I asked him one time if he was having trouble remembering the correct details of the event as they had occurred. He replied that yes, he sometimes didn't recall everything correctly because it was so long ago and he wanted to tell it the right way to me. I loved the old man and trusted him without any doubt to share the history of our ancestors and our immediate and extended family. But…I know that there was more to his reluctance to speak than that, there had to be. Generally, he was a fluent speaker and was a man with confidence and intellect when he was speaking with my parents or other adults. It was only when he spoke to me of the homeland and stories of our family and grandmother that he closely guarded his words, pretending that we had never had any turmoil within the family unit. However, on many occasions, I could read that he was not being completely truthful when telling me these stories, and sometimes I could feel it so strongly that it would make me shiver when I was listening to him.

Grandfather was a non aggressive, insightful man who really didn't approve of warring with the other tribes or with the army. He felt it was not necessarily the proper way to retain possession of the lands which had been theirs through birthright and occupation. Every now and then grandfather would fall into various lingering stages of deep depression. He wouldn't eat, he would leave the dinner table and go to his room and lay on the bed. He would sit slumped over in his chair, like he was waiting on death to come and claim him. He no longer wished to go outside and sit under the trees with me, where he had made a daily ritual of making up stories for me based on how the clouds looked each day. He would apologize again and again for drawing the last prayer stone and taking me away from all of the other family members that we had once spent so many happy times with. He would sob until his tired eyes lined themselves in deep red. Inconsolable, he had to wait until his weary eyes were completely void of tears, and then he would return to the surface around him and slowly come back to be himself.

As I grew older, I wondered how long it was that I had not noticed that he was becoming an unhappy man; it seemed that as he aged, his expression was most often one of sadness. He had grieved so harshly for the death of his wife, of leaving behind his brothers and their families and the loss of independence and land he once rode upon freely. He resided with my parents and me for the rest of his life, but nothing replaces the loss of one's mate. What had begun as an arranged contract had evolved into a great, fulfilling love with my grandmother. Ignatious closed his eyes to life as a very old man one evening in his sleep and appeared more peaceful that at any time that I remembered him to be. Perhaps, he knew that he would soon be rejoined with his Gentle Flower once again now.

Chapter Five ≈

THE QUIET ESCAPE

I am standing by the railroad line in Havre, Montana, picturing the trainloads of supplies brought here for miners, trappers and the military stationed at Fort Assinniboine, after the railroad was built in 1885. But I have disembarked here for far more than the history of this town and its historical significance. This location holds memories of an earlier time in my childhood, when so many crucial events took place in my life, my family's life and that of the entire Nez Perce tribal unit as well.

As I stand here on the edge of the Buffalo Jump, I remember my grandfather telling of how this place and many others were used in the massive harvest of the buffalo before winter. The tribe did not want to be away from their families and villages for very long, due to the increasing threat being placed upon them by the invasion of the settlers coming to stake claim to their lands. They would gather the buffalo herd together and steer them towards the steep cliff and leaving them no place else to go, they would jump off of it. Some would die, some would be maimed and then shot, a very few others would escape (for now) their fate as a food store for the winter months. When the hunters returned home, there would always be a celebration in honor of the buffalo, making it possible to sustain them where they were for an entire winter. Some years were not so lucky, and they relocated several times before they found a place that was rich with bounty. Travel in the winter months was extremely difficult and took a toll on the tribe as a group, usually losing several tribal members due to the bitter cold and extreme wind chills, particularly the elderly. And then they would need to remain where they were at least several days to have a proper burial ceremony for those who had passed.

The revered and respected leader of the Nez Perce Indian tribe, Chief Joseph, had surrendered his family and freedom to the white man after extensive battles with them. They had not given up easily, only after losing so many people and not being able to carry on with the fight did they resolve to stop running away. They would be sent to live on several reservation sites dictated to them for the remainder of their lifetimes after leaving here, a truly sad story for all involved.

There had been a plan devised to safely harbor a portion of the Blue Dove tribe, but due to the luck of a drawing of the prayer stones, grandfather and two of his brothers, Vincent and Leopold, had drawn badly and would never make it to that safe harbor in time. They had not chosen to give up their rights roaming their countryside with their people and living by their own means and resources, they had been forced to do so. Now, they needed to find new territory to rebuild their lives; lives that would not be consumed with fear each moment of every day; there must be such a place to harbor them. After careful consideration, it was agreed that Canada would be their only hope for real survival and where the tribe could thrive and rebuild once again. It would be their only defense against those who wanted them to be herded like the buffalo in massive numbers off a cliff. In this scenario, they would be driven onto a reservation where every moment of their lives would be controlled until death rescued them.

When attending trading celebrations, where other tribes were present, they would hear of Canada with its rivers with abundant bounties of fish, and remote areas where the buffalo and other animals had not been depleted. They decided that the tribe would pack as little as possible to travel light and swiftly, and food would be rationed, and to hunt would be the only option on their hasty and grueling progression northward.

It would be crucial that they travel on the most intricate and treacherous passes through the steep, jagged mountains running along the Seven Devils Mountain and Hells Canyon. The trails and rivers that were decided to be their course would be dangerous and ice covered in some stretches and may take many months to realistically achieve their goal. They were not going to be able to cover a great deal of distance before they were discovered missing, or the Army with the benefit of horses, would be sure to catch up to them. Their advantage was the small number of Nez Perce slipping off into the night; likely they would not be noticed missing for several hours. They would need to exercise extreme caution and adhere to absolute silence and have have to burrow in tightly once they found an adequate yet unpredictable cave or rock formation... and wait. There they would remain and not dare to even peek out of the confinement of their lair. If they could just make it west into Hells Canyon, just on the other side of the prison which once was home, they could easily hide in the massive rock formations of their native homeland. After a week had passed, one scout and only one would sneak out to investigate the conditions. They would have to determine that the Army wasn't out there somewhere waiting them out before venturing outside.

That was what the brothers had planned before the Army forcefully persuaded them at gunpoint to accept their invitation to be grateful guests of the government with so many promises made to them. The chiefs and elder tribesmen were responsible for the decision to decide the welfare of their immediate families, and they each felt that they had let their families down by not acting sooner and avoiding capture. My cousin Steven, Leopold's grandson who had lived on the reservation in Oklahoma, was interviewed on his life, and his recollections were included in historical publications on the Nez Perce War and its results. There have been many, many books written on the wars and legends of that time. It is there that I have been able to partially fill in the blanks of the scenarios as they played out after we lost all contact with Alphonse, Vincent, Leopold and their families.

Neither Vincent nor Leopold knew of the intricate plan to separate them from each other until they actually had begun their journeys in tow of the Army soldiers. When it became time for the groups to no longer travel together it was then that separate destinations were revealed to them. Chief Vincent's family would be taken to a reservation in Nebraska and Chief Leopold's family to Oklahoma. They had been tricked and misled; they would not be living out the remainder of their lives with each other's presence. The government felt the chance of an uprising would be less likely if the two were unable to communicate with one another. The passiveness with which they had been following along behind their captors was over. Vincent would not stand for any more trickery from the Army. If they resigned to this, what would follow? Would they indeed be going to a reservation or perhaps to be locked in leg irons and chains for the remainder of their lives? Or would they be destined to be slaves for the white man as the black people had been forced to be? It was time to make happen the attempt which had been thwarted by capture to seek new territory in which to once again live free and peaceful.

So, with a horrendous storm like no one here had ever witnessed about to rip through the valley, Vincent and his family seized the opportunity and fled their encampment on foot with barely anything with them. They each had a small water pouch and meager rations of food when they left the lockup area. They had intended these items as emergency travel food for the imminent relocation journey, but this was an opportunity they had to risk. It was as if all the good spirits that they had worshipped all of their lives were on their side. They felt as if they were there with them, guiding them with this miracle that they had beseeched the gods for. Beneath the torrents of rain and severe winds bearing down on them, my great uncle, Chief Vincent and his family were forging their way toward the Canadian border. He had confided in his brother, Chief Leopold and wanted him and his followers to join them, but he refused. He said he would rather give up peacefully and live on the nice reservation that the Army was providing for them, than risk their lives in a foolish escape attempt in foul weather. Chief Vincent said that he did not believe a word of what the white man had been telling them, everything they had done to them past and present had turned out poorly. And that was the last that anyone heard about them. The rest of the family could only hope that the gods of protection and safe journey were watching over them. Perhaps some time far into the future, some word of what had happened to them, might possibly filter down to those on the reservation.

My parents and grandfather had told me the story of our escape from capture many, many times, and I in turn have shared it with my husband and children. My children, as I did, hung spellbound on every word of the destruction of the Nez Perce families and legacies. Frederick and Ignatious gathered up our small party of five family members shortly after dark in November, 1905. With an ensuing major storm about to hurl heavy amounts of wind and rain, it was the most opportune time for us to slip out, and preparations were made to leave during the night. We would only be taking food, bedding items, and the heaviest of clothing to withstand cold, cruel elements. Traveling in November at the start of the winter season guaranteed that we would be walking straight into the worst conditions. The belongings left behind and shortness of food items would not be a strange situation to any of us; life had treated us harshly in the past and we had not forgotten those meager times. The knowledge that we would probably not reach safety very early in our trip would stress heavily upon all of us. But grandfather and father would persevere and push us hard toward our goal of freedom, certain that our lives would be replenished once we were far enough away and felt safe from being hunted down by the government. It would be a straining, grueling endeavor to finally reach a place where fear was not our most recurring feeling. And to give us a new home, but especially to begin life over again for me; but I never understood why they phrased it exactly that way. But I knew in my heart that there had been a reason that I did not want to live in another town or another state. Even today, when I think back on the story, I feel an uneasy sickly pain of loneliness when I think of our home, family and friends that we never saw again. But I also feel guilt and can't explain it. Grandfather said that it was such a great sadness that the Army was forcing our families to split up and hastily flee in mortal fear of being killed or imprisoned.

The night before we left was only the beginning of the inclement weather. As daybreak came and the day began it worsened considerably. The rain was like none that we had ever witnessed in our lifetimes. It was coming in sheets across the valley from the east, slapping against Schoolmarm Peak and over its top. Trees were being flattened, and anything else that was in its path was being dragged down the west side of the mountain like a massive waterfall. It was November and this kind of tornado-like weather was usually reserved for summertime, and then it was still atypical for the weather here.

Frederick and Ignatious both agreed that despite these life threatening conditions, it was time to go. They had made an alternate plan to those escaping underground. It was quite probable that our family would not have time to make it, and that is exactly as the situation played out. And now it was definite, we would not be coexisting with the three other families in the Blue Dove line; each would be driven out in different directions. Those who had already relocated deep within the cave system were truly the lucky ones; they were among the uncounted ones. The Army now had taken a roll call and had announced they would be pulling out soon, with their hostages in tow. We were listed on their charts, but our loved ones in captivity could easily cover the absence of the five of us. Fortunately for us, they had allowed a time frame of three days for everyone to choose what belongings to take with them. That would give everyone a fair chance to say goodbye to their friends and neighbors in Riggins and their land of Idaho.

At dusk, the five of us quietly left our precious Allison Creek homestead and headed northeast toward the old Florence town site. We should be able to find an underground mine in which to hide and rest a bit. The distance traveled would not be great, but the squalling conditions would prevent us from going any farther for now. My grandmother and I were not capable of

62

moving on our own. I had contracted smallpox they said, and was not showing any signs of recovery, so I had to be carried, and grandmother couldn't keep up with her tiny weak frame and her age an extra factor. The intensity of the storm increased and we struggled across the wind, forcing us onto the ground at times to crawl through the mud. But this was the course chosen to allow us to live out our lives as free people. Actually, it was what everyone else but I had chosen for life's journey. I know that before I became so ill there had been a different world waiting for me; I have felt it my entire life.

There was to be no convenient spot to stop until we actually reached the town of Florence. When we arrived we were drenched and muddy, but grateful to see buildings still standing in town. The old saloon was before us, the men knew that there was a cellar harbored beneath its floorboards. We could hide inside awhile and get the break that we needed from the weather, and we should be able to dry out and clean ourselves before moving on. The storm had ripped through Florence, and the saloon had sustained heavy damage-part of the saloon had collapsed. That would work to our benefit it wouldn't be at all noticeable that we had tracked mud in or tore additional boards up from the floor. It would gain us additional secrecy with the old settlement being terribly ravaged and its historic significance destroyed.

The saloon was a long narrow building with living quarters in the back. Despite the fact that these buildings had been abandoned years ago, some furniture still remained. My father carried me in and settled me onto the one bed, and my mother and grandmother heaved their wet bodies down next to me onto the torn and tattered mattress that lay on the bed frame. We would need a brief respite to catch our breath and to stop shaking from the chill that had overtaken all of us. The men located the trap door to the cellar and began the climb down the ladder to see what kind of conditions the underground cavity held. It was dampened of course from the rain, but there was no standing water or debris hindering us from making it our home for awhile.

My father and grandfather started to take our food and packed clothing items down and set up a livable space for us. They would use the devastated buildings as supplies to build the necessary pieces of furniture we would need to get by. They rounded up all the boards, chairs, tables, anything that could be of use to us and lifted them down into the hole. They found blocks of wood that, stacked uniformly, provided a base for the bed, topped with boards running crosswise, made them fairly stable. Some straw had been found blowing around, they piled it under the sparse mattress found upstairs and laid our still damp bedding over the top. Then they made another bed, minus the mattress layer, it served well. Perhaps more straw or even hay would be found to add to it after the winds stopped.

My mother and grandmother had rested some and were ready to help create the temporary living quarters themselves. They unpacked all of the wet gear and began to hang it around the saloon; it would surely have time to dry out before we needed to be completely sealed into the crawl space. They made a shelf for our food stores and laid them out also to dry from the time spent in the rain. We ate a rationing of bread, honey and a little milk, this would most assuredly be the last milk that we would taste in quite some time. But what they had brought along would keep one more day in the cold, dampness underground.

I had been lying in the upstairs of the saloon while the cubbyhole in the floor was being readied for habitation. I was too weak and exhausted to move on my own, they were increasingly worried that I would not last out the journey with my fever still spiking and declining again. This had been recurring for several weeks now and no amount of spiritual praying, rituals or remedies had taken hold and brought me back. And now that we were actually and on the road traveling, there would not be anything special they could do for me now except to make the herbal tea that contained the herbs brought by grandmother in her special pouch. Everything was dark and hazy, and I was so disoriented that I truly realized nothing, oblivious of the fact that we were even on the move. This crucial step in our existence was one that I would never be able to recall or recount to future generations. I had to rely on the memories of grandfather, mother and father for all of the details of this horrible mess that had become the greatest nightmare in anyone's life.

All of the preparations were made by nightfall and we were hidden well amongst the rubble. The heavy, wooden double swinging doors from the entrance to the saloon were pulled over the top of our opening, and provided a secure roof for us, rather than just nailed down floorboards. And with that accompanied by various debris collected and carefully teetered on top of the doors, we felt reasonably safe. The men were afraid to close their eyes but only for a few brief moments, one man at a time, the others nervously aware of what was taking place outside. But at this point, with the severity of Mother Nature continuing on with her tantrum, we had to be securely sealed beneath the saloon before the storm's end. We knew that the Army would be marching our people south of this town, but doubted they would actually venture north just for the shelter of Florence, especially so early in their journey. We imagined that they would limit their stops if they were going to reach the reservation before the harshest portion of winter set in. We remained in waiting for two days while the winds howled and torrential downpour continued outside. Then the sky began to clear and we knew the storm was passing through and this would perhaps be our last peaceful night here. Our cover would be less invisible then, and the chance of unwelcome visitors threatened more with each cloud that moved on.

In mid morning of the next day, we heard the dreadful sound of horses, many, many horses. And as they continued to approach, we could hear the squeak of wagon wheels, and prayed they would pass through quickly. If not, we would be in extreme danger in our earthy dugout, and we would not be able to breathe or attempt to move for fear of discovery. But they did stop; we shakily huddled together and held each other not knowing what the next moment would hold. And then we heard the creaky wagon stop. "She's buried deep," one of the soldiers hollered. Another responded yelling, "We're gonna need some manpower and some blocking to get her out." It was quiet for a minute or so, and then we heard what we believed to be the captain shout, "Get some of those strong Indian boys over here to help us dig this sunken wagon out." The soldier walked around and finding the natives that looked in the best shape, started choosing and pointing, "You, you and you," and continued until he had singled out six young men.

The braves looked from one to the other, their minds beginning to form suspicions that being ordered to help so harshly made them feel like slaves. Maybe the true nature of this relocation is all a hoax; perhaps they are indeed going to be sold into slavery.

They would be very alert of everything that is said and done as not to fall into any kind of a trap that the Army had planned for them. There was so much shouting from the soldiers at the men urging them to dig out the stranded wagon, shouting that was less than friendly. What could be heard from inside our dugout indicated that the Army personnel were barking out orders, never dismounting from their horses. Again, perhaps this wasn't a friendly little escort to the new lands, where the Nez Perce would be the "grateful guests" with the government as "the amicable hosts." We could hear the frustration as our people worked feverishly to free the wagon from the sinkhole.

They could not work it loose as heavily laden as it was; they would need to empty the supplies from the wagon first. Once again, only the Indians were tending to the wagon unloading. Shortly thereafter, we heard the sounds of the boxes being unloaded onto the front porch of the saloon. We wanted to reach out and touch them, tell them that we were hiding in here, but we knew if we were caught, it would be the end for us. We had defied the orders given to evacuate and march with them to the reservation. So we remained tucked in tight, but deathly afraid we might be found out; they were working right outside our rubble filled trap door. And grandfather, father and mother were praying that neither grandmother nor I would groan, or sneeze or cough giving all of us away.

At that, we heard heavy boots walking over the top of us, the prickle and sickness of fear ran through our veins where blood and fluid used to. We froze like little animals caught without their mother to protect them. The sound of their voices sounded close enough that we could physically touch them, sending deadly chills throughout each of us, paralyzing us to our beds. We feared severe punishment if caught, they were certain to make an example of attempted escapees. They would not kill us though, we were sure of that. It would be detrimental to quietly dispensing all the natives to the reservations. A soldier above us yelled back out the door, "Hey Joe, come in here and see this." Each of us crouching in the hole in the ground glanced at one another, each thinking the same thought. Had we forgotten something upstairs? We thought we had completely hauled everything down through the hole in the floor. They couldn't have spotted us, with all numerous pieces of rubble and timber in addition to the large doors we had pulled over us. The man spoke again, "Look here. I found us a bottle of whiskey, no fun to drink alone." His pal said, "Hey, now that's a real treasure, we'll just be keeping it between us." "Yup, shore will," the first guy said, and then laughed.

And that was all of the conversation between the two soldiers that we could hear. They turned and started for the entrance, dragging some boards behind them, no doubt to be used to shore up the entrenched wagon. If we could view their faces, they would more than likely be wearing big grins, knowing the two of them would sneak off and share that whiskey later. We certainly wished that we had found it. It would have been beneficial for Grandmother and for me with our declining health issues. Or just for some added stamina for the others during this nerve shattering experience that was keeping them revved up with horrific fear.

Fortunately for us, they got the wagon out without too much further delay, once it had been emptied of its contents. They pulled it onto a flat area and carried the supplies to it and reloaded it once again to continue their journey. Soon, the command was given to pull out. They turned around and the caravan passed through without further incident and left

Florence. We let out our deeply held breath and relaxed our taut muscles; the experience had completely drained us. The Army must have felt pretty confident that they had rounded up everybody that they had started out with, as there were no further searches heard above us. It had been discussed long ago, that when any sort of head count was taken, if someone had slipped away, their count would be covered. A simple "here" chimed in for those not present would virtually go unnoticed in a cast of 150 people, which was the approximate total of people being moved. With our five people and the estimated twenty that had gone underground prior to the roundup the Army performed in Riggins, it would be fairly easy to cover for us. We wished that we could thank them for this glorious moment of freedom for us. Knowing that we would never be able to repay them would weigh heavy on our subconscious.

With weather that severe, it would be easy for the Army to veer off course in another direction. with the storm conditions likened to a tale of a hurricane. Our little group discussed the route that the Army would likely pursue after getting back on track from the unfortunate trail that led them into Florence. When they reached the North Fork of the Salmon River it turned south in the City of Salmon. Then they would be leaving the Salmon River as their guide and take the fork southeast on the Lemhi River. The biggest hurdle of this venture was about to confront them; they were approaching the Lemhi Pass with an elevation of 7,373 ft. It is now more commonly referred to as the Lewis & Clark Back Country Byway, and is also where they crossed the Continental Divide. The rest of the Army's trip could only be left to guesswork; they had many options once across the mountains.

We would remain within the confines of the dirt cellar for a few more days, should the Army come back looking for anyone discovered missing from the ordeal in Florence. If no one came, then we would feel safe that they had traveled a good distance from us. And also, the rest would hopefully help grandmother and me renew our strength somewhat and prepare us for the next portion of the journey ahead of us. We had been reasonably warm, dry and safe nesting in our underground haven. When we emerged into the air above, a deep cleansing breath was welcome from the damp and musty smelling earth below, but our light-deprived eyes were blinded by the brightness of the daytime sky. We would not leave Florence until this evening, but we felt secure enough to move about in the saloon the remainder of the afternoon. Everything that we had brought with us was now repacked and ready to begin our travels once more.

Chapter Six   ≈

WITH THE HELP OF FRIENDS

We had very little food left, and my mother was beginning to worry about our resources when the men told her of the next plan that they had made. It seems that they had been preparing for this escape for quite some time and had purchased three horses and a wagon. Arrangements had been made to pick them up along the Salmon River in Lowell, 50 miles from where the money had been paid for them. My parents had friends of many years, Ellsworth and Barta that lived on the north end of Salmon River Road in Grangeville. They were cherry orchard growers and provided the fruit at markets in a radius around them. My mother had met Barta at an ice cream social in Lucile many years ago, and they had become friends quickly. They introduced their new husbands to one another, and soon they were visiting each other's homes as often as possible. They were the only people that had been taken into confidence as to what our plan was and what direction that we would ultimately be seeking to travel. But that is where the knowledge stopped for everyone. While we knew we would go east, we had no specific destination in mind. There were so many factors to consider: the failing health of two members of our party, the winter weather about to befall us and how much difficulty it would require to pass through the mountains.

We set out from our comfortable lodgings in Florence and went straight out the north end of town. It was felt that there would be much less danger of being noticed if any scouts might be lurking around the area. The Army had gone straight east after turning around and would be following the Salmon River, which puts them just west of Salmon, Idaho after a week's travel. It took several days for us to crawl through the mountains, hills and valleys in our pathway. Crossing with difficulty the North Fork of Slate Creek, grandmother and I were certainly slowing down our escape, as she had been steadily becoming more ill each day. These rainy conditions had dampened more than just her spirits; the fear of pneumonia was on everyone's minds. And I was in and out of my delirium, but still burdening them with my full weight. Once we reached the rendezvous point with our friends, grandmother and I would be able to lie in the wagon, when the landscape would allow for it. Hopefully, we would find an abandoned cabin here and there and be able to harbor ourselves there when the severity of winter attacked us. The terrain now was mellow compared to what lay ahead of us, encountering Lone Knob at 5,295 ft. Gratefully, it had a fairly used trail through it; it would help to aid us through more effectively than blazing one of our own. We were certain that we would still be presented with difficult terrain to stunt our climb numerous times.

When we arrived at the planned upon meeting site in Lowell, we found our friends and saviors waiting there for us, just as they had pledged to be. Accompanying them were three of the sturdiest work horses to be found along with a good sized wagon. My father and grandfather had sold everything that we had possessed to make the purchases of these steeds that would carry us to our free life. We wouldn't have any room for furniture, dishes or large cooking pots, and these were not necessary to our travels anyway. We only took a couple cups, plates, utensils, coffee pot, a skillet and one cast iron pot with a handle for over the fire. Only a very limited amount of precious items handed down for generations would be allowable for us to remember and cherish our heritage. The wagon space was needed for our food larder, clothing, bedding and only a meager amount of them. Each horse was outfitted with saddle bags containing tools, first aid items, shotguns and their shells.

Ellsworth was a tall, sturdy man with slightly graying hair mixing with his dark hair and complexion. Contrarily, Barta was of small frame and barely five feet tall, giving them the difference of a foot and a half in height. They looked comical together, mother had said, but had most likely been drawn to one another because of their even tempers and eagerness to help those in need. They were both happy to have been able to help us, but were deeply saddened to be losing us as friends and equally saddened for us being forced to abandon our homeland. Ellsworth and Barta were not in the same position as us, they were not of Nez Perce descent and in no danger of relocation, or they would have been happy to have accompanied us on our journey. They had been camping out there a couple of days now and each night in anticipation of our arrival not knowing exactly when that would be; they would have a fire ready and waiting to welcome us. They would spend the night here agaie with us now, and we would say our goodbyes in the morning. They had a fire already built with excellent coals for roasting with an aromatic cauldron of simmering stew awaiting our arrival. Barta had also prepared fresh baked bread and delicious cherry sauce for a succulent sweet treat and put fresh coffee on the campfire when we arrived. This would be our only hot meal for a long while, and they were glad to provide it for us as our last dinner together...forever.   They had formulated a plan should anyone come along: we would sink out of sight and they would answer any questions that the strangers might have. They would cover for us by saying that they were relocating which would logically explain the four horses and supply laden wagon. Two to pull the wagon and two to tow along behind them for when they chose to ride, would be their story. Actually, we were taking two for the men to ride, one for our wagon and they would keep one for theirs. Our dear friends were very giving in nature and had added a substantial amount of their own goods from their winter larder to sustain us through the mountainous climb. If there had been any possible situation by which we could live safely in their dirt cellar, they would have been ready to harbor us.

However, our family would not involve them any further; our consciences would be blackened if any ill should befall the two of them on our account. They had risked enough trekking to Lowell for our convenience and worrying there on whether we would make it or not. This location was chosen because it would put us at the Clearwater River, which would be our guide to and through Lolo Pass. This pass is treacherous and we expected to spend most of these next few months encased by its various crevices and peaks. Lewis and Clark on their search for the Northwest Passage had followed the Clearwater River and charted the Lolo Pass. That charting would be our only guide to lead us through to the other side of the mountains and on to a new homeland. The distance the men estimated that we would cover after leaving Lowell and up through the pass, and we reached the Montana side, was approximately 125 miles. If we were fortunate enough to make it through everything that would challenge us along the way.

We arose in the misty, foggy hours of the morning to the pleasant aroma of coffee, smells of food cooking and a hot inviting fire. Ellsworth and Barta had awakened earlier to make sure that we would have something hot to eat before we left. Biscuits and gravy and that wonderful smelling coffee were the perfect traveling farewell meal. When we had finished our breakfast, we added the rest of our things to the wagonload of fresh items that they had brought for us. They were willing to risk allowing themselves to run short of food for the winter. They knew that they would get by; they were not being forced to leave their home. They were healthy individuals who would survive on daily, reduced food consumption. Aside from the run-in that Ellsworth had with a puma that left a gash across his stomach, he was fine. Along with a gracious amount of jerky, fish, cherries, and huckleberries, Barta had also generously given us a good share of her winter's stock of camas roots as well.

And then it was time to depart, time to say their painful goodbyes. Grandmother and I were arranged in the wagon on top of our bedding and clothing and the supplies around us and prepared for the long journey. Barta began to cry and my mother and she clung together and sobbed into each other's shoulders. Barta said, "Oh, Isadora, I will never forget our friendship of all these years." My mother replied shakily, "And I will always remember you as my special friend and all we've shared together, both our laughter and our tears." Barta tried to speak but was unable to be audible above the uncontrollable sadness she was feeling. Isadora, her voice equally unstable managed some control and spoke, "Good friends don't fade away; they live within your heart." Barta nodded several times, still not able to speak her feelings. They pulled themselves apart and Barta reached into the wagon and gave me a comforting pat on my back and a kiss on the forehead and likewise with my grandmother. I was told that she brushed the back of her hand across my hot and sweaty face and said she would pray every day that I would recover. The women had discussed their fears the night before, that pneumonia was setting into grandmother with our escape into the rain and that very likely would cost Annahah her health and possibly her life. And it quite probably had added another affliction to my already fragile condition. The men shook hands, firmly and gripped with emotions. They looked each other hard in the eye; each knowing it would be for the last time. Our little wagon train started off, the women and men both holding tears in their eyes as they said goodbye and waved until we were out of sight.

The Lochsa River and Lolo Trail would be our road map toward freedom for a long time to come to the east. The river branches off of the Middle Fork of the Clearwater River at Kooskia and extends all the way across the state to Powell Junction where it curves downward to the southeast. The beginning of our journey will take us to Lone Knob with an elevation almost equal to the region that borders Idaho and Montana, called Lolo Pass. Lolo is a Chinook word which translated means "to carry"' so we will have faith that we will be carried to safety using the Lolo Trail. After the Nez Perce acquired horses in the 1700s, it became the main thoroughfare from the Weippe Prairie to harvest camas roots to the prairies of Montana to hunt buffalo. For now, this area lying ahead of us is open and will be a fairly level trail for awhile, with very few encumbrances. But then, travel will become increasingly difficult with downed timber, boulders, steep grades and snowstorms until we clear the Lolo Pass. The family had estimated that it would likely take several months for us to cross over without any emergencies to delay us. Even if the plan executed itself perfectly, it would take a miracle to reach the other side in any amount of time less than late springtime.

Chapter Seven   ≈

THE NIGHTMARE ENSUES

Our progress on that first day went extremely well, and we were about halfway onto Lone Knob when dusk came. We found a small clearing in a densely wooded area and felt that this would be the best we would find tonight. Building a small fire would be alright, just enough to be effective; we did not want it to be seen from any distance. It would warm and soothe us from the day's travel as well as heat our supper. The men justified it with the thought that we wouldn't be at risk from discovery while we were here on the mountain. They felt that the Army would have expected us to push straight north into Canada, on the plains, the easier route of escape. It would probably never be considered that we would dare to tackle such a dangerous area to make our way to safety.

After a short night of sleep, we took up the trail again in the morning; we wanted to get as high as possible, as soon as possible. Things went smoothly for awhile; we had picked up a logging trail that had been used recently, indicated by the familiar drag marks cutting a path. In mid afternoon, we encountered our first bit of trouble; there was a huge boulder blocking the way that we wouldn't be able to deal with. We stopped for a rest break then, to contemplate what should be done next. There was no opportunity to go around it. We had a solid rock wall on one side and the steep edge of another cliff on the other. We had to go back down the mountain two switchbacks to the left. There were plenty of rocks to challenge us along the way there and there would be plenty of delays and other issues for us to deal with. But most of the rocks could be dragged off the line of travel with one or two of the horses pulling them without too much strain. We made it to what we felt was the tip of Lone Knob, and my mother told me that father and grandfather laughed around the campfire that night. They were very happy that the first leg of the journey had gone fairly well, and were hopeful that we were under a sign of luck the remainder of the trip. Mother said she did not feel much like laughter. She looked back and forth between my grandmother and myself and wondered if we would both make it.

Lone Knob provided no more issues for us; we climbed over it without too much time delay. The small encumbrances that presented themselves to us were easy for us to handle. We hadn't found any indoor shelter yet to spend the night, but our ancestors were watching over us and approved of what we were doing to save ourselves. We always found something to shield us from the wind, or hide us from the snow that was beginning to fall. My parents and grandparents truly believed that those who have passed on before us would help to carry us to a new world.

My mother was scanning the area as she rode up front in the wagon being handled by Grandfather. It had been snowing for two days now and we desperately needed to find somewhere to stay that was out of the cold and was dry. She sighed relief at the sight of the open area spotted above and the gentle slope of the approach. Arrival up there was swift and when we reached the clearing, things became even more accommodating; a cave entrance lay dead ahead of us. This was without a doubt the best of the stops for overnight stays for protection from the winter elements. A fire built inside the dry cave would be hotter and last longer, we would truly sleep comfortably in the warmer temperature. The blessing of the spirits had provided this safe haven for us, and the decision was made to remain here awhile, at least until the snow stopped falling. We would be able to thaw out our stiff, frozen and aching bodies and prepare for the second half of mountainous climbing over the Bitterroots. The men were a little concerned about the smoke swirling around us and making us ill or disoriented. They set up our fire ring about half in and half out of the opening of the cave and our sleeping area directly behind it, imagining that this would be the most logical method. Most caves have cracks, holes, or passages, which would allow the ventilation of the fumes somewhat. They had been researching this issue for the real possibility of finding just such places to stop and refurbish ourselves.

During our restful stay in our stone encased home, supplies were abundant to be gathered. In the mountains you can be buried in snow and then turn the corner and find green grass and plants waiting. Mother had found numerous varieties of roots, flowers, herbs, bark and fruit buds at her disposal. She had been able to make tea, medicine, and flavorings for broth, stews, and meat. And to pass the time riding she would grind the fruit buds to make enough soap to last our journey. The oversized saddlebags of the horses would be stuffed with these items; they might not be so lucky to find much on the mountaintop. The men were able to add several rabbits and squirrels to our menu and ensured they would remain frozen for later use on the trail.

My mother made some healthy soups and stew's while in our home of nature's rock and was able to feed her two sickly charges and try to build our strength some. She was an amazing woman with many talents, she could handle anything thrown at her, and could use everything found in the wild to our advantage somehow. Whether it be for food, clothing, lodging, she could always be counted on to come through with the littlest amount of means possible.

Grandmother was barely uttering a word now, she was becoming listless and more tired each day. Mother believed she was digressing into the deep stages of the same fever that I had been battling for months now. And while I was young and could battle it out, she most likely would not be able to. But grandfather believed that if she hadn't mentally felt as if our world had ended, she would fight to recover. She needed to be reminded to remember those of us still present in her life and with her on this quest for new lands. She was a frail, wisp of a woman to start with and this time spent in the cave would hopefully boost her spirits as well as her physical condition. Annahah was so broken hearted over leaving her homeland and the members of the dear families, that it affected her health gravely. My mother also was lonesome for her comfortable home on Allison Creek, and the once peaceful existence they had all known and loved. This long, cross-country excursion would toll sadly on all members of this family; my mother had felt it almost as soon as it was suggested for their course of action. Having to disassemble the tribe and divide up all of the families was a gruesome step in itself, but now having Josie so ill and grandmother falling prey to such a deadly virus, was too much sadness for five people to suffer. My mother's instincts were usually right ninety-nine percent of the time; if only more people had made it into the tunnels, perhaps we would be among them now.

The Army would no doubt realize that two different branches of the family were missing once their journey to the reservation came to a close. But it was most improbable that any attempt would be made to locate them now that the December snowstorms had begun. But in the spring, they would assuredly be pressing hard to round up the escapees. They could not allow themselves to be thought weak for losing them and would be seeking their revenge. By then, Alphonse's family would be the only ones they would even have a chance of finding, and they had taken precautions to remain underground in the caves at least one full year. They would need to sneak a few strong, crafty people out to hunt, trap, fish, and gather wood and supplies without being caught. If it was absolutely necessary, someone would be allowed to leave and travel north for the purpose of trading, but only as a last resort if they were running low on things that they could not live without. They had even thought before the move of the fact it may be difficult to keep the smoke from their fires from escaping. But because of extensive tunnels, the smoke would be drafted through a mire of vents and lost in the cave system without notice from the outside. And once actually occupying their rock fortress, they could further work on creating a habitat beneficial to them.

We no longer felt at risk for capture so high up in the majestic rock formations of Idaho. If the Army had any notion that we had gone this direction, search parties would assume that we had frozen to death along the way. They would think fools of us, that at least we would be alive if we had allowed them to take us with all of the others to the reservation and warmer climates. They wouldn't search for us up here, and Father said that was the crucial reason for my family to choose to encounter the most intricate and treacherous passes through the steep, jagged mountains running along the Lolo Canyons. If we succeed in our mission to cross over, all risk will be justified.

And so the nightmare began, tackling crossing a mountain was difficult enough, but towing a wagon would make it an unrealistic expectation. But where there is determination, there are results, and both of the men and my mother were certainly stubborn enough to not give up without a desperate fight. Our first upward grade steadily increased as we pursued what looked like remnants of a trail to the left. That was a good choice as it took us from left to right and back and forth in a series of several switchbacks. The Spirit of Good Luck seemed to be working closely with us in our endeavor up the mountain. We had reached a steep cliff at the end of the switchbacks, we stopped for a lunch of water, jerky and bread while studying what lay before us and contemplating the next move. It was decided to backtrack about 200 feet, where they had noticed a break between cliffs. We entered the crevice; it was barely wide enough for the wagon to pass through, but they managed to squeeze it to the other side. We were only about one quarter of the way up and it had been easy going, but soon it would become much, much harder to maneuver.

The snow had started now to add to our difficulty, the rocks were slippery and the ground was frozen. After we passed through the crevice we were left with nothing but steep sides no matter which way we chose to go. We would stay here tucked into the crevice's sharp walls, with its one overhang keeping us free from the wind and leaving us reasonably dry. The men struck out to scout the area for firewood and a new route once again; there was simply no way up from here. If this was to be the constant progression of things, we were in for a long and grueling climb. The wood gathered was sparse and we would need to find all we could to mix with our dry supply. If we did not gather some each day, we would run out quickly. And our survival up here in the mountains depended on the warmth of a daily fire; freezing to death in the mountains was a pretty common occurrence. The men returned with their arms loaded down and smiles on their cold, red faces. Not only had they found a new way to go, but also they could see a definite opening up above where it appeared it would become easier for awhile. So our wagon was wedged back through the crevice again and we started in the direction of our new trail.

Thus far Grandmother and I had been able to be wagon bound most of the time, and now I was beginning to show signs of slight awareness, I was told. A great feeling of relief came over them all. It is very rare for anyone to survive smallpox, and for as many months as it had a grip on me, they all felt that my death was imminent. It was then that my mother noticed my fluttering eyelids. I wasn't opening them, but she said there was definite movement under the lids. Mother told me that I began moving my fingers a little as she was warming me in front of the fire that evening. In addition to each of us sleeping with a hot rock from the fire, my mother also warmed our bedding that way. She labored to keep us as warm as was afforded during travel time. With me being in a coma and grandmother slowly sinking into dangerous health, we had no circulation flowing within us, so our risk of frostbite increased one hundred times. My mother was diligent in her duties and was our constant nursemaid and protector. When she wasn't warming us, she was attempting to get water for hydration into us and coffee for additional warmth. She was becoming pretty exhausted herself; this trip was weighing heavily upon her, trying to keep alive the two most important women in her world.

Morning came and it was getting much colder, but today was clear, no sign of any perverse weather, which made travel easier, allowing us to get an early lead on what was yet to come. Camp for the night was at the mountain base in another cavern. This one was much larger than the last, allowing them more space to move around and re-organize everything. Frederick and Ignatious stood before the mountain and tried to imagine a way over her largeness. The men had plotted a sketchy map based on topographical information of public knowledge before we had set out. That was the only thing helpful in aiding them to design the new route. Because they had chosen not to inform anyone in any of the other families, no one knew they were planning this mad escape route. The benefit of their knowledge of this area was lost to us. And here we are, just such a tiny fraction of the family trying to get away from capture. And now we were faced with the impossibility of reaching the crest with only three people capable of anything, and burdened by two incapacitated persons and a heavily laden wagon. They had discussed all the possibilities that could be seen by them and drew it out on writing paper, but nothing scribbled on paper is quite like the real thing. Several drafts were drawn before they formulated the course that they felt would be the most feasible, and prayed it would lead them over the top of Lolo.

Within our days of protection in the cave dwelling, the men had been preparing for the rugged task awaiting us. The wagon had been disassembled and they had attached rope to the pieces, and our supplies were bundled up, too. Then they had hooked our fine work horses to the parcels or wagon pieces to transport everything up to the top of our first difficult hurdle. They had slipped, skidded and started over, but they accomplished the task set before them. Animals can show complete dedication to their masters when called upon to do so. It had not stormed nor were there any high winds to hinder them, and they were able to work steadily during the daylight hours. All that was left to task was our bedding, and that would be bundled around the two of us who could not make it on our own. We would be strapped onto the horse, and my parents would risk injury to themselves to ensure that we would not fall off the horse. While the horses lunged and struggled to keep their footing on the slippery surfaces of the rocks, they possibly could be dragged along by the horses. It was a dangerous, yet very necessary risk to take, and injury to those riding or leading the horse was quite probable in the icy conditions of the landscape awaiting us.

The next few trips up this ice laden landscape, the cargo would be more precious and fragile than the supplies were. My grandmother was hoisted up first, and my mother and father accompanied the horse, one on each side, with rein in hand to keep the horse on a straight path. Grandfather waited with me below, fearful that one of the three would be seriously injured in the attempt. The horse jumped for the first ledge of rock, but could only get his front hoofs up on it and slid back off of it. Perhaps feeling the weight of a person's body was different from the items the faithful horse had dragged up there earlier. Mother and Father got above the horse and gently urged it to keep going and lunge for the next shelf. The horse tried and slipped sideways nearly knocking my father back off to the step below. But they both regained their footholds and tried it again with better success and reached the top. My mother started to slide down from both ledges and picked up quite a bit of momentum and was jostled and turned around and landed nearby to grandfather and I. She said she was unharmed, but grandfather had seen her somersault down the icy rocks between the two ledges and land hard. She was only a bit dazed; the body would likely not suffer until later when swelling and black and blue bruises would be prevalent. But still, she was physically intact, which was a lucky break, one more invalid would have immobilized our group.

It couldn't be risked that there would be any more accidents; they would have to change their method now and not use the horses again for help. Mother and Father aided my grandfather in his climb up the sharp incline, but tied ropes around his waist. In the event that he should slip, they could control it somewhat. This went much more smoothly than the dangerous method my poor, fragile grandmother had been subjected to, and in hindsight they realized what a terrible idea that was. My body was limp and uncooperative, so I was wrapped in blankets to cushion me from the pointed edges of the stone and ice. It was the least degree of difficulty of the three maneuvers. They spent quite some time wrapping and padding me tightly before moving me. My father climbed back up on the first ledge and with my mother steadying me from below, pulled me up on to the first narrow lip. My mother then hauled herself onto the ledge next to me, and then they performed the same routine again until we were all safely on the same shelf. And thankfully, only one of the three of them had fallen and mother was not injured seriously.

That had been excruciating, grinding work on their backs and muscles and set their hearts pumping fiercely. The two of them lay there in the snow trying to regain their strength and composure and just looking at each other wondering if they truly were doing the rational thing. Too late now though for regrets, there would be no turning back; there couldn't be, they would just have to go ahead with their plans to eventually cross the Rocky Mountains. It was hard for them to not remember that just a couple of weeks ago, we had all been in our cozy house on Allison Creek, awaiting the departure, warm and comfortable, and certainly not anticipating this much difficulty. They knew that it would be complicated enough to be traveling with me in my weakened and sickly state, but no one foresaw that grandmother would also become ill.

When everyone had rested a bit, it was time to forge on to shelter. This process had lasted the whole day and we would remain here for this night. Things would be a little simpler for awhile now. We were as high as we needed to climb, and we would now start east around the mountains. There would be no more cliffs to tackle now and the distance around was shorter because of our height. The decline on the other side had to be less challenging. They could not repeat the incidents of today, and going downhill was often more treacherous than going uphill. When first light came, the men reassembled the wagon, and it had been reloaded with our things as well as grandmother and I. We would follow the ledge that we had fought ourselves onto and should progress about halfway around if the landscape should be that accommodating.

Once there we found a mass of downed trees and a multitude of brush piles that would provide our shelter for that evening. Moving things around a bit created an opening in the center for us to bed down for the night, and we piled some brush high to protect us from the force of the winds so prevalent in higher altitudes. The next day raised no more challenges to face and it was a smooth, pleasant couple of days of hiking in the Bitterroot Mountains and toward our destination. From our viewpoint above, we were able to see downward fairly clearly and it did not look like our descent would be insurmountable. All of the extra time that was provided by the flatter surface of travel would help aid us down to meet the Clearwater River once again.

The sooner we made it safely somewhere into civilization, the sooner help could be obtained for the two severely ill and declining females. Grandfather was becoming increasingly worried about us and the strain was visible on his weathered face. He was afraid that he was about to lose two of the three precious women in his life, which would deeply sadden him. He had been quite adamant about striking out on our own and leaving Riggins far behind, and he didn't want this to become something he would regret for the rest of his life. They told me that it was at this point in the trip that they felt that I had progressed enough, even as slowly as it had been, that they knew then that I would indeed make a full recovery given time. The warm blankets, hot soup, tea, medicine and all the diligent care my mother had tediously performed had brought me back to life, brought me back to them.

The canyons that we were winding through had been cut by glaciers long ago, and Lewis and Clark had trudged through here on their discovery quest. The treacherous Salmon River of No Return pushed them back, they had and crossed at Lolo one century ago in 1805. After they had announced to the world that they had found a fairly navigable route to the majestic, towering Rocky Mountains, this area had been well traveled. We had expected to run into people eventually and were surprised that an encounter hadn't happened yet. We were hoping that we would be able to cross the border in two months time, if we did not experience any delays. Hopefully, we would be able to find a place to settle in for the rest of the winter, and acquire and stock food items and begin traveling again in the springtime. There possibly could be a logging camp operation somewhere around where Father could find some temporary winter work for money to help with our relocation.

The men felt confident to have chosen this route; Lone Knob had been quite mild. They had feared that Lolo would be so treacherous that they may fail in their attempt to scale her. But, the next portion of the journey around was uneventful and the winding trails and rock surfaces were kind enough to present no great obstacles for us. So uneventful that our little party of five was reassured that they could take whatever following the Clearwater River through the Lolo Pass would present to them. Other people had traveled both directions through the Rockies and survived. Today there are millions of acres undeveloped such as the Gospel Hump Wilderness and Frank Church Wilderness in Idaho that the United States has declared to remain untouched. The Macgruder Road Corridor snaking through the various elevations from Idaho into Darby, MT, is also one of the land rich areas preserving the wilderness as well. Being stubborn and determined, they would make it through any wilderness confronting us, they would not give up and all five of us would make it to the Montana border. We would all be present, but doubtful that all of us would be alive. They had previously feared it would likely be me in my poor health that would succumb to death. But, now that my fever had broken and I was showing definite signs of recovery, it seems that Grandmother Annahah will not make it to her sister's home in Fort Assinniboine in Havre, Montana alive.

Finally, we found a welcoming little cabin shortly after we began to ascend this beautiful landmark. The snow is beginning to fall hard up here, and we are desperately in need of shelter for this evening. We have been traveling for days now without a proper covering for us to eat or sleep, harboring ourselves in any protection of trees, rock formations, anything that would get us away from the wind and snow's harm. When we turned a corner and saw this sturdy looking structure, my mother said she cried with relief. She was so cold that her emotions were right at the surface. She was sure they would all freeze to death. No amount of bodily contact was working to keep each of us warm and our blood circulating within us, and today she felt as if we would all freeze to death. This place saved us for now, and each capable person began to develop a daily routine" mother of warming and feeding grandmother and I properly again, and father and grandfather caring for the horses, hunting for fresh meat and seeking wood for the fireplace in the cabin. It would not be necessary to go through the difficult task of cooking over an open fire outside, the cabin had a wood stove for that as well as for warmth. This was the first actual house-like structure that we had enjoyed thus far; we will certainly appreciate each moment spent in this little home that had been abandoned. We would remain here for some time. To feel the protectiveness of a roof and four walls to shelter us properly was an opportunity not to be passed over. We had been fortunate enough though, to keep coming across something that would serve as a covering of some sort. We were most definitely being looked after by the spirit world at the end of each day. Or perhaps the families in the other encampments were thinking of us and performing ceremonies in our honor and for our safety. Not knowing what happened to us, where we had gone, how we had left; that must be haunting them.

Grandfather told me that after we had been squatting in the cabin for a couple of weeks, I showed my most significant increase in mobility to this point. My eyes had opened one morning, and I was able to move my body somewhat and shift positions slightly. My mother cried over me with relief, for now she was certain that her little girl would someday be their lively young lady, ready for a new, full life. We moved along slowly now, trying to cover ground, but constantly attending to grandmother and trying to keep her comfortable and alive. Mother pleaded with the men to reconsider leaving this homelike dwelling in solitude and dig out in the spring. But all they talked about steadily was plodding on until they were over the Idaho border into the neighboring state of Montana. It did little good for her to present her case to these dedicated, hard driven men. Remaining here was not in their realm of thinking. But grandmother was continually spiraling downward at a rapid rate, and the fear of losing her had now become a certainty. My mother had tried the same methods of medicine and healing rituals as she had performed on me, but someone much older and so very fragile had just too many strikes against them. Her fever was high and she was in about the same condition that I was in when we left our home on the creek, and she had fallen now into a coma of her own.

Another shelter was not found for our next night's respite. We had no alternative but to stop for the night under a cluster of trees, which was unfortunate as the temperatures had been quite frigid today. The three of us women huddled together in the wagon for collection of our body heat to keep the blood in Grandmother's veins from turning to ice. The men had pulled the wagon around for the back opening to face the heat and kept it hot and blazing all night. The men slept close to the fire, taking turns feeding it throughout the evening and replacing our hot, sleeping stones when necessary. It was imperative that one person remain awake at all times. Should the fire be lost, we would all freeze to death. The morning brought promise of sunshine and indeed it was with us most of the day. It served to lift our spirits as well as warm us throughout, and we thanked our ancestors for watching over us on that particular night.

Our group needs to remain on the south side of the River to go through the Lolo Pass with an elevation of 5,233 feet, almost 2,000 feet less than Rhodes Peak on the north side, which is 7,950 high. For anyone to cross over and go that route would be a huge error, the extra height would present more problems to face and more time of travel. We need to stay focused on this course; it will lead us to our final destination in the end. Directly after we pass through Lolo, there is a natural hot spring that our people have been bathing in for generations. Its rewards are so great that it is said to have tremendous healing powers, and people return many, many times for various ailments. There is a hot spring pool in our former home, possibly this could have aided in my recovery after experiencing the warm steaminess and the power of the healing waters. My parents and grandfather prayed to be guided safely there before they lost grandmother. They were hopeful that perhaps she would be saved if we experienced the waters of the great ground spring and recited our ceremonial chants.

After further travel, we found another shack in these mountains to serve as our temporary home, but this one wasn't quite as accommodating as the first one. There wasn't much left of it, it had so obviously been abandoned long ago. Nevertheless, it was under cover. The sky was indicating severe weather on the way, and we could already feel the threat hanging in the air of a blizzard. We needed to be indoors somewhere, anywhere, tonight. It was a small place, but it did have a partial cellar underneath, which added a little insulation to the building. There was nothing else to provide even a little bit of warmth to us. We would have to rely on each other; there would be no fire tonight.

The men found pieces of boards here and there outside that had probably been blowing off for years. And the wind was howling and swirling around outside, while they were collecting enough to patch the holes in the walls and windows which had all been broken out. They struggled to get them inside the cabin and nailed them over all openings exposed to the winter storm. Once that was finished, the cabin would at least be free from snow and wind for our stay there. Whoever had moved out of here had taken care to completely gut the inside of all possessions and furniture. All that remained were a couple boards nailed from one end of the cabin to the other to form a bench or perhaps it had been used as a narrow bed. It was sturdier than the rest of the place and my father carried my grandmother to it and gently placed her on upon it for this night; at least she would be off of the cold wood floor. And my mother said she had lain with her to provide body heat to her now immobile body. Most of the floorboards were rotten, and the men gingerly crept in and positioned our bedding on the floor for them and me for this long, cold night. Fearing that too much movement might find us falling through the weak layer of worn boards to the ground floor of the cellar, our sleep was strained and sparse. It was necessary to concentrate on remaining absolutely as motionless as was possible to do so, which made it difficult to keep our circulation moving. But, sleeplessness and a cold winter night would not prevent tomorrow from coming and bringing with it a very important day in the saga of our escape to the Bitterroots.

While lying there awaiting slumber to overcome us, I woke up and asked where we were. Each of them, as we lay in the decaying structure, with tears in their voices, welcomed me back to them. My father was laying on one side of me with my grandfather on the other, each reached over to touch me to reassure me that this was not a dream world. They said they had been waiting and praying for this to happen; the gods would not punish them by losing me. This was the real thing; I was there with only them, cold and shivering in a dank, empty hovel high in the Bitterroot Mountains, far away from any form of civilization. My mother was cuddled together with her mother on the wall's bench, and she greeted me back into reality from there. She told me that grandmother wasn't feeling well and she could not leave the makeshift bench for fear of falling through the weak floorboards. Grandfather took my hand in his and squeezed it hard and told me gently to lie still, and when I woke up in the morning, his hand was still there. And then mother warned the others that I was still too weak to fully grasp the situation and would need plenty of time to adjust and understand. And with that brief amount of information, as I was falling back to sleep, I heard my mother, say, "Frederick, I hope this does not send Josie back to her coma. When she starts remembering on her own, she may not want to be here." What did she mean by that? Why would I want to be anywhere else except here with my family? Unless, she meant that I had to give up the rest of our family as they did, and my friends, home and surroundings. Yes, that's what she must have been talking about; we had left everyone behind and gone our own direction.

Chapter Eight ≈

THE DEVASTATION OF THE NEZ PERCE

The expression has been widely phrased, "When Indians and horses roamed the lands." And that is precisely how life used to be for the Nez Perce tribe as well as every other Native American tribe living peacefully on a chunk of land. Their only inhibitor was the other tribes desiring to encroach upon their land when their own resources had been depleted. Then usually a war between them was inevitable, the goal of one to retain their territory and the goal of the other to claim it as their own. These attacks most often resulted in brutal massacres which were carefully planned to wipe out the inhabitants of the area desired. But still there were numerous tribes who were content to live where they were born and respected the boundaries of the others. It is those people who are easily persuaded to give up what they have and fall prey to broken promises. Recorded history has taught us that this is precisely what happened to the Nez Perce tribal community.

In 1855, a deal was struck in the form of a treaty allowing the Nez Perce to occupy and roam on ten thousand acres in northwestern Idaho. But when gold was discovered in Pierce, Idaho in 1860, and the Idaho Territory was established in 1863, the Nez Perce were pressured by the government to revise that treaty. It would require them to reduce the size of their reservation to a meager twelve hundred acres. In May of 1863 at Fort Lapwai, a council comprised of military and government officials and some of the chiefs was conducted. Among them being Christian Chief's Lawyer, Timothy, Jason and Levi. They agreed to the reduction in land size and placed their signature on a document stating thusly. They were not overly concerned by the issue because scarcely any of their own land was involved. Chief Joseph and the other chiefs who would be robbed of their venue became very angry with this situation and went home to their respective villages.

The government attempted to hold the argument that the signatures that they did have should account for all members of the Nez Perce tribe. But Major Wood, the Adjutant General who investigated the problem for General Oliver O. Howard, declared that not to be the case. The non-treaty Nez Perce were not bound by the treaty and should not be deprived of their locations. But the treaty was never ratified to reflect this finding of Major Wood and any promises made or payments promised went unfulfilled. When Old Joseph was dying, his son, Young Joseph vowed to his father that he would never sell any of their lands to anyone.

The reverence felt between members of the same birthright is the most extreme example of monogamy in history. The measure of disrespect that one Nez Perce felt for another is approximately one in one   hundred thousand. They quite simply did not revolt against each other and their loyalty is deeply dedicated to the protection of each member from infant to aged. They will kill for or die for another without a moment's hesitation. Their existence became complicated with the introduction of the white man into the equation. The whites attempted to employ several tactics to persuade the red man that he was uncivilized and uneducated and they regarded them as indigent savages.

The Native Americans were found living a life unaccustomed to and unheard of by the white man. They were told they needed to be as educated, governed and Christianized as the people living in the eastern portions of the states were. But they were, in fact, proficient in all three of these areas already. Each person was taught the ways of the Indian from birth and steadfastly continued these teachings throughout their lives. They had rankings of stature beginning with the chief and ending with a newborn destined for greatness or leadership. Beliefs were present and practiced in everyday life and the reverence held for those above and their ancestors were of the highest element of worship.

But no one viewed these newly found people appropriately. They were told they needed to change and conform to the ways of the white man. The Europeans introduced them to alcohol to drink in celebration and changed these passive human beings into loud aggressive individuals. There had been no severe illnesses or afflictions present in their world prior to the exposure to the smallpox which between 1780 and 1810 killed one half of the native population. Many recordings revealed an intention to do so by offering contaminated clothing to them as gifts for the sole purpose of infecting them. The Indians were clean people who bathed regularly in the lakes and rivers, while the Army personnel never took the time to. But because of their skin color they were treated as the dirty creatures. Most of the traditions were regarded as foolishness and unfounded: how could people possibly believe that holding events in honor of something do any good? Ceremonials dances were performed for protection from harm, in support of a good harvest and hope for abundant game to feed their people.

It was also thought that each individual had a good spirit looking out for them to guide them through life and nurture them in the skill that he or she possessed. Some of their intuitions have proved themselves to have had merits in many situations. On Lost Trail Pass there is a tree named Medicine Tree. It has a ram's horn stuck in it eight feet off of the ground. The Indians believed that passing by it would give them premonitions, and after passing it in 1877 on their way to Montana, several people had visions of a battle to occur. Four days later in the Battle of Little Big Hole, ninety Nez Perce warriors were lost. How dissimilar are these beliefs from the beliefs of the white man in his worship of entities or items placed in a position of respect?

After old Chief Joseph died, Young Joseph took up his position as Chief of the Wallowa band of the Nez Perce in the state of Washington. Even though he and his followers had never agreed to give up their country, they eventually realized they had no choice anymore. So they started out for Idaho with their destination the reservation at located in Lapwai. But they never made it to be incarcerated on the little area at all. Perhaps that would have been a better fate than the one that would befall them.

In June of 1877, on their journey, three young braves decided to seek some revenge on some local white people. Chief Joseph and the others fearing the worst, flew a white flag immediately and signaled that they wanted to speak with the commander of a cavalry unit of about one hundred soldiers camped down in White Bird Creek. The flag was ignored and the cavalrymen attacked the surrendering Nez Perce, and even though the Army outnumbered them, the Army lost thirty-four men and the Nez Perce didn't lose any. Now they were forced to flee and fight, so they headed northeast hoping to reach their friends the Crow tribe in Montana, or even Sitting Bull, who had fled to Canada the year before after the Battle of the Bighorn.

But it was Chief Joseph's time to fight, and it became one of the most incredible wars in all of our American heritage. Covering one thousand, seven hundred miles and lasting almost four months, the Nez Perce fled across the state of Idaho. They performed many acts of elusion and disappearance baffling General Howard who was pursuing them tightly. When he finally caught them at the Clearwater River, the Nez Perce warriors kept six hundred soldiers at bay while Chief Joseph escaped. He led the old men, women and children toward Montana and away from the fighting. Feeling that they were in the clear, they began to travel slowly. They struggled over the treacherous Bitterroot Mountains via the untamed Lolo Trail and believed they were out of reach of the Army now. But they were not; the camp was attacked by soldiers from Fort Missoula in Montana on August 9. The Nez Perce lost many people but slipped away again, and it was a little over a month before the Army caught up to them again. On September 13, the Nez Perce took victory once again in a bloody battle, but were saddened to see that their friends the Crow had been recruited to ride with the Army, thus ending that friendship and increasing the size of the enemy's forces considerably.

They had to reach Sitting Bull in Canada now, where he had fled after the Battle of the Big Horn devastated his tribe. They had exhausted all other options; they had to manage to get over the border to freedom. On September 30, beaten down by the chase and still running, they stopped by the Snake Creek on the northern edge of the Bear Paw Mountains. With just under thirty miles to travel, they were again assaulted by troops from Montana with Colonel Nelson A. Miles in charge. The Nez Perce took down sixty cavalrymen, and the result was a draw between parties. The chiefs argued for five bitter, winter days, and Chief Joseph's decision was to surrender. But seventy year old Chief White Bird did not share that decision. He took two hundred members and quietly passed over the border into Canada during the night hours.

On October 5, Chief Joseph mounted his horse and rode into Colonel Miles camp to announce his reluctant decision to give up and give in. He was scarred by bullets about his body and had bullet holes in his clothing; he had been close to death himself many times. He decided it was best for the remaining four hundred of the tribe's people and himself to stop the fighting. The results of their efforts had been costly; they had lost many in their struggle to roam freely about the land. It is quoted that he said this to Colonel Nelson A. Miles upon surrendering:

> "I am tired of fighting…The old men are all dead…The little children are freezing to death. My people, some of them, have run away to the hills and have no blankets, no food. No one knows where they are… Hear me my chiefs! I am tired; my heart is sick and sad. From where the sun now stands, I will fight no more forever."

In recent years however, a linguist of the Nez Perce language assembled written evidence that Chief Joseph's famous speech was never given. It is believed that this was a ruse assembled by Major Wood for a magazine publication of that era. Whether the speech was given or not by Chief Joseph himself, it correctly stated the situation of the plight of the Nez Perce from his standpoint.

Colonel Miles comforted Joseph by promising him that they would be returned to their Idaho reservation. But General

William Tecumseh Sherman superceded Miles in authority and ordered that they be sent to Fort Leavenworth along the bottomlands of the Missouri river in Kansas to be held as prisoners.   Almost half of the people contracted malaria. Twenty-one people died there and no one ever adjusted to the hot, humid and unhealthy temperatures there.   They were then transferred to the Quapaw Agency in Indian Territory which is what we call Oklahoma today.   That was seven thousand acres of sand and sage brush where approximately fifty people died, they were relocated three times within that same territory and the death toll continued to rise.   Over one hundred children alone perished, one of them being Chief Joseph's own daughter. In 1881, an Indian Agent Thomas Jordan recorded only three hundred, twenty-eight survivors and concluded that it was not the fault of the Indians.   He said that unless something was done to save them, they would soon be extinct. He further vindicated them by saying that they were careful people in relation to their health and logistics were the blame of their deaths. He was quoted as saying that "They are cleanly to a fault...They keep their stock in good working order, and are hard working and painstaking people."

The Nez Perce remained incarcerated there for seven years and it was finally made possible for the remaining one hundred and fifty people to return to the Colville Reservation in the state of Washington.   Chief Joseph had relentlessly petitioned the government to allow their return to their home reservation reciting the promise of Colonel Miles made to him in 1877. He was allowed to travel to Washington, D.C. and spoke eloquently before President Rutherford B. Hayes, members of the congress, cabinet members and other important dignitaries who were anxious to meet the famous "Indian Napoleon" as he was dubbed. He delivered his final argument on that day in January, 1879:

> "You might as well expect the rivers to run backwards as that any man who was born free should be contented penned up and denied liberty... Let me be a free man— free to travel, free to stop, free to work, free to trade, where I choose...free to think and act and talk for myself."

But they did not honor his request even with the testimonials of Colonel Miles and General Howard who both interceded on his behalf and pleaded for his return home. Chief Joseph and his followers remained on the Colville Reservation, and he passed away peacefully sitting in front of his teepee in 1904. He had been allowed to visit his father's grave in the Wallowa Valley in 1900, and while he was there asked a group of white settlers to set aside a parcel of land for them. Their response: "You are not welcome here."

As in all confrontations between the government and all Native American peoples, in the end, the natives were forced to succumb to the will of the white man. All the Indians were guilty of was occupying land desired by more powerful individuals who greatly outnumbered them. They did not deserve the treatment extended to them and the denial of any right to ownership to their birth lands.

Chief Joseph or "Thunder Traveling to Loftier Heights," (Him-mah-too-yah-lat-kekht) as was his tribal title, had an iron will that would have made a worthy adversary to any authority in the defense of his people and his country.

Chapter Nine

MY ARRIVAL IN RIGGINS

The beauty in this area of the country is breathtaking and compares to nowhere that I have ever witnessed before. I fully realize the agony and despair at having to leave this picturesque place. With its river's rocks almost strategically placed to show off the spectacular twists and turns, as the Salmon River flows mystically on and on. The reaching mountains lining the river majestically show themselves from all turns of the head. It is much different from the flat lands that I am used to in the Dakotas, where you can see for miles without obstructions. I believe that being a young person while living here did not allow me to fully grasp the significance of my surroundings. Now that I have reached an age of appreciation, I can truly see that this is a place to be admired, awed and hopefully preserved for generations.

It has been a successful trip traveling out here and into this beautiful state and I am happy to have had the opportunity to have attempted it. If not for the letter from Arnold that arrived in total astonishment for my family and me, I would never have dared to dream that I would attempt to come all of these hundreds of miles alone. This is part of the reaction I received from my children, but I reassured them over and over that this was the chance of a lifetime, to know what really happened in and to my life. I always wanted to go back to Idaho, but no one had the time to go with me, and it did not occur to me at that time to try to it alone. Rose will tell me any details that I think have been omitted from the tales told to me by my family once in North Dakota if I can find her. Perhaps she is still here with her family as I would have been had we remained in Riggins.

She was a blend of Nez Perce and Spaniard; consequently her darkish skin and hair allowed her and her mother to pretend to be full Spaniard and elude capture. I have so many good memories of Rose. She and I were inseparable, and at times our parents said they didn't know whose daughter was whose. We were very mischievous little girls and loved to play pranks on people. Once we waited by an upstairs window for her brother to walk underneath it. When he did, we dumped a pail full of water onto his head. He was plenty mad, and we ran as fast as we possibly could to my house to hide out until he got over it. One time we filled a gunny sack with horse droppings and left them for another friend to find on her doorstep in the morning, only it backfired and the girl's dad found it first and was whopping mad at his daughter, and she had nothing to do with it. I have missed not having my best friend in my life; so many things we could have experienced together over all of these past thirty years. I hope that she still resides here, but if she does not, I certainly hope someone will be able to help me find her.

I finally have arrived in the town of Riggins, tucked neatly into a valley between Schoolmarm Peak and Preacher Mountain. There seems to be a gathering of sorts at the north end of town. I think I will walk back up there and join them after I am settled. I will try to strike up a conversation with some of the townspeople, and begin my informational query right there. And perhaps I will learn something about some of my family that went into hiding in the caves that are probably still here. Some of the elders may have passed on, but my cousins in Alphonse's branch of the Blue Doves are all about my age. Perhaps some of them have families here now also; I am so anxious to meet any one of them. Just to have a sense of belonging to a large entity of generations of people that I have missed growing up around and with. I am overcome with shivers of excitement just thinking about becoming reacquainted with the remnants of my childhood.

I came upon the sign for the Riggins Motel with a vacancy sign hanging out front and need look no further; Arnold's letter told me to stay here. It was every bit a home, painted white with green shutters with little trees silhouetted into them. There were groupings and beds of carefully planned and placed flowers to show each one's exquisite beauty to its fullest extent. That beauty being flanked by perfectly tied climbing vines and berries each at a consistent height and all of them meticulously groomed. The aroma of theses gardens alone captivated me and pulled me into them, and I forgot for a moment where I was or why I had come here.

I walked up the steps and into the small lobby area, anticipating meeting the owner of the motel, because anyone here could be a relative, friend or former neighbor. There wasn't anyone in the room, so I rang the little brass bell neatly placed on the desk. A man came out and introduced himself as Alfred, and when I inquired about a room, he was very gracious about helping me. I paid him the money that we agreed upon for my stay for two weeks and told him I could perhaps be staying longer. He took me to my spacious accommodations, which included a sitting room, bedroom and a bathroom. This would be a luxurious stay for me; we do not have any indoor plumbing yet, it is just beginning to be installed in a few homes in Spring Brook. Alfred helped the driver get my things from the top of the stagecoach and carried them into my quarters.

I don't want to seem over anxious, but I can't wait to ask about Arnold and his wife, I'm sure the motel owners will know where they live and will be able to give me directions. In a village as small as this one, I'm sure that everyone knows everyone else. Why does Arnold not seem familiar to me? Yet, he apparently knows a great deal of information about me. A man who sent me a letter talking about my relatives and friends and hinting that there were some hidden truths to be uncovered here in this little place. When I think about Arnold, it feels so comfortable, as if I'm thinking about a comrade who has done me a great service, why is that? And why didn't he just tell me where to find him, or his wife, or his house? Why leave all that to chance when I arrived, unless perhaps he considered that fact that I may never come, or may wait years to finally decide to? Or had he told me to stay here so that Alfred could contact him if I ever did check into this motel? Perhaps that is the real reason for the secrecy in not being able to locate him or contact him.

When I was settled in and had unpacked my clothing and travel accessories, I wandered back up to the hotel lobby. This time there was a woman sitting and talking with Alfred. He told me that this was his wife, Doris. She stood up and apologized for not being able to welcome me earlier when I checked in. And they invited me to sit with them and offered me a cold drink of lemonade to quench my thirst from the long stagecoach trip. I took a deep breath and explained my story to them, I told them who I was, who my family was and where I lived and told them I had been away a period of thirty years. And that I wanted to locate my surviving relatives and to learn what had happened to all of them back then and where they all were now. They looked at me as if they were frozen in place. What I had said definitely stunned them. They weren't sure how to answer me, so I spoke to them again and told them that a man named

Arnold Able had written to me and invited me to come for a visit. Their faces softened a little, perhaps in belief, perhaps in disbelief, I couldn't tell for sure. They said they weren't familiar with a lot of the history of this town; they had only lived here for ten years. They had moved here from the Midwest to escape the hot and humid temperatures so common there in the summertime. They appeared to be very happy with their choice and praised their new hometown and surrounding area thusly. The two of them were both bubbling over with cheerful personalities, and they hung on every detail that I told to them. I believe it was not with the deception of something to hide from me, but with true interest in my amazing story.

Alfred said that Arnold is a traveling salesman and that he and his wife are probably both out of town. Arnold is traveling his business routes during the weekdays and Mrs. Able is away at her workplace a couple days each week. She is a caregiver down south of here in New Meadows in a large facility filled with elderly people, and she stays there when her husband is away. She is not comfortable staying alone in their big house with nothing but the dogs for companionship. I guess I would have to wait a little while to meet them, since they had no way of knowing when or if I would arrive in Riggins, so I could hardly expect them to be there to greet me. I thanked them for the information and told them that their graciousness would be remembered.

I walked back down to the north end of town where I had seen the large crowd of people gathered together in the park. Most of the crowd had left already but there were fifteen to twenty people left yet, so I started my inquiries right away. I approached a group of five people and introduced myself as Josephine LeClaire, the name by which I had gone thirty years prior. They just looked at me and managed to say a meek, "Hello." It was said with a question mark in their voices, and then they waited for me to speak again. And I moved on to another group and asked the same questions and received the same negative results.

I am convinced that as I was probing about my mother, Isadora Blue Dove or my Father, Frederick LeClaire, that a couple of the older people did in fact know who I was referring to. But no matter how politely I posed my inquiries or worries, they just shut down while I was speaking. It appeared that no one wanted to commit to have known them or had heard of them over the years. They said that they didn't remember me or anyone in my family, not even my grandparents. How could that possibly be true? Some of these people had probably been born here and the chances were good that they were relatives to me themselves. Some of the people were clamoring together, pointing and whispering, and I know that there has to be a reason for all of this rudeness.

It was then that the first inklings of a deeper, more complex story became present to me. I could feel that I had sparked an interest by the reaction on the faces of those I had questioned. Most hesitated before answering me, but I could see that they all had one thing in common: they were lying to me. The more I persisted, the quieter they became and just listened to me explain my life. Eventually, not a soul would speak to me; it was as if I wasn't standing right in front of them at all. I'm quite certain that there will be some discussion amongst the townspeople as to whether or to tell me the truth about what I am asking. There are definitely things to be learned here from these secretive people, and I am here now, and I intend to find out the truth.

I certainly hope that this narrow path that I am taking will expand greatly as I am able to gather some new facts. Right now, the leads are slim and I believe that this endeavor may be much more complicated than I could ever have predicted. I'm feeling strongly that my knowledge of the issues of my parent's marriage is a twisted tale that was only partially correct and the truth. I believe large portions were painstakingly omitted and others covered up and tucked away in everyone's mind hoping that their subconscious would be able to bury it away so deeply that it would never surface again. But my entrenched feelings of hidden personal tragedy had surfaced over and over my whole life and the time had come now for me to discover what it was that haunted me so. The outcome of talking to the people in the park was to leave me feeling somewhat discouraged, but I had to give them the benefit that perhaps they really didn't know who I was or anyone else that I had asked them about.

I'm going back to my room and rest awhile now. After the very long, bumpy ride by coach out here and the excitement of beginning my search, I was exhausted. After a restful nap, I was hungry, so I started walking up the street looking for a restaurant and came across the Seven Devils Saloon, where I had a proper meal and felt ready to start searching again. As I was sitting there looking around, I felt as if I was being watched. As I scanned the room gradually, I saw a man out of the corner of my eye; he is not out in plain sight, but certainly present. At first, I was uneasy. That I may be in some danger crossed my mind and then I reminded myself not to think like that, I would never find out anything if I became afraid. Is he the one who wrote the letter, who identified himself only as Arnold? No, the motel people said he was out of town during the week. I'm going over there and tell him my name and ask him his and see what happens. I turned around to pick up my purse and push out my chair but by the time that I had stood up, he was gone.

The stranger was what I would judge to be of a medium build, the color of his skin was darker than mine. I was only one half Nez Perce, while he appeared to be full Native American. His dark hair was not long, just a short, shaggy cut that I imagined would be fine and soft. He was dressed in an outdoor, comfortable, rugged style with sturdy work boots. These were indications to me that he most likely has a job that requires safe footing and rough-wearing clothing. Perhaps he is a logger or rancher or maybe a builder, some occupation of a rigorous nature. But more importantly, he could be someone from my past. If that were true, I might be able to put to rest some of my nightmares. I have continually experienced violent, near death nightly interruptions of my sleep since regaining consciousness after the fever of the smallpox in my seventeenth year. There is a man hovering in my dreams, seemingly ready to pounce at me, but somehow never does attack me, as I fear that he would.

I'm reasonably certain that there will be plenty of odd circumstances happening to me here, so I cannot get upset about any of them. Or I will lose my courage to forge on and find out the mysteries of my youth and reasons for those mysteries.

Chapter Ten ≈

<u>CAREER CHOICES</u>

After I settled into my rented room, I walked up the street to the home of the woman who ran the telephone switchboard and I placed my scheduled call to the children. I told them of my safe arrival in Riggins and that my stagecoach ride was pleasant and uneventful. My trip began with boarding the North Pacific passenger train the "Alaskan" with service from St. Paul, Minnesota, to Spokane, Washington. I met a nice couple on the train and enjoyed visiting with them beginning when we boarded at the train station in Mandan, North Dakota. I had to get off of the train in Post Falls, Idaho and transfer onto a coach for the remainder of the approximate two hundred mile journey south to middle of the state. I laid over that first night in Post Falls before starting the trip by stagecoach and again in Potlatch and several others before arriving at my final destination and birth home of Riggins.

I can't believe that it will be probably be two months or more before I see any of my children or grandchildren again. I have never been away from any of them for more than a couple of days, and still that was spent with one of my children's families. I feel the pangs of loneliness for them, especially being here without Allen by my side to reassure me that I am doing the right thing. No, I am doing the right thing; I'm searching for my life, one that I know is out there. There is a whole separate chapter that I feel, but do not know. I didn't really have anything to tell the children about my family yet, my search has not begun and won't until I have had a good night's sleep. I told them that I had spoken with the people who own the motel though, and they didn't seem to know who I was talking about when asked about the Blue Doves or the LeClaires. I was content to just listen to an update of each family's story about their lives and careers and how things are going this week for each of them.

Anna and Lee are under some heavy pressure right now to abandon the success of the creation of their efficient small town newspaper. The City Council is strongly urging them to join with the other small newspapers in the surrounding towns to syndicate with the Williston Ledger and form one larger news piece. They will fight them every step with all the effort that they possess in their attempt to abolish the smaller community informational source. The Council members feel that it is time to have the national news included in their weekly printing, and while Anna and Lee understand the concept, they have something that they produced, and it will be hard to let go of that. At present they hold the positions of owner, editor, reporter, manager, all of them, but who knows where they will be needed, if at all at the Williston Ledger. Anna has lived up to her native translation of Brilliant Fire; she has quite a commanding presence, especially when it concerns her life's accomplishments. She and her husband will not be overthrown easily in this attempted takeover of their newspaper they have struggled to build.

They have been receiving some "hate mail" recently that has contained some strong suggestions that could be construed as threats to their safety if they do not concede. Life could become very challenging if the majority of the public sides with the city government and no longer supports the operation of the Brook Valley Journal. Anna and Lee don't believe that the people realize just what they are really giving up; their intimate publication of the communities in the surrounding area will be destroyed. Simple things such as paying for their ads, which were available to them for a small fee in the Journal, will now be charged by the word in the large newspaper. And there is the possibility of not having articles printed subject to the approval of the larger and more impersonal editorial staff who are not familiar with the people here and what is of interest to them.

Allen and Beth have found what they have been searching for: they have purchased an old inn on the Missouri River. Its former distinction as the Missouri River Crow's Nest will now be known as Liadva's Looking Glass. The inn was tightly tucked into a grove of trees that also lined the road up the gradual incline to the Inn at the rear, hiding it from full view until you actually arrived. A few houses dotted the shoreline here and there, but no neighbors that could be seen or heard, even from the river access below. While sitting on the veranda you had an incredible view of the water and its numerous inlets and outlets and the occasional boat or barge passing through. You could see for miles down and around the river through a telescope mounted on the front porch and a straight line shot of the lighthouse teetering on another of the river's cliffs. The Inn was perched on the edge of a cliff as well, with a sharp drop down on the front side of the place, claiming the peak as its own. It was a very stately mansion, and from the water it appeared that it rose up four stories into the clouds. It looked like a chest of drawers with four drawers along each side with a narrower four running down the middle. In the center of each was a door opening up onto a small terrace off each floor. From the river's enchanting picturesque view of the looming Inn, the doors looked like knobs with which to pull open the drawers in the center. These middle rooms were sitting rooms for the guests with the bathroom facility directly behind them on each respective floor.

The two of them had made a good real estate purchase, they had bought it for about half of its value, and it was completely furnished too. Why would they have left everything just as if they would be back tomorrow? All that was missing were their personal effects and clothing. Pictures remained on the walls, and all of the antiques were in place just as they had been by all of the previous owners for almost one hundred years. The Inn had housed sixteen owners since it was built in 1810; no one seemed to stick it out very long. Allen and Beth hoped they would be able to live there a lifetime and turn the Inn into something extraordinary. A place where the guests would feel at home, as they knew that their family always would and that it would be handed down from generation to generation. According to the ledger of the previous owner, it was always at least half full which was enough to make it prosperous. The Inn was a very interesting place to tour and stay with its grandeur and intriguing history and to relax with its gorgeous view. It was not necessary for any refurbishing to be carried out, it had amazingly remained in the same meticulously beautiful demeanor as its grand opening in 1812. Apparently, each innkeeper had taken a solemn pledge to honor this grand place and keep it immaculate and sparkling. Or was it the innkeepers who were responsible for the Inn's spit and polished appearance? There is a legend that goes with the Inn; it has been told that the original owners of the place had passed away in their sleep there. What makes it a spooky tale is that they died on the same night, in the same bed, holding hands with peaceful smiles on their faces. The feeling is that they never really left, but have watched over each new owner and their beloved establishment. Each proprietor since then has said the place is haunted with good spirits, the kind that cleaned, polished and lent an aura of pleasantness floating through the halls.

Mae and Jack needed to live relatively close to the dam, as Jack was on call always, like the job of a lighthouse keeper. They found themselves the perfect spot and they live in a cozy log cabin just big enough for three. It is several miles up a steep grade, on a winding, rocky, shale covered, one lane road, which is sometimes impassible, rock slides and washouts are a constant hindrance to travel there. But the road to the dam site is a straight shot from their cabin, which he could easily hike if the road was blocked, rutted or washed out. Jack is responsible for alerting the area residents of any possible flooding during its pre-construction gouging process should a large storm arise that would threaten them. He and a crew of several other men have been doing work in preparation for the official construction of the massive earthen dam that has been scheduled to begin in 1947 to control the flow of water more efficiently on this portion of the Missouri River. It will be named the Garrison Dam and it is scheduled to open around 1953, barring any large setbacks in its structural solidarity and resistance. When they open the dam, they plan to flood a portion of the reservation and create a lake which will be name Lake Sakakawea in honor of the revered Indian scout Sakakawea.

Mae wasn't always able to make it out and up to Garrison to work at the orphanage, but that was acceptable in areas where the weather plans things for us sometimes. She did not necessarily need to keep any sort of regular hours; the children lived at the Fort and were ready to learn from her whenever she arrived. Madelyn was always welcome and happily included in the lessons with the other children. Each time she was there, she listened in awe of the experiences endured by these young people and shared with her and Madelyn. Upon hearing their stories, she felt grateful that she had been fortunate enough to have parents and siblings to share her life with. And she prayed that her little Madelyn would never have to face an unimaginable situation, such as one of being all alone in the world.

Chapter Eleven ≈

THE MIRACLE OF LOSS

And now for the first time, I am beginning to be somewhat aware of my surroundings, although I do not know how I came to be here. Mother told me what was happening right now and of our location to calm me from my upright outburst demanding to know. I was quite shocked to learn that we were in a falling down shack in the mountains of Idaho, escaping from the Army and running away from our home. So far from our home on Allison Creek, this is a place people only talked about; that Lewis and Clark had explored this pathway between states. Mother said that I had sat straight up and screamed out Rose's name. I do not recall asking for Rose, but it would make sense that I would ask for my closest friend. I settled back down and tried to relax as they were speaking to me, but as I was slumped there I was thinking it was not Rose that I had been calling out for.

When I awoke in the morning, I hazily remembered that I had awakened from my coma last evening and a few of the words of explanation that I had been given for the situation that we were going through. I recall happy words from all of them that I had come back to them at last and a reminder to lie still, that we were in a cabin in the mountains with a no-so-stable floor beneath us. And now that it had become daylight, Grandfather and my father chimed in to tell me parts of the story from the very moment that led up to our flight from home, to where we are now. I was stunned and even shocked by the descriptions and hair raising details that I was hearing and understanding that we truly had left Riggins and our life there was over. It had actually happened, we had split off from the other Blue Dove families and had taken off totally alone, just the five of us. We would have no more contact with them or those that went in other directions or remained in Riggins.

No, that would mean my dear friend Rose was left behind too, and I don't remember if I got to say goodbye, I just don't know anything that happened. We were to be best friends forever, be present at each other's wedding and raise our children together. Even though Rose and I had known that we would be separated, we thought it would be just by the distance of a mountain, and I was promised that after a year's passing it would be possible to see her. But now, that hope was destroyed, taken from me while I was near death. I feel stabbed in every part of me and my heart feels as if it has been blasted into little pieces, never to be patched back together again. Is this my destiny? Am I to have little pieces of me strewn about, from my precious homeland into our new world and life? We were leaving behind so many people, not just Rose, but I had a sense of another loss, a deep, empty feeling that I had lost a love, possibly the love of my life. Young people most often don't think that the worst things will happen to them, so there is no real preparation for it. I broke into a full heartbroken cry now and just covered my head and myself and sobbed into my pillow. I was much too shaky to withstand such emotional thoughts yet and the memories that joined in to sadden me. There was more; I was giving up something of greater importance. I knew it, it was evident by the knife in my heart.

And the rest of my life, where was that to go now? I am all alone now with my entire world consisting of my parents and grandparents, but no one my age to confide in: not my cousins, not my friends. I hadn't really thought to ask about anyone else yet, just worrying about my own childish needs and desires right then. I asked my mother what had happened to me, why do I feel so weak and cannot stand up. She explained in her definitive tone all that had happened to me, contracting the smallpox disease that kept me ill, near death, for months. When she spoke to me, it was in a voice of facts, with an air of truthfulness. She was stern but caring, and had never lied to me previously, so I would believe every detail she expressed to me. I nodded and listened to the accounting of my illness, which had occurred in the midst of the turmoil with the evacuation. Apparently, I had become ill just a couple weeks before we left, but the chance had to be taken, despite my health. Then I was gently, quietly told how close to death my precious grandmother was, and all other thoughts that I had been selfishly thinking left me in a humbled state of regret and shame.

The plan had been that after we had crossed over the Rockies, we would we trudge northeast into Fort Assinniboine near to Havre, Montana. Grandmother had ties there and hoped that after we arrived there, we would find some remainder of her tribe still residing therein. Her sister had married a man from there and her parents had accompanied her to this new land and she had not seen any of them after they moved away. Her parents were long since deceased, but she hoped to find her sister and her family well and still there. And she was genuinely praying that she could possibly persuade the men to settle down there and create their new life in her sister's territory. It would be easy for her to feel at home there and to make her loved ones feel the same way and find that it would become a friendly, accepting venue to start their new life. It was a widespread area filled with many resources, where it wasn't necessary to venture more than a radius of twenty miles or so to hunt for game. There was no need to pull up roots every so often and seek out new territory to live on as some natives did. But grandfather had his reservations, believing that the area was probably inhabited now by French Canadians and wondered how welcome we would be if there were no Native Americans.

Our first hurdle has been overcome and here we are, ready to step into Montana for the first time. None of us had ever been on that side of the Bitterroots before. This endeavor has been a tremendously grueling effort to save our little family, and we finally feel as if we can breathe a little easier. The word "Lolo" means to carry, and thus it would. It would carry us across the Idaho border to search for freedom. The Lolo Road did not claim any of our lives; there was no death as a result of frostbite or injury. My grandmother's illness began as we started out, and I have been recovering very slowly from mine. And now, it is painfully clear that grandmother will not be experiencing our freedom, she is slipping away from us a little more each minute that passes. And, I now partially understand what is taking place. We are searching for a home, one in which we can flourish and feel protected from tyranny. I will grow up with my family in an open environment, which does not include life within the constraints of a piece of land - a piece of land designated for our existence and from which we will never be allowed to leave. I guess that story was designed to make me feel safe and happier about our self-banishment to a new state hundreds of miles from home. But in spite of all the convincing arguments, I know that pieces of me would be left back in Idaho, and I will never completely be a whole person again.

My grandmother did not fare well on our hasty, grueling progression across the state, over mountains, and through deep canyons. It was more of a strain on her tired little frame than it could endure and she gave in to the spirits that called for her to come home to them. Annahah Blue Dove died on the journey crossing over the Lolo Pass connecting Idaho to Montana. But she knew her life was to end soon and she would never make it to see her sister or the burial grounds where her parents lay. She timed it to relinquish her hold on life while still in Idaho, just short of the state border, where she had begun her life. We were overcome with sadness and guilt feelings; we felt a deep, dark, damp pain within our hearts. She was gone. Physically, she had left us, but spiritually she would be with us always and eventually we would join her in her world upon our death. We were left with an enormous aching that we had perhaps sacrificed her for our freedom, along with all of her dreams of rekindling family bonds at Fort Assinniboine.

It was a gloomy, foggy, rain filled day, and we had sought refuge under a covered bridge. I had never seen one of these bridges before, but had heard about them from people up north. They have been in existence as early as 1850, and with the covering overhead, it doubled the lifespan of bridge. These bridges did more than serve as a means of crossing the rivers, they were used for gatherings, dances, rallies, and for lovers to meet under. But sadly, we would remember this structure for an entirely different reason; it was where my grandmother took her last breath. I had been lying in the wagon with grandmother, staring at each other, neither of us capable of movement. Instead, we communicated with our eyes, sad eyes, filled with love, respect, pain and a partial degree of regret. I remember her exact last moment, her eyes flickered, opened wide and looked at me, one last time, and drifted peacefully into her final slumber. I was still pretty shaky, lapsing into sleep on and off due to the exhaustion of the illness and the trip, but grandmother's final breath will remain a vivid memory until I take my final breath. Our tiny web of five suffered severely with her loss, we were all that each other had, and to lose anyone of us so precious was a difficult blow. When anyone intricate to your existence is taken from you, a part of you is also taken and there is no replacement for a loved one.

It was still a long road to reach Havre, certainly at least three times the distance or more than we had already traveled. The rivers will be our pathways to our destination. They really are the only steadfast guides documented as a means of travel across the United States. We progressed east following the Blackfoot River after clearing the Lolo Pass to cross the Rockies at a fairly narrow vista point. We managed to stay on course. The Big Belt Mountains did not hinder our travels because they were to the south of us and not in our path. The Blackfoot River ends a considerable distance from Holter Dam, so we had no access to a river for guidance for awhile. But once we arrived there, we were able to hook up with the Missouri River and twist and turn with its drastic hairpin curves. It wound us up into Great Falls and beyond another couple hundred miles until the river turned south at Virgelle, Montana. The next waterway that we followed was the Big Sandy River, and once we reached that, we were so close to our destination that it was decided that travel could slow down some. Just slightly northeast lies our destination, Fort Assinniboine, which the men estimated to be a couple days ride from there.

We kept our decision to just stop for awhile now and calm ourselves. The worst of our difficult endeavors was over. We were almost there. All these months of traveling over dangerous terrain had brought us close to our goal. We had no fear anymore, we had been through a lot of bad situations to get here, and we could take whatever was presented to us now. We were just fatigued, mentally and physically, and really needed a few days to settle down in one place and rest ourselves. We will do so when we arrive at the Fort. It had been a long time since we had been a part of any civilization, and it would be good to converse with others for awhile. All of us will remain with guarded tongue; we do not want to reveal any reasons for our trip to any persons in an official position. But we would seek out Grandma Annahah's family and tell those persons remaining there our story and of grandmother's passing and wishes.

We set up camp for the evening on the banks of the Big Sandy River. My father and grandfather said that we still have approximately one hundred miles to ride yet. While I was inside the wagon that evening I heard them talking outside about the events that had taken place on our long journey. Mother asked the men, "How much of all that has transpired do you think that Josie will remember?" Father said, "I doubt that she will remember much of anything before she awoke that night back in the cabin. She was ill for so many moons now that I think we're safe there." Safe where? What were they talking about? I listened closer now, hoping to catch some explanation. Grandfather added, "I think she will be so bereaved over losing Annahah for a long time and that she will not even think to ask about anything else. She knew that we had plans to leave our home one way or another and I don't think that she is all that surprised that we raced her out of there." "Yes," Mother began, "but Father, if she recovers her complete memory of last year and the time this year up until we fled in November, things could get very complicated." My father spoke now, "We cannot discuss this any further, she is well enough now to pick up on what we are saying, and if we don't want her asking questions, we need to be silent. It's bad enough that we will have to fabricate certain things to make them fit into the time frames we agreed to tell her." Wild thoughts race through my mind, nothing able to be clear right now. What? What are they talking about? What does all of this mean? What happened last year and this year before we left? They are planning to tell me lies about something to explain what? If I am hearing properly, things aren't as they seem, or rather, weren't as they seemed.

When we awoke in the morning, our campsite was completely surrounded by Army personnel. They had moved in last night, probably a quarter mile's distance from our campsite. We had heard them come in: we were much better scouts than they were, which is why so many of us were hired or tricked into guiding them. They had artfully encompassed us and had left no path by which we could even attempt an escape. The river was behind us to the west, crossing that in the dark was not an option for us. Having no alternative but to face them, we just remained around our campfire and prepared breakfast. Let them come to us. By panicking and trying to scurry out of an impossible situation, we were just inviting injury to ourselves. Better to just remain calm and see what the soldiers had planned for us now that morning sun had peeked through and they would move in. I didn't know what the men would say to them, but I know that they would not be lying to them when they told them that we had come to bury grandmother in her birthplace.

My father took me firmly by the shoulders and looked intently into my eyes. I knew that this was going to be a crucial matter, he had done this with me before in serious times. He said, "Josie, I know that you are beginning to feel better, and seem to understand some of what is taking place. But right now, I need you; we all need for you to pretend that you are back in your comatose state." I stared at him confused, "Why would I do that?" He replied, "Because I believe that when the Army comes into camp shortly, it could make the difference between going with the Army and going on our way." "Oh," I squeaked, "Why?" Father explained, "I believe that when the Army sees that your grandmother has passed on and that you appear to be next, they won't question us too much. They will see that we are hardly any kind of menace to anyone, and will allow us to continue on our journey to return grandmother to her place of origin." "What do you mean?" I queried. "We aren't from Montana." Father continued on, "Grandfather and I have prepared another small lie to tell them too." He was grinning like a big brother about to play a prank on his little brother and get away with it.

Despite members of the Crow tribe joining sides with the Army, our Nez Perce tribe had friendly ties with those who remained loyal to the Crow tribe in Montana, and we hoped they would help us should we get into any trouble with the Army. We felt fairly safe spending time here, knowing that they would be ready to identify us as tribal members, should the need arise. And if we should so choose, we could remain disguised as Crow and they would help us earn a new start here. Father spoke again, "Our good friends the Crow will be helping us out once we reach them in Chinook, and we are going to start now to pass ourselves off as Crow to get up there. We will tell them that we are relocating from the southern portion of the state. Our lands have been overpopulated and our tobacco resources depleted to the point that we have had to seek out other territories to survive. The northern Crow have told us that the tobacco crop is abundant on their lands and we are welcome to settle there with them."

Tobacco is the key to many, many things, and also held sacred. The belief was that as long as they grow tobacco, the tribe would flourish and have only good luck. Furthermore, the belief is expanded to include healing the sick, handling the weather, warding off all evils and even serving as a truth serum. It was believed that one could not lie while under the smoky effects of the tobacco leaves tossed into the fire. Sitting in a circle around such a glowing fire, was how many hunting expeditions, warring parties or special celebrations were planned. Everyone was allowed to speak freely without inhibitions, feeling relaxed enough to bring forth new ideas.

"A highly believable saga, don't you think Josie?" he asked. I shook my head in full agreement. It was a good plan and I had faith that it would work quite well. I hadn't realized until now that our clothing was completely devoid of any recognizable symbolism of our membership in the Nez Perce tribe. Again, Grandfather and Father had planned this far ahead and oh, so perfectly. Our safety was their priority and nothing would fail them in their attempts to relocate us. The Army would never place us as escapees from the roundup all the way back in Riggins, Idaho, from many months past now. We're just a lonely group of five people, one of which is now deceased and searching for the Crow family that she began her existence with. I truly believe that they have taken every precaution to ensure our passage northward toward a new life, and the Army would forget all about us.

We arose before dawn and all sat around the fire having morning coffee and breakfast, waiting for the soldiers to ride in and pay their visit to us. I was completely confident that things outside would be handled quietly and with no trouble for us at all. Frederick LeClaire and Ignatious Blue Dove were smart men and had thought out all of the angles. I heard the horses approaching and stirred slightly, but needed to remain immobile. I would now be pretending to be near death once again. And my recently deceased grandmother was lying in the wagon with me. It was a little eerie having her there with a sheet covering her from head to toe. But it was also comforting to have her there beside me for a few days yet before I had to say my final farewell to her.

Father must have stood up to meet the horsemen; his voice sounded farther away than it had been at the fire. But I heard him say, "Good morning, can I do something for you?" The reply was, "We're just checking on people who might be camped out to give them a warning." Grandfather said, "Oh, what kind of warning, Captain?" The Captain spoke, "There has been a pack of wolves running up and down the Big Sandy this spring; they're hungry and that means they're mighty ornery. We don't want any folks getting hurt or even worse, if we can prevent it, so if you can travel some other direction, it would be a good idea." Father told him, "We'll be on careful lookout, sir, and we'll go further on east away from the river." And then came the big question, "Where are you and your family headed?" The man inquired. Grandfather shakily, and in tears said, "I've lost my wife to the pox and my granddaughter is not far away from death herself," nodding in the direction of the wagon. "We're trying to get my wife back to her homeland to place her with her elders." The captain dismounted and asked to look inside the wagon - that was my cue to play comatose. I'm sure I looked pretty terrible, it's been a long time, since I've had my hair combed and my face free of the damage from the outdoor elements. Later, my family told me that he had taken off his hat and touched it to his chest in a gesture of reverence and nodded to the three of them. Then the Captain asked them, "If your homeland is north of here, where are you coming from?" So the explanation was given about the marriage between the two Crow tribal members and that Grandmother had left her birth home to live with my grandfather's tribe in the southern portion of the state." And that was it. He mounted his horse and said, "Good luck to you now and watch out for those wolves." He tipped his hat and rode away. We were safe now; they didn't care much about us one way or the other. Father said that he thought the story of the wolves was just an excuse though to come into camp and question us. And we ignored the warning and we did continue to follow the Big Sandy River as we had planned.

Many memories and stories had been revived while we continued on to Fort Assiniboine after her death. She had never left her birthplace until she and my grandfather were bound together in marriage and then still just south of Lapwai, but still in Idaho. It would be impossible for us to lay her to rest in Lapwai now, but at least she will be with her parents in Montana, and grandfather is confident that she would approve of her final resting place. Grandmother passed on from us before I could learn even more from her as I matured into adulthood. But I at least had seventeen precious years of her knowledge and expertise to carry with me forever, and to share with the generations yet to be born. It is very important to share these legacies with your children; they will always carry a part of you with them in their endeavors as well. For an only child to lose her grandmother at an early age is a devastating plight. But I had to accept that it was her time to be with her own grandmother again; as well as her parents and her grandfather. And in turn, my mother would take up the privilege of being a grandmother to my future children and guide them in this world, as my grandmother had taught me. I am grateful to her for the detailed instruction in shaping my imagination and turning it into finished creations and true works of art. Giving to others of oneself of things made with our own hands puts authenticity and love into each accomplishment. And she had instructed her daughter, my mother, the techniques of her great craft, and I learned from both of them how to develop that skill even before I was able to understand what I was doing.

We experienced no further delays or mishaps, and the spring weather was mild. Some spring rains had fallen, but only a fair amount and it had not hindered our travels. Arrival in Havre had us longing for something good to eat that had nothing to do with trail food. And a bath and a real bed would feel so good, a mattress and fresh clean bedding to climb into. It had been a long time since we had experienced even the simplest pleasures of the life we left behind in our home on Allison Creek. Once we had placed our precious cargo onto her resting place, then we would seek out fulfillment of our needs.

We did not want to hurry the process of leaving grandmother here and we wanted to spend some time remembering our ancestors and the important events on this site. We visited the ceremonial area where the rocks were positioned in alignment with the stars in the sky to predict the changing of the seasons. I had not had the privilege of seeing a medicine wheel or calendar wheel before, as these were so named. It was quite an extensive system, cylindrical in shape, fashioned after what we would see as a wagon wheel with spokes. The rocks were placed in varying positions, and the seasons were counted by the shadows that fell and in what directions. It kept very reliable track of the days and the months. The new month always began on the day of the crescent moon, and how many days until the next was kept track of with small rocks, sticks, or anything that would visibly record each day as it passed.

This was the first time that I had ever witnessed Father and Grandfather in tears, silent drops of water filling their eyes and cascading down over their worn, weathered faces. It was a very solemn, emotional moment for each of us. A portion of our history is here, even though we were hundreds of miles away when it took place.

We turned around and went west of the battlement and sought out the burial grounds nearby. And then we paused for a prayer in front of the sacred network of wooden platforms that had been erected to honor those who had been placed there. Since birth I had been taught that the roles that family play in your life and that of others, the family traditions, family positions are all things to be greatly respected and revered. It was of great honor for her to be placed near to her mother and father in death, and grandfather made us promise to bring him here after he expires, so that he could be with his precious Annahah. My mother and father made him that solemn promise, to return him to this very burial site to reunite with his wife. The men built scaffolding with space enough for two people, as was traditional in our culture, and positioned her upon it, to wait for her acceptance to the next life. Mother and I looked on sadly as the men lifted her onto her final resting place. She was dressed in her wedding ceremonial finery, which was the one garment of Nez Perce origin which she had not been able to part with upon relocating.

Along with her we placed several items of significance on her person to take with her into the afterlife, so that she would take a piece of each of us with her. Grandfather took off his belt that grandmother had especially stitched and beaded for him as a wedding gift from wife to husband. He wanted her to know that he felt that they would remain married forever, and he would return to this place to join her and wear it once again when he passed on. My mother left her dream catcher to keep grandmother safe once we left her and continued on our quest. We believe that the air is filled with good and bad dreams and the dream catcher filters those dreams for us. The good dreams are allowed to pass through the center hole and the bad dreams are trapped in the web, where there they perish at the first light of day. Father left her tiny portions of each variety of our food supply, as an offering to those who would watch out for her now. I could not give to her my one possession that I have with me, my water pouch, which she had made for my fifth birthday. It was beautiful, made from buffalo hide for insulation, covered with beaver fur, with a fluffy, white bunny's tail dangling from its bottom. I would need to have that beside me always to remember a woman and grandmother as wonderful as she was. Instead, I decided that I would part with something that I had made myself and wanted to share with her. I am a girl of seventeen now and traditionally should be preparing to enter into a marriage agreement soon. But we are embarking on a new life that is anything but traditional, so I will leave with her something that she helped me to create.

It was the winter of my fourteenth year, and together, Grandmother and I had cut a strip of deer hide and pounded it soft. We were fashioning a headband for me to give to my intended husband on the day of my marriage ceremony. We had scalloped the edges with a rock that had been ground into a point that was used in cutting edges for clothing and teepees as well. The strands with which to tie it were difficult to cut and I had stained them with my own blood toiling to cut them just the right thickness. I had practiced many times on different articles with her, but she felt that this was something to be solely designed by me. And lovingly detailed in such a manner in which I would be proud to present it to my mate. My mother grabbed my hand before I could lay it upon Grandmother's forehead, she said nothing at first, just shook her head negatively. Then she spoke, "She would not want you to leave this with her, she would want the headband to be worn on the day that you are united with whom you have chosen." I reluctantly withdrew my hand from Grandmother; I really wanted to leave something with her. But she was right, it should be saved for that special day, but I somehow feel that that day has already come and gone. Why would I possibly think this way? I have always been with these same four people, haven't I? No, no, there is something nagging at me, something very important related to this beaded headwear to be worn at my betrothal. So, I left nothing of a material nature for Grandmother to take on her journey. Mother said that she would know that she had a piece of my heart that would always remain hers.

And now, laying her to rest beside her parents, she will forever be at peace in her afterlife. But sadly, Grandmother will not be reminiscing with anyone she had hoped to see again, relatives and friends left behind here many, many years ago. If not in life, then in death, she shall be reunited with her family. Our ancestors from their placement in the sacred burial grounds are consistently watching over us from above. They will always take care of things, I have always been told. I remember repeatedly hearing the phrase, "When one light burns out another is lighted." Which translated means that when we lose a loved one to death; that it provided room for another person to be born into the world. And most certainly we were being held to that long believed philosophy, it was coming true for us right now. For, I was given back to my family, and my grandmother was lost to them.

My grandfather, eyes still glistening with the water of tears glanced over at me and said, "Josie, it's real important that you have a legacy to pass on to your children, that the Nez Perce not be forgotten. And the personal history and legends of your ancestors is equally important. It is a part of who we all are and have become. I will tell you many things of the history of the Nez Perce peoples, and grandmother would like you to meet her family, if they are still here."

Chapter Twelve   ≈

OPPORTUNITIES

Allen Jr. was the first to come on the line this time when the switchboard operator hooked me up to the Spring Brook office. He was excited to tell me that they would be able to start moving into their new place any day now. Allen and Beth were anxious to open the new "Liadva's Looking Glass" and show off their new home. Their living quarters will be on the bottom floor so they will be available for late night check ins. Beth would take care of the baby and run the business affairs of the Inn, with a small staff for cleaning and cooking duties. Allen would see to the yard, the outside of the Inn and the carriage house, which was large enough to use for several horses and the wagons they pulled to be stabled for the guests and themselves. He felt he should be able to handle those duties as well as those of managing Curtis Timber. I reassured Beth that I would be home in plenty of time for the grand opening and would be able to help her in any fashion that I could be useful to them. And to spend some time with their son Joseph, my youngest grandchild, just talking to him and reacquainting myself with him if he has forgotten his grandmother in the time that I am away.

I believe that I will be quite content to be home again and sit on their luxurious front porch reflecting on my joyful reunions and viewing the wondrous Missouri River and her constantly changing flow. In the near future, I will be selling my now much too big house that Allen, Sr. and I had lived in for most of our married life and raised our three children in. Allen and Beth have invited me to live with them at the Looking Glass and I am happy to be doing so and be relieved of the burden of caring for my house alone. I will occupy any one of the rooms at the Inn that I choose, so I have picked out one in the back and one of moderate size as well. I am free to roam the vast expanse of the mansion at any time and I can enjoy the overlook of the cliff any time I wish, so there is no need for me to occupy a large room or a riverfront one.

Allen asked how my search was going, and I told him I still hadn't found the answers I was looking for. My next quest was to seek out Papoose Cave, the safe haven for my relatives that had gone underground. I was hopeful there would be someone who would know of the Blue Dove family.

Anna wanted to speak to me next, and she asked how I was and if I was feeling optimistic that I would make some more progress today. I said that I was hopeful, although I hadn't found anyone willing to talk to me about the Blue Doves just yet. And, as I told her brother Allen, I was hopeful that I would have more news to share after my visit to Papoose Cave. My subconscious tells me it will be the beginning of my fact finding mission. My heart tells me that I will find the answers it needs.

Anna said that their scuffle with the local townsfolk that wanted them to turn themselves over to the larger newspaper was intensifying. Not only were they receiving hate mail, but people were throwing garbage into their yard and at their house, and it was messy garbage, eggs, tomatoes, rotting fruit and the like. She said that she and Lee and Michael were not going to run and hide from them, they would only target the newspaper office next and follow them wherever they would be staying. They only hoped whoever responsible would stop this crazy behavior isolated to just simple garbage and that it would not escalate into something far worse - damaging or life threatening.

The mail they had been receiving so far had just involved name calling on their selfishness in wanting to stay with the local news and nothing further. Michael had been teased by some of the kids at school about his parents, even though the kids really didn't know what they were taunting him about, they had heard their parents talking. Would they ultimately give in? I asked her. She replied that it would be sad for Lee to give up his life's dream of having begun the paper and hers of joining in and keeping it going. They would rather that the people work with them as a team to keep this merger from happening. Or perhaps they should consider the merger as joining another team, one with larger resources. But there is still that fear that they will be tossed aside if they agree to the merger. On the other hand, the Williston Ledger's owners should be wise enough to want to bring Lee and Anna's talents to the table to produce even better news articles.

Life does not always travel on the course that you have planned, and can change in the flicker of a candle wick. Jack, Mae and Madelyn's lives were forever altered on that day when the rain would not cease and the lightning's luminescence sprinkled the heavens and the thunder's drumming sounded out disaster. Jack had made his rounds and delivered his usual warning in a crisis such as this one and then went directly to the dam. He and a crew were sandbagging on the dam trying to keep up with the washouts when Jack was struck by lightning. It was never determined if he died from the actual bolt of lightning or from drowning as he toppled into the water. The volunteers were unable to locate him in the blinding storm and with the unforgiving river twisting and turning in the night.

After Jack's passing, Mae and Madelyn moved to Mandree to the reservation, so they wouldn't be living in such an isolated location. Jack's parents still lived there and they would be able to help her with Madelyn when she needed them and she would only be two hours away from us in Spring Brook. At first she lived with them until they found a nice little house close to them and within an easy walking distance from the Fort. Mae dealt with her grief by teaching the children longer and longer hours and soon her work with the children became invaluable. The tragedy seemed to accelerate her desire to spend more time with the orphans and the less fortunate children. She was fully aware now of how quickly her own daughter could be put into the same situation as they were without parents to turn to. Mae began instructing them on every aspect of daily living from the simplest tasks of grooming yourself to the more difficult ones of protecting a home from predators. Her teaching methods were easily accepted by the people in charge, and they offered her a permanent position there for money, instead of the voluntary basis on which she had begun. Good for Mae; that gives her something satisfying to concentrate on and build on. And Madelyn now feels she has a whole bunch of brothers and sisters, as she calls all of the kids she see each day, and learns and plays with. And quite often, more than one goes home with them at the end of the day to spend the night at her house. I am grateful to hear that they are both doing so well, since the drastic change that entered their lives so unexpectedly.

Our time to talk for today has ended I told them, "I miss all of you and I'm sorry that I am not there to help any of you. I should be there for you all, but I know that I am not wasting my time here. I will find something; I feel it more than ever now that I have actually set my physical presence down here in

Idaho. When I call home next, I will have found some link, some connection, I know I will."

Chapter Thirteen ≈

PAPOOSE CAVE SALVATION

There is little doubt for me that there is something very wrong here. The people to whom I introduce myself and give a brief explanation of my interest here are very aloof and turn away from me before finishing a sentence. They usually allow me only a brief word or two and only of the negative sort of response. And that is certainly no help with any answers to my inquiries, leaving me to go on to the next person to again ask the same questions over again. Consequently, asking where any member of the Blue Dove tribe resides, worked or otherwise spent their time has become impossible. I will just have to strike out on my own and begin to look where my memories of our history here will take me. My mind is just not very clear on what took place when the turmoil began; I was under the influence of the fever deeply by then. Also, my memories are somewhat limited, because I was only seventeen when we left, and because of that age, I wasn't paying much attention to the situation. I had other issues to be worrying about. I don't recall them exactly, but I know and sense that there were some things happening to me personally. But my grandfather and my parents told me enough of the plans and locations later on that I know where I shall start, but I do wish that I could recall more of the events of that time to work with. Grandfather's reminiscences had told me that Papoose Cave saved the lives of his brother Chief Alphonse, his wife, children and grandchildren as well are other families who were with them. He was a rich, rich man, grandfather would say because he was able to smuggle out each and every person in his family out of Riggins. Careful planning and execution of that plan allowed

Alphonse the good fortune to live out his life with all of his descendants present.

Papoose Cave is where the families entered into as a hiding place and escape route when the tribe felt that trouble was imminent and their existing ways of life were about to be terminated. Papoose Cave provided an excellent seclusion from all the elements of inclement weather as well as any and all intruders that may be seeking them. The cave is one of the deepest in the United States, with depths ranging from 600 feet to 945 feet. It is composed of limestone and has more than a mile of passages and vertical formations from 15 to 65 feet in height. Some of the extensions in the caves offer many choices of diversions off the main hallways to massive caverns which were easily adaptable for use as living quarters. Also, this cave is one of only a few in the entire state of Idaho which contains a water source flowing throughout. This would be of extreme value to their incarceration within the rock walls which would be their new home for an undetermined length of time.

Fortunately for all of them, their actual point of slipping out of town and into the cave was never discovered, so they didn't need to take any more action to preserve their unit. An escape from their haven of hiding might have been possible by traveling west out the back of the Cave and crossing the vast forest. Then they could have headed for the Snake River for direction, and forged their way upstream into the thousands of acres of hunting ground. This area was so immense that they could have disappeared for quite some time and had enough wild game fish, plants and roots to sustain them endlessly. Another option would have been to cross the forest, portage across the Snake River and disappear into Seven Devils Mountains. On the west side of the mountains it drops into

Hells Canyon, and they could have attempted to climb down into the colossal emptiness. They could have split up into individual families or remained united if they chose, to, but either way the possibility of eluding the Army for awhile was likely. But these were felt to all be drastic measures to choose. The Nez Perce had enough of life on the run and being chased, and it had come to a tragic end resulting in the destruction of masses of people.

The story of their departure totally unobserved is an amazing tale of courage and perseverance demonstrating the Native American people's determination to survive. One whole group of Nez Perce about to be absconded successfully fled into Papoose Cave and had never been exposed by the Army. They had snuck into the "Old School" house in Riggins, where a tunnel out of the cellar had been well secured and hidden craftily beneath the storage bins. Everyone was aware that this war was escalating and they feared for their lives and their futures should they survive. They had intuitionally prepared for the escape into the cave systems. Supplies were smuggled into the school with every teacher and child that entered the building for nearly six months prior to the beginning of the escape. When that fateful period of time was growing short, they began the process of leaving through the "Old School" cellar. The members of one family would go each day until the family was complete on the other side, thus keeping that unit whole. When the ordeal began, several complete families had nervously slipped away without a single hint of Army suspicion lurking in that area to hinder the operation.

The cellar under the school was used as storage for many items: coal, wood, potatoes, squash, dried roots and seeds and many other food items that needed to remain cooling in the dirt bins for a winter source. Although the children brought their lunch to school each day, there were times when the children were boarded overnight at the school during times of inclement weather. So, it was necessary to store food there for that purpose. The dirt also served as extra insulation and preservation for the labor filled garden produce, and made an amazing natural cover for the exit through the floor of the school out into the caverns. After the persons chosen for the day had slipped out to safety, those remaining behind scuffed the dirt around, put the coal or produce back, and no one would have any clue that such a well planned operation was taking place there. It was not an area that would ever have had a clean surface, as it had always been used for the same storage purposes. Supplies were replenished by members of the community each year at harvest time and enough coal and wood for the schools needs was brought in then also.

The Nez Perce had long ago discovered the mire of caverns under Preacher Mountain, named for Preacher Hess, his wife and two children who homesteaded the peak. They only needed to burrow a connecting tunnel to link the cave and school for their retreat to asylum. Although the mountain has an elevation of 4,645 feet, the solid limestone chips away easily, making the task far less problematic than any other kind of rock. It also decays and falls off in sheets as it ages, which would require constant maintenance; but the immediate merits were the relevant ones. It took them only a span of one year to accomplish this task and equip the tunnel for the evacuation. Each night, several men would enter the cave on the far side of the mountain and work throughout the night, towing building supplies in with them. The midnight workers brought shovels, tools and wood planking for shoring up the passage, all things of a construction nature that would not arouse suspicion. The Nez Perce had set up a camp out off of Squaw Creek Road by the creek for the butchering, skinning and tanning of wild game. The meat would be smoked and dried for storage and a large portion of it would be stashed away just inside the caves entrance; it was one less thing to have to be transported from the beginning point of the cellar. There was absolutely no mistrust of the location of the butchering camp; it was a logical place to do it where the mess and putrid smells of rotting meat would be away from town. No one caught on that some of the members of the "butchering crew" were actually working in the cave all night hollowing it out from that side of the mountain.

The hope of evacuating the persons several at a time each day to reach the new site was that they wouldn't be missed so readily. When an entire family had vacated their home, members of another household would split up and some would move into their house, so that someone was always occupying all of the dwellings, giving the appearance of daily life as usual. This would be done until so many of the people had gone underground that it would be impossible to do so. The number of Nez Perce tribal members that inhabited this area was about two hundred and fifty persons. There were also many Canadian, Spanish and Caucasian people residing here also, and those who had married natives, raising the number to about 500 total. So, if 250 people had actually made it, there would still be 250 to cover as the families submerged. There would always be second thoughts no matter how many people had escaped, wondering if it would have been possible to send double the amount each day. But they had not wanted to risk the exposure of the perfectly planned escape route to freedom, and it was indeed a good plan.

The Army had never taken a census of any kind in any of the surrounding small towns or outlying areas, so they really didn't know how many people they were actually going to be rounding up. That was poor recordkeeping on their part; thankfully for us the less they knew the more we could get away with. If necessary at the bitter end, a mass escape would be attempted, but only if it was absolutely certain that it would not jeopardize the safety of those who had already gone into seclusion. They would allow themselves to be captured and tortured before allowing the Army any knowledge whatsoever of those who had been secured and would have the possibility to begin their lives anew. For those who had been successfully rerouted to the reservation, such a day would perhaps come that would provide them with the opportunity to slip away from the reservation that they were being forced to reside on. It was conceivable that some individuals could make it to a location free from persecution and pursue the same path that other tribal members had taken to avoid confinement within defined borders. And hopefully that they would somehow one day be able to reunite, and once again live with the Papoose Cave family members of the tribe.

The order of the families that went and those that did not was determined by a drawing of prayer rocks presided over by the oldest living member. He was considered both their spiritual leader as well as their healer and would hold the sacred rocks in his possession until his death. My grandfather, Ignatious Blue Dove was that very elder who was dispersing the families, which was his appointed duty by being the oldest of the brothers. One by one, the family orders were drawn, ours being the stone which was left, so we would be the last family that would enter Papoose Cave. It was a ritual agreed on and witnessed by all and deemed to be unanimously fair by the entire population concerned. All residents, regardless of their race, were in attendance at this solemn ceremony where lives were at stake and fates would be decided. The likelihood of the last families in the drawing order having enough time to make it into the school before the Army conducted its mass departure was only a slight one. That's when Grandfather and Father decided on an alternate plan for us; or so I had always thought was the reason for parting from the other Blue Dove families.

Prayer rocks have been used for many things; praying for health, safe hunting, food, spiritual direction, and laying out the future. The ritual that the tribes prayer rocks were used for this time was to decide the order of the families entering into seclusion. The rocks weren't really anything special or unique in looks or features. But they were significant from the fact that they had been handed down from generation to generation. The rocks were placed in a raging fire built at daybreak one morning and left in the hot flames for three hours. Then at random, the head of each family chose a rock and laid it in front of their family in the sacred circle the people had formed. This was done until all the rocks were distributed to all of the families and all the tribal members were seated again. Then there was nothing left to do except to nervously anticipate which coal would die out first, because the last rock to lose its red hot coal glow would be in position number one to go. They all sealed their fate on the gamble of which rock held its heat the longest according to the agreement they had set forth to handle their disposition. The chain of descent would begin with the mother and youngest child, then the rest of the children and the father ending their family. They felt that would hold some protection for the children, if the movement was stopped part of the way to completion; the children would have a protector and provider on each end of the spectrum.

Today, I'm heading for Papoose Cave to see what remains there. I am anxious for what I will find, but not allowing myself to feel too optimistic that anyone actually still inhabits that area. I think that I would feel that while Papoose Cave had given them back their lives, it also had been a prison for a year or more. I would have felt eager to reposition my loved ones and break out from living inside a rock to the green, lush forest region not very far away. And conceivably that could be exactly what they did, and I would not find anyone at all, just scattered remnants of a lost generation.

I didn't get an early start like I was planning to; it was a grueling task to drag myself out of my cottage after a horrendous night of restless sleep. I tried to distract myself by reading a light hearted book last night, but that did not help. I just couldn't get those people at the park out of my mind. But while I was tossing and turning, I think I put some matters into perspective concerning why I am being slighted here. And as a result, I've changed my perception of it somewhat and perhaps I should step back and view this from another angle; their angle. Perhaps it's not all protectiveness of their people or disbelief that I am real and standing here in front of them. Instead, if my story was indeed real, we had made it - survived the rules and regulations dictated by the government on the reservation to those transferred there that they loved and sympathized with. In that case, I wouldn't blame them for being cautious, even to the point of rudeness towards me. I finally just resigned myself to sitting there in the dark and waiting for the first light of day and the birds to sing forth a new morning.

While trying to revive myself by sipping a cup of coffee at 'This Old House Restaurant' on the southern edge of town, I contemplated and wondered what the days search for my lost extended family would yield. Hoping that it would be a productive and happy experience, I hired a horse for the day and started out. Before venturing onto the road and riding back into the area where the butchering camp and cave were supposed to be, I stopped before a road sign. It stated that I was on Squaw Creek Road and I could continue straight on to ride up the hill twenty-two miles to a landmark known as Heaven's Gate. It is located on top of Seven Devils Mountains with the very peak of this grand formation being 8,429 feet. The view from the summit I have heard is supposed to be indescribably beautiful but it is twenty two miles of narrow, winding roads to reach it and would require several days to go up and back down again. Traveling by horseback or burro is about the only way to attempt the hazardous upward climb on the rocky, rutted trail with very few outlets for passing, which would make it impossible for a wagon to attempt such a trip. There is little room for error riding up or down the road, with a mountain wall to the right and to the left there is danger of diving off the cliff into Hell's Canyon below. Hells Canyon is the deepest gorge in North America, the rampaging Snake River having cut through its rough, black basalt walls. Its depth is 7,913 feet from He Devil Mountain down to the Granite Creek at its base. I could see that portions of the trail were blocked here and there with rock slides, and wondered if anyone had ever been killed by the unfortunate timing of the dislodging of debris from the right side. And even though I have heard of the incredulous beauty from up there, I will simply have to picture it in my mind's eye.

It has been said that Heaven's Gate was named so because it is the closest one can get to heaven while still on the earth. And you can witness the corners of four states from up there, where Oregon and Washington border each other and the tip of Montana over the Bitterroot Mountains to the east and of course, I am physically standing in Idaho. I could picture the mountains rising high, tipped in their snow caps, sharply dropping or sloping down to generous forests and valleys. I felt absolute seclusion and complete freedom as if I was actually standing on top of the world amid nature's breathtaking wonders. I remained perfectly still, just calmly resting and letting the wonders of nature free me from all of the anxiety that was inside of me. I felt a surge of inspiration and would never let anyone hinder my exploration here in my birthplace.

I turned onto the road to Papoose Creek to search for the cave where Grandfather had told me that it should be, and I didn't see any signs of civilization. I kept going and came to the butchering encampment that had been used for processing of the animals long ago. I would have expected it to be abandoned and grown over with sage brush by now. But it appeared to be fully operational and its hardware was surprisingly up to date looking, indicating to me that it perhaps was still in use. Besides that, this area remained undeveloped and natural as it was in my family's time of occupation; nothing had taken over this wonderful wilderness and desecrated its habitat. Up the road a little farther I saw a historical marker and dismounted my horse so I could read it and see what piece of history that it was paying tribute to. It was the 'Legend of Seven Devils' and is quoted as follows:

*"Many, many moons ago the Indians made annual hunting trips to these mountains. On one of these trips, an

Indian brave – one of the best hunters in the tribe – was lost in these mountains. He wandered around trying to find the other members of the tribe, but became frightened because he saw a devil looking at him. A little later, another devil came around from behind him. As time went on, more devils appeared until the total was seven. When the members of the tribe finally found him, and he had recovered his strength sufficiently, he related his adventure. Hence, the mountains were named Seven Devils by the old prospector to whom the Indians told the legend."

I had finished studying the legend and started thinking about the way that our Native American ancestors felt about things. Their whole way of life, and that of their families and tribes was often put completely and trustingly into the hands of the alignment of the planets and the stars. Spirits and ancestors, prayer rocks, dancing ceremonies also had a big role in determining everything, from how they lived, where they lived, if they lived and how they believed. The passing of the traditional pipe of peace, the strong teas, the mystical fire of the sweat lodge often decided matters of such importance as entire relocations of the tribes. Or simpler matters such as hunting or harvesting trips and when they should move to higher elevation into the winter lodges in the winter. The elders taught our people to always look to the heavens for spiritual guidance and help in selecting the pathways that would be followed by all.

I stood there daydreaming some more about our traditions and how fortunate I was to have them instilled in me, so that I would realize the importance of passing them on to my children. And then something stopped me cold. My stomach felt as if it was invaded by butterflies and my heart had a short, dull stabbing pain that left me as rapidly as it had started. And then, my body froze, but with excitement and anticipation, not with fear or dread. I could sense someone standing directly behind me. But I found that I did not feel threatened in any way; whoever it was, would not harm me. I turned around to face the stranger and I was stunned and mystified by who I saw. For in front of me stood someone so like me, that it was as if I was facing myself.

*(Source: A Walking Tour of Riggins)

Chapter Fourteen   ≈

GENERATIONS UNCOVERED

I froze solid, but not with fear or alarm. I simply could not fathom what I was seeing. Am I asleep and dreaming all of this? Am I actually standing here looking at a portrait of myself? The woman before me has the same details on her face that I see each day in the mirror. Each of us, standing there, pondering whom this duplicate could be and where had the other come from? Neither of us could utter a single word, we just stood there and stared at each other, while visions of family ran through our minds. The memory scanning went back to childhood, until we both hit upon the only conceivable possibility. We each thought that the other girl looked about the same age, so there was little doubt which relative we each were. Our looks of confusion and incomprehension turned to ones of undeniable recognition and ecstatic surprise.

After which we pitched excitedly toward each other with arms extended to embrace each other heartily. I started the identification with, "I'm Josie, remember me?" To which she laughed and said, "I'm Sharon, remember me?" Anxious now and grabbing hold of each other, almost knocking each other over with excitement, we spoke in unison, "You're my cousin!" Again, the exuberance was timed as we both resounded with an emphatic "Yes!" We held each other tightly, giggling and crying; each of us relishing in our newly found relative.

Sharon and I as young girls highly resembled each other, and truthfully, we could have been sisters. Both of us had brown hair with reddish hues and were thin to the extreme, with bones protruding from anywhere that there were bones to protrude from, with a stick-like frame. Now the two of us have grown to maturity, and while still of moderate frame, show characteristics of women in their late forties. The hair on each of our respective heads has turned various shades of white, gray and silver, the same identifiable trait that my mother and her father's lineage also possessed.

Sharon and I climbed into her wagon and put my horse in tow on the back and drove the couple of miles or so toward the little village which they had been so fortunate to achieve as their new world. Upon entering, a quiet little park with picnic facilities came into view first with rows and rows of ponderosa pine trees in the background. We unhitched the horses and took off their harnesses so they could rest and put mine in the corral with hers. Then Sharon and I went to bask in the peaceful tranquility of this quiet piece of unchanged and undeveloped landscape. We mused over memories of our youth while taking a leisurely stroll through the tall pines and green meadows skirting the village. She pointed things out to me and explained that what had started out as a matter of life, death and survival had miraculously resulted in this wonderful place where everyone was happy, safe and free at last.

Beyond this wall of woods was a meticulously groomed small town, positioned at the base of the mountain. Experiencing freedom from persecution they unanimously had named their new village, "Salvation." The safe haven that they have built was carefully planned and reflected as much in the building structures and positioning. Every family had their own home, each modest in size, resembling a scattering of cabins but still in close proximity to one another. They had only acquired electricity in their village about five years ago, still leery to allow the outside world to know that they were there, and invade the privacy they had fought so hard for. They still lived without any running water indoors yet, but there were several runoffs from the mountain where the water was fresh and clear.

The sun was setting and it would be dark in just a few hours. She said that it was pretty late for an announcement as monumental as my return. She would sneak me into her cabin for the night; tomorrow would be soon enough to reveal my presence to the family members left behind so long ago. And she winked at me, and said, "Besides, I don't want to share you with anybody else just yet!" We walked around the perimeter of the beautifully landscaped area into a small entrance through the pines that was hardly noticeable as a path. We were just behind the cabin which she shared with her husband, Francis and her dogs and cats. We set one of the dogs to barking ferociously, but she assured me that it was only a tiny little creature. She said Francis was away visiting his family and we would have the whole place to ourselves to reconnect with each other.

We spent the evening talking and learning about each other and our lives. Sharon and I had been separated somewhere in our first ten years and had not grown up with each other and knew very little about the other one. We knew that our mothers did not speak to each other very often-sad but true, and neither of us knew anything more than that. When asked, they did not disrespect or have bad feelings toward the other one; each simply said that they did not have much in common. No matter how hard we pressed them as we became older, no further explanation was even considered due to us.

I told her the story of my life as I remembered it after we left home for new territory. I detailed the passing of our grandparents Annahah and Ignatious and my parents and my husband Allen. And I shared with her that Allen and I had been blessed with Anna, Allen, Jr. and Mae, and our three cherished grandchildren, Michael, Madelyn and Joseph. And I learned that she and Francis did not have any children, but she had been caregiver to many in Salvation.

After we retired to bed, Sharon asked me what had made me return to Idaho now to search for the Blue Doves who were lost to me. I told her of the letter from Arnold Able that I had received and that I had to follow up this lead even though I did not remember who he was. I let her read his letter, and she just nodded her head as she was reading it and said, "Yes, Josie you have so many family members and friends here to catch up with and it will be a huge shock that you are here." And then she beamed widely and nodded, silently remembering Arnold and his wife and what it would mean to them to see Josie again. "What are you smiling about Sharon?" I inquired. "Have you seen your friend Rose, yet?" she asked. "No, I haven't, how is Rose? How does she look now?" I asked her. "She is fine and she looks pretty much like we do, thirty years older than when you saw her last," she said grinning. Sharon said their paths do not cross often. She remains here in Salvation the majority of the time and Rose is in New Meadows a lot. "I was hoping you could go with me to New Meadows to see her," I said. Sharon replied hesitantly, "Sure, I'll go with you down there, we'll check and see when she is there first, though; we might not find her there for a few days yet." "I don't want to wait very long!" I said. "You'll get to see her Josie!" Sharon answered.

Somewhere after I reached adulthood, I should have taken a chance and at least written to Rose in an attempt to locate her. I have carried a significant amount of guilt with me for not doing so. The last thing I remember of her is that we were digging camas roots together on Weippe Prairie in the fall and then we left in November. No, that can't be true; my mother said that I had been sick at least six months prior to our escape from here. That would mean that the bulb gathering that I remember would have been the year before. How could that be that I have no recollection of that long span of time in between? Where did approximately a year of my life go? Had my wretched fever from the smallpox caused a memory loss of that enormity? That seems almost impossible, but it had undeniably happened that way to me. My memory had been wiped out, and I know there were important things to discover here, not just reuniting with my loved ones. I need to stop myself from these bitter thoughts and questions that have plagued me for now and enjoy this phase of my reunion here in Salvation.

I was saddened and told her that I had missed everyone and had always felt horribly guilty about not contacting anyone or coming out here sooner. But I was told we were in hiding and would be for the rest of our lives and that we could not jeopardize our safety or that of anyone in Riggins. I was too young to attempt any kind of trip back the first few years we were in North Dakota, and then after that I married, had a family and Allen and I had a business to run and a return trip wasn't feasible. It had been deeply engrained into me that punishment and serious repercussions from the Army would always be a possibility no matter how many years had passed by. We laughed together and cried together many times that evening, just talking about the days of our youth, good ones and bad ones.

Now, of course, the era of terror has passed and the fear of the Army riding in and squelching their existence has been put away for many years now. So the ability for Sharon and the others to live comfortably and freely in mainstream society has been possible for about a decade now. But each and every descendant would remain closely guarded when it came to matters of their lineage and ancestors. When in town this last week buying supplies, someone had heard that there was someone searching for their relatives bearing the same tribal last name of Blue Dove. And they had been unable to figure out who or where I was to speak with me, and now here I am coming to them. And still after all this time, they were suspicious of my motives upon inquiring about their people who were my people too.

Sharon said that the families that had made it to Papoose Cave took a new last name as symbolic gesture and the need for secrecy. They had no intention of letting the outside world know that they were there, but sooner or later some of the clan had to venture out, especially the younger ones. They had decided that their surname would be "Bewer," which would remind them constantly that they would need to always be alert and "beware" of anything or anyone even slightly suspicious. No one must do anything to jeopardize their well hidden solstice under the mountain. They had always referred to the relatives that did not make it out through the school as "the lost ones," which our family was among. And these last thirty years we had all been living out our lives without any knowledge of the others' survival. We had been fine in North Dakota, and they had thrived well in their encampment in Idaho. And hopefully, the same could be said of Vincent and his family, if they had reached their destination and been able to live out their lives in safety as well. Alphonse's family as well as ours felt great sympathy for Leopold and his followers who had been led under false pretenses to dormancy on the reservation lands. For fear of discovery there was no attempt made between the four families to contact one another. Better left unknown than to bring harm to someone simply for the sake of knowing.

For the past three decades there had been absolutely no word of what had happened to Ignatious and Annahah, or Frederick and Isadora and I. They certainly did not want to believe that we were all dead; a party of five would be no match standing up against the Army seeking our independence from them. So they prayed that we had found refuge somewhere, had started over and lived free, fruitful lives. They had been under the assumption at that time that either we had been part of the roundup of remaining Nez Perce that went to Oklahoma with Leopold's clan or escaped with Vincent's to Canada. Until, that is, Steven, one of Leopold's grandsons, had surfaced here in Idaho, much like I have, looking for answers. Then the story of the incarceration to the reservation in Oklahoma was revealed and that we were not among those people transported there. That being the case cut our odds of survival down greatly in their eyes. But Grandfather Ignatious and my father; Frederick had decided that the trail of Blue Doves sneaking into hiding was moving along too slowly and not everyone would be able to escape that way. The decision was made to just take off one night, enlightening no one to the secret plan they had developed. They felt that waiting our turn to enter the school and slip under the mountain would be too far away to be counted on as sure thing. There were still many family tribal members huddling together nervously awaiting their evacuation time from the village. I had heard them talking about it over and over again, if they in fact had made the correct decision. They feared that they may never be forgiven for not including other families in the separation of the brothers and their children and grandchildren.

A whole new world of the Blue Doves had been established here, and the outside world had no knowledge of their existence. The Army had been in the area from time to time, but they really didn't look at the village as members of the Nez Perce tribe. They more or less assumed that they were miners trying to scratch out a living in the mines under Seven Devils Mountains. They had hidden in plain sight, and gotten away with it. They never had to use the lie that they had devised that they had come inland from the Oregon coast and settled here, members of a tribe that the Army had no quarrel with. Now the time of danger had relatively passed and they now lived openly at Papoose Cave, but they still handled themselves guardedly. This new home had provided them with shelter and seclusion when it had been imperative to their needs, and they dedicated themselves to protecting this home they had built in the name of freedom.

The Nez Perce once again flourished on their native lands and they had resumed some of the lifestyles of their ancestors as well as acquiring a few new skills from the new world outside them. At first, life was pretty primitive and very difficult; they needed to remain isolated in the cave. Any form of existence in the daylight was impossible. There was only one section in the cave that provided enough height and ventilation for them to have a wood fire, and then only at night for the least possible risk of discovery. They remained contained in their rock fortress a little under a year, and then only let a few people go out into the field for short amounts of time. People were reacting poorly to the living conditions, and finally they just took the chance to go out and exhale some of the cave dust. They began feeling better immediately after they were able to inhale the fresh air and soak up some natural light and the sun's warming rays.

Sharon was bubbling over that she couldn't wait to take me to our family and have everyone guess whom I might be. We resembled each other greatly, and truthfully it would be undeniable that this duo shared the same family genes. I was thankful that there was an entire parish of kinfolk alive and waiting for me to rediscover the family unity we had once shared. There certainly would be plenty of pleasant confusion and exuberant questions when we first arrive and everyone is alerted that a family member has come back with Sharon. It would have to be. No one else has been or will be allowed in their camp, they had always lived their lives that strictly guarded.

Sharon went and knocked on all of the doors up one side and down the other and told everybody to come out and meet in the park at 11:00. She had something astonishing to tell them and they wouldn't want to miss it. When I walked in through the trees toward the gathering of people, they just looked at me at first, not knowing what they should be seeing. As I walked up closer to them with Sharon, she excitedly squawked, "Look who I found!" No one reacted at first, until Uncle Herman stood up with his mouth gaping open and eyes wide and gleaming. Then he began to cry and laugh and said, "You little imp, did you come to let my chickens loose again?" I ran into his arms and we hugged each other so tightly I was a little bit afraid that we would crush each other from the intensity of the embrace.

The rest of the crowd moved in around us now, they knew exactly who I was. That story was among the many, many stories that Herman had told in his reminiscences of his loved ones lost to him. He had been deprived of his mother and father, brothers, sister and nieces and nephews all in one horrendous moment. But he did have his family. His wife, son and daughters were with him and many other relatives had successfully made it out with them underground.

Uncle Herman always had a fabulous sense of humor. He was a jokester, and played plenty of practical jokes in his day. I suspect that's where my cousin Mary Jane got her love of mischief and daring to do what her mother would be mortified to know that she was doing. He proudly announced to me, "I'm the Mayor of Salvation," to which I threw back my head, laughed and replied, "I wouldn't have expected anyone else to be." Everybody laughed with us then, they knew it was a title of respect, not so much one of duties performed.

I started to relay to them the saga of our Quiet Escape to safety. They listened intently, for this was a portion of family history that they did not know about. We were an absent branch of the family tree, and they were hungry for information about us. I tearfully began telling them that Grandma Annahah died after we fled, but I was so wracked with fever that I only foggily remember her passing away. But I had realized the full impact by the time we laid her to rest. That was another effective tool that my parents could use in trying to prove to me that my inklings of another life did not take place.

The only three people of my generation who had ventured away from their new valley home and pursued life in the mainstream were Mary Jane, Roger and Luanne. It was necessary for some persons to earn money for things that were not available within their resources of the land or from trading the old fashioned way. Roger had sought employment at the Rapid River Fish

Hatchery south of town just to the west of the Little Salmon River. They mitigated the Chinook salmon runs after the Hells Canyon Dams were built. Sharon said she had been there and Roger showed her the life cycle of the salmon from the egg stage to the smolt stage when they are released to go to the ocean. Mary Jane worked at the library in town, she had always been obsessed with learning to read anything that she could, and when we were young, reading material was rare. Now she had access to as many books as she could possibly read in her lifetime. Roger and Mary Jane were brother and sister and lived together up on Bean Creek Saddle, north of Riggins. Luanne was a sister to them and she and her husband owned the Cattleman Café in Riggins. I had eaten there this morning and had no idea that the person serving me my breakfast was actually a relative.

On Sunday morning we went to my room to obtain fresh clothing for me and then on to the Cattleman to see Luanne again. We entered and seated ourselves at a small table in the farthest corner in the back of the room. When Luanne came out, she and Sharon greeted each other and she asked Luanne if she knew who I was. Luanne replied, "You were in here yesterday, weren't you?" I nodded that I was and just smiled at her. Then I said, "Do you recognize me? I'm your cousin, Josie." And she dropped the tray with the glasses she had brought to our table and made no move to catch them as they fell. Luanne's face was flawless and she reddened easily, I remember that now. She had more lightly colored skin than I despite her full Nez Perce bloodline. She blushed crimson and sat down with us without saying a word at first. When she recovered herself she said, "My god Josie, we all thought that you were dead. How? How did you survive?" I gave her a brief summation of the facts of our escape and journey to North Dakota to which she listened intently. Luanne and I had not spent a great deal of time together as she was about ten years older than I. She looked at Sharon and asked her if I had met my family yet, and Sharon told her about the meeting in the park on Saturday. And then she said that we were heading up to Bean Creek Saddle to see Mary Jane and Roger now. Luanne questioned, "Is that all the people that you've seen so far? No one else?" To which I questioned, "Who else is there?" Sharon and Luanne looked at each other and didn't say anything. I was confused and wondered how many other people they thought I needed to rekindle with and who could they be. Sharon just grinned that same grin as when she asked me about Rose on Saturday night; is that who they're talking about? I wonder.

Mary Jane and Roger had the same reaction as Luanne to seeing me standing before them in their doorway, alive and well. Just thirty years older than the last time we were all together. Mary Jane and I remembered instantly the bond that we had shared from toddler stage up through our teenage years. Then we had been ripped apart when the terror was beginning to engulf our village and the likelihood of ever seeing each other again was miniscule. My mother, along with her brothers and their families, had faithfully celebrated every tribal ceremony and numerous special events together. In spite of the large number of the relatives present we had been the closest to them, so the separation from us was painfully difficult.

I also remember one summer that my mother had become so violently ill that it was necessary for me to move in with Uncle Herman and his family. I was thrilled to be living with my cousins, Luanne, Roger and Mary Jane for a time, while my mother was recovering. They weren't sure if she was contagious and so had been placed under quarantine by my grandfather, the healer for all in our village. I was removed from the household not only so I wouldn't contract whatever illness had sickened my mother, but also because she needed complete bed rest, and having a small child at home was not restful.

Mary Jane and I were mischievous children and we managed to get into trouble for many things. There were mud pies thrown at the milk wagon, using her mothers sewing quills for arrows, (they should work, shouldn't they?) We had heard about people digging for gold and gave a try at that too in the most inconvenient of places, of course. We were climbing up the gigantic piles of corn fodder being stored for the winter in the barn, and I lost a moccasin and I remember how mad everyone was when we couldn't find it. My Uncle Herman did come across it however. When he gave it back to me he told me that a cow had eaten the fodder and the shoe and had returned it in the form of a cow pie. We used to dress up in our Grandma Annahah's clothes at our house and listen in to the adults having a conversation in the native Nez Perce tongue. We understood some, but they spoke so fast and fluently that we could only pick out a few words, usually.

Roger was a little older than us and put in a place of responsibility already and very seldom accompanied us in our childish pranks. But he appreciated the humor of our indiscretions and did laugh with us at the outcome, but denied any involvement every time, regardless of how guilty he may have looked or been. He would occasionally play baseball with us, which required a nice thick stick and a few rocks, and we played with him awhile like that until we realized that he was hitting the rocks straight at us on purpose. We continued playing with him, but with a substitution of corn cobs for the painful stones. They didn't fly as far, but they certainly hurt a lot less and didn't leave bruises behind.

The oldest of the three, Luanne, wasn't allowed to come out and play with us at all; she was in the house, or in the garden working steadily with their mother. And she was only allowed to cease her duties at the very end of the day like the other adults; after supper was a time for reflection and sitting on the front porch with all of us present. Luanne would read to us then. She was very gifted in her ability to speak well and had a natural talent for reciting poetry.

I was returned home two weeks later, after my mother's symptoms had lessened, and I spent many long hours tending to her while she was still recovering. But she told me repeatedly that I was rapidly speeding her back to good health. She believed I had been bestowed with the "healing powers." She had regained her full strength after four weeks and had credited my caring techniques for that rapidity in her recovery. Grandfather told me that my gift had saved his only daughter's life; such a grave illness of unknown origin could very well have been fatal. It was never truly discovered what had sickened her so severely, but in the end they concluded it was an insect bite that had poisoned her.

"Me, too, I've been blessed with the power to heal others," Sharon blurted out. "I've been healer to the ill and injured in this village since we went into the caves. My first patient or 'victim' I guess," she teased and went on, "was one of the children that had gotten lost in the caverns and was breathing stagnant air. When he was found, I took him directly to the air shaft and source of clean water. He was able to get fresh air into his lungs, and the cool water soothed his physical being, as well as his mental exhaustion. After that, I was regarded highly as the gifted one in my generation. With Ignatious and Isadora gone, we truly believed that we were left without a source of healing powers. We didn't know who we were going to turn to for either medicine or instruction in the ways of spirit healing. And it turned out to be me in our family branch of the Blue Dove tree."

We had all undergone destruction and devastation of each of our individual family's lives. There would be stories of joy, laughter, heartbreak and also tears shared while reacquainting ourselves with each other. Some were tears of thankfulness, for this reunion and some of regret, that we had been separated as very young children. I repeated the stories that I had told to everyone in the park yesterday about the five of us who crept away into the stormy night. They anxiously awaited every detail of the sudden disappearance of us from their lives and I filled them in with the best that my memory could offer them.

I wasn't the first Blue Dove to return home looking for answers. They told me that Steven had returned from Oklahoma and told the story of their trip there, life there, deaths, marriages, births, etc. And Steven had lived it; he was a young man of fifteen and fully capable of remembering the details accurately. He then gave them a firsthand accounting of the events that occurred for Vincent and Leopold's families on their last moments of freedom. And then as he grew to be an adult, he decided to seek out his relatives lost to him in a difficult separation. He had heard the closely guarded secret of the underground evacuation from within the confines of their sad, but new home on the reservation. And he had read the numerous history books written on the legends and fates of the Nez Perce. The stories of Old Joseph and Young Joseph, and those of Leopold were facts recorded for all to peruse.

Steven first had made sure to tell them that all of the family members in his Grandfather Leopold's following had all arrived safely at the reservation. And that his sisters, Linda and Sandra were still residing in Oklahoma: Linda in a neighboring town and Sandra on the reservation. No one had been left behind, killed or encountered any trouble whatsoever. They had simply accepted their fate and decided it would not be in their best interests to rebel in any way. The people who had not been able to complete their plans of escape from Riggins and the Army had been herded like the buffalo that they hunted. They had been forced with rifles into one of their own winter lodgings on the second ledge of Seven Devils Mountain. Soon all members of their family branch that had been captured had been encased in the lodge and guards posted within arms lengths of each other. Once the hysteria and struggling had ceased, it was time to try and devise a plan to wriggle out of this once peaceful den-turned-stockade. The Nez Perce once protective surroundings was to be an encampment for their misery. They had now become backed into a corner and the trapped animals of the army.

The lodge was almost completely hidden in a densely wooded mass of trees wedged in and among many boulders. This cozy winter respite from the elements had now become a quite effective prison. Rows and rows of trees blocked the winter winds whistling off the canyons. There was a very narrow avenue of escape as two thirds of the area was directly atop the steep mountain. In their cold weather solstice, they felt perfectly safe, as the area leading up to the lodge was always well guarded. The Army seldom bothered with them or wanted to war with them during the cold months; they preferred warmer climates for themselves as well as their horses and mules packed with supplies. Sleeping on the frozen, ice encrusted ground with snow on it did not appeal to them.

Steven said that they were sure that it must have been a tornado that swept in that night. He saw straw pile up in a single, square column, like stacked mats. Then a wall of water came up, but they were high enough up to watch this phenomenon without the fear or danger of harm. The dry canyon filled with the flying horizontal sheets of water, anything that had been down there didn't have any chance of survival whatsoever. The Army waited it out for a few days until the weather calmed somewhat, even though the terrain was full of mud and difficult to pull their wagons through. When they were all lined up, they carefully surrounded them and then pulled out for their new land of promise and carefree living.

Chapter Fifteen

<u>DECEPTION'S FACE</u>

Sharon talked me into spending another night in her quiet cabin in Salvation. It would allow me the opportunity to visit further with my family with which I had thankfully been rejoined. Looking back from today, I wish that I had taken the time out of my busy home life and workplace to make this journey a lot earlier in my life. I would have been able to fill portions of the void which became deeper as my life grew on. It seems as though I left my birthplace and my roots worlds ago, with my desire to know things constantly picking away at me. I had been accustomed to being surrounded by family and yet, spent countless hours creating memories with this extended family each week of my life until my seventeenth year.

Undoubtedly, that has molded me into the woman that I am this day. I'm very conscious that one moment you are encompassed within the circle of relation and friends and the next moment they are all gone. Vanished; not only left behind in an escape from authority, but also an abandonment of the ties that bind you together and make you a whole human being. I kept my husband close to me in both my physical persona and my mental and emotional structure. I was not overprotective of my children but very aware that it could end in an instant and consistently made that known to them. The opportunity before me today is a precious one indeed, and I will cherish each moment spent reuniting with my uncle, cousins, their children and grandchildren.

When morning arrived and we had gathered ourselves ready for another day of reminiscing, we walked back to the little park, and I was surprised to see Uncle Herman sitting there in a chair all by himself. We exchanged hugs and a kiss on the cheek and then he grinned his grin at me again, which always made me laugh. I was excited to talk to him further about what had happened in everyone's lives after their successful escape to this haven. When we left them for the unknown in that unrelenting storm it severed us from them and our loved ones only to be reunited with them now. I was anxious to hear of births, deaths, illness, I wanted to know all of it, good or bad. Herman and Sharon were equally as curious to hear the personal stories of Ignatious, Annahah, Isadora, Frederick and myself and my family. Or so I thought that is how the day would progress.

Sharon pulled our chairs close enough so we could touch each other, which I thought was very strange for her to do so. When we sat down she gently took both of my hands in hers and Herman put a hand on my shoulder. Sharon began to speak, "Josie, we know that you have traveled a long way in search of the secrets and truths of your past life here. And also truths about other generations that caused the ruination of some parts of yours. Uncle Herman and I are going to reveal to you some indescribably shocking events that occurred in this family which left everyone reeling and scrambling for answers." Sharon was beginning to struggle for her words now and I could see her mouth going dry making it more difficult for her to articulate her words. Herman spoke and almost whispered, "Josie, we're sorry this is going to be so difficult for you to hear, but we must tell you some pretty hard facts."

Very seriously, Sharon said, "We're going to tell you a story of something that happened before you were born, between a man named John Ray Mon and your mother." "What?" I exclaimed. Sharon began again, "He set his sights upon her and began to attempt to court her.   And without her consent he announced that she was his girl and that he intended to marry her." She took a long pause before continuing on, "Your mother did not reciprocate those feelings and she did not trust him at all. He had a history of being a troublemaker and had been involved in some shady deals. She let him know that she did not appreciate his public speech about her and that she wanted no part of a man like him and rejected him coldly.   Isadora said he immediately lost control and he began to breathe loudly, and his chest heaved in and out in rapid movement. His eyes turned black with anger, and he gritted his teeth at her, and she could see his rage escalate while standing before her. He lunged at her and started pulling her hair and told her that she was going to be his. She screamed back at him that she would not and slapped him across the face as hard as she could.   This infuriated him further still, and he pushed her down, and he started to hit her, and hit her, and hit her." "Are you sure about this?" I asked. Could I believe this story? I had never heard anything about it; could it be true? John Ray Mon? Beat up my mother?   Sharon was attempting to control her emotions, she was struggling to finish the story, and I could see her choking back her tears. "Josie, I'm sorry, I guess she never wanted you to know while she was alive, but now you need to know some things about this."   She continued, "John Ray Mon beat her quite severely and just left her laying there when he was finished." I was stunned and could say nothing, just sit there and sob listening to this terrible story.

Uncle Herman, his bright grin gone now, spoke, "I found her Josie; helplessly, almost lifelessly, unable to move and her speech frozen. All she could do was look up at me pitifully with tears streaming down over her bruised cheeks and into her lovely hair. I sat with her until she could move some and then I carried her home in my arms. Fortunately, with rest and privacy she recovered eventually with no apparent physical scars left behind. But the shame of John's profession of love that turned into an evil display by a wretched, selfish man was visible on her pretty young face." Herman shook his head in negativity, the poor man; he was reliving it while telling it to me. I felt as badly for him being the one to have found her like that as I did for my mother who had lived through it. I hugged him and just held onto him for awhile. We both needed the comfort of embrace right now. I asked them feebly, "But she was alright, wasn't she, I mean it sounds like she recovered from the beating, didn't she?" "In some ways, she did, and in other ways, she never would," was his response. "We have more to tell you, Josie, and there is no way possible to prepare you for any of this, so we're just going to tell you all of it, all of it…so much to tell you," Herman said.

Herman spoke somberly and continued, "John Ray Mon was lacking any real emotion for another human being except for himself and had been hard and obstinate his entire life. What happened to Isadora was a cruel and twisted act of obsession inflicted upon an innocent young lady guilty of nothing except being a kind, caring individual. He was a man crazed by a need for the total domination of another person to prove his superiority to others," Herman heatedly said and continued. "For John Ray Mon to exert such forceful rage and exhibit such blatant disrespect for another human being was without question an unforgiveable act. At first, he denied all wrongdoing, saying that Isadora was lying and that she must have been meeting some other man somewhere. He further stated that he had no part in what had happened to her, still professing to love her and didn't so much as blink when questioned. But no one believed him, given his volatile personality and everyone, including his own brother, turned on him. He was thrust out of the circle of protection within the community by all, not just those directly affected by the debauchery." I was spellbound and listening intently, waiting on what would follow, and Herman started again. "Isadora's brother, Hubert, my brother, confronted John and a vicious fight ensued which ended horribly. John killed Hubert in another display of human disregard." "Hubert? Hubert who? I didn't know that my mother had a brother named Hubert; why didn't I know this? How could I not know that I had another uncle?" I screamed.

Sharon spoke again now, after being silent for so long, "It all happened before you were born, it changed the lives of everyone thereafter and no one spoke of it after it occurred. The grief took an irreversible toll on Ignatious, Annahah, and Isadora, and in order to go on, they buried the atrocity when they buried your uncle, Hubert," she said. My mouth gaped open in shock and uncertainty. This had all happened within my family and I had no hint of it growing up? No, I must be inside another of my frightful night dreams waiting for the ghostly man to spring out at me. I was mortified, "My poor mother; what a tumultuous ordeal for her to endure and how guilty she must have felt for having such a man enter her life."

Then I asked them, "What happened to this John Ray Mon? I hope he was hung from a rope by the villagers and my family." I stammered out, my blood pressure rising thinking about this evil man and the everlasting horror inflicted upon my family members. After such a cruelty, causing a scandal into their quiet, reserved lives; when they had done nothing to warrant such behavior; he didn't deserve to live. Herman said, "Ray Mon was lazy and always looking for an easy way to get what he wanted no matter how dirty and underhanded it was. He disappeared, just plain dropped out of sight. Speculation was that the men had gathered up a lynch party and took care of him somewhere, just like you said." Herman shook his head in disgust. "He was never seen again, so if he wasn't dead, he was smart enough to take off." Stunned, I hung my head, partially in disbelief of this whole thing, and partially in absolute pity for my mother, her brothers and their parents. I wonder, is that why my family was always so sad looking and emotionally detached? All photos of them are so straight faced with no joy in their eyes, no spark or light, just blank stares. No doubt each of them was remembering the empty place in the family photo where Hubert had once been seated among them.

I asked Herman, finally, "Tell me about my Uncle Hubert, were all of them that ashamed that they would deny his existence? They must have destroyed all the photographs ever taken with him in it too, I have never seen any." "Yes," was his reply, "They did. The impact on them was so grave that they could not live with any reminders that he had been in their lives at all. So they just wiped him out of it, like he had never been born to them or lived with them for twenty years. Hubert was a happy youth who brought laughter out in everyone, no matter how stone faced the subject was," Herman answered with a hint of a smile. "And with him gone, so was the gaiety from their lives, and they were never able to carry on lightheartedly from that point forward." "What else do you remember of Hubert?" I asked him. His mouth twisted up at the corners and said, "He had this poem he used to run around rhyming all the time, catchy little tune, too. Let's see if I can remember some of it. Hmm, I think it goes like this:

'In winter I get up at night,   And dress by yellow candlelight,' Herman and I recited it together now, and then we stopped and I burst out that my grandfather used to recite that poem all the time about the long work days. He had told me that a little boy had made it up and used to say it every night before bedtime. I continued, "But grandfather said he didn't recall who that child was. How sad that it was his own son and he wasn't able to share that with his own granddaughter. That little boy was remembered by his father after all; he had kept him alive through his poem."   Herman asked me, "Josie, do you remember the rest of the poem? I can't seem to recall any more lines." "Yes, I do," I chimed.

'In Winter, I get up at night;   And dress by yellow candlelight.

In Summer, quite the other way;   I get up by the day.

But still I hear people's feet;   Trampling on the street.'

"Grandfather said that the poem meant that no matter how early a person got up, or how long he worked, there was always someone who got up earlier and worked longer still."

But the reality of the facts which I had just been told jolted me back into misery. I silenced myself to ponder on all of this family history again and just looked back and forth from Herman to Sharon and back again. These two deliverers of such repulsive news; it had been as difficult for them to bestow all of these details onto me as it had been for me to receive them. And then I began to tell them the story of my nightmares that I had experienced for many, many years now. I believe now that the persistent intruder into my slumber is not my

174

ghost, not at all, but my mother's. A horrible man waiting to lunge at her and not at me; not something that was threatening to me but to her. This horrid dream was not meant to cease until I found this episode of my life and learned of the confrontation which was its devastating cause. But I would have to suffer awake at the cost of discovering the catastrophic stream of horrors that my mother had been through. Ones that had altered her state of being and that had cost the life of her brother. It would take quite a period of time for me to process these enlightening details and put all of the incredible pieces into place in my mind.

Sharon and Herman glanced at one another in obvious uncertainty and nodded, and Sharon's lips slowly formed the words, There's more, Josie." My heart plummeted, what else could there possibly be? How much more did these people I thought I knew withhold from me? I feel as if we are talking about complete strangers here today, not my grandparents and parents whom I trusted and believed in. My voice barely gurgled out a reply of, "What more?" Sharon inhaled deeply before speaking, "When my mother Shirley became ill of health about ten years ago, she called me over real close to her one day. She looked up at me from her sick bed in the loudest voice she was capable of and said, "Sharon, the time has come for you to know some things, some facts-important facts-about your life." Sharon stopped quoting her mother, to say, "I was surprised that my life was any different than I had believed it to be, much like you are feeling right now." And then she continued, "She told me all about the tumultuous relationship between John and Isadora and the improprieties and repercussions which had resulted. And then she said that she had a confession to make, one that would affect me and change things for me, forever." Sharon said that she had thought to herself then, "How could I possibly be involved with the tale of the Ray Mon and Blue Dove hatred for one another?"

Sharon moved closer to me now and said that Shirley had then told her a heartwarming story, one of an ultimate sacrifice in her life and her husband's life. Sharon continued, "When John Ray Mon beat your Mother, it did not only leave behind cruel emotional scars, it also created permanent physical changes for her to struggle with. The pounding on her body had left internal scars which would never heal as the outside wounds had," she sadly told me. "Isadora and Frederick were never able to conceive a child, and it was concluded that it was because of the beating that Isadora had withstood." "But…I…me," confused I ranted, "Who gave birth to me?" I demanded. "Who are my mother and father?" I demanded and moved closer to the edge of my chair, almost falling into Sharon's lap. She smiled now and I sensed that it would be a pleasant shock that was to follow. She said, "Your parents are Shirley and Carl, Josie, you are my sister; we share the same birth parents. Which is why you and I are so similar to each other and look so much like each other too?" She gasped for air and said in her next excited breath, "You are not just my sister either, you are my twin sister!" She reached over and grabbed onto me and pulled me toward her in a silly kind of embrace, which was half comforting and half joking. My mouth gaped open and my eyes bulged, and I only partially returned the hug, still in an immense state of shock. "You are my twin sister? How did this happen? Was I just given away then?" I asked her. "Well, yes," she whispered. "But in a caring protective act of humanity," was her response. "How could this be true? You and I are sisters and were separated never to know about each other? How can that be humane?" I cried.

Sharon explained herself then, "My mother could not provide enough milk for two babies, and they had not the means to provide for double the amount of children which were expected. Isadora was so saddened by not being able to bear children that my parents decided to give you over to Frederick and Isadora to raise as their own daughter." Then she elaborated, "It was all done at the moment that we were born. It was decided that the first child born would be kept and the second child would be given; you are younger than me by just a few minutes. Only those present at the birth knew of the twins, and they were sworn to absolute secrecy, which they adhered to. All were touched by the sincerity of this gesture and happily honored the promise they made that day. Even though we were together at certain times throughout our childhoods, it would never have been thought by anyone or us that we were anything other than cousins," she said. "You mentioned yesterday that you thought that our mothers weren't very friendly toward one another. They were; they just didn't want the secret to be discovered if we spent too much time together." I could say nothing for awhile, just letting these inconceivable facts settle in a little bit. When I was finally capable of speech again, I said humbly, "What a brave, unselfish act of compassion for your parents to give one of their newborn daughters to someone unfortunate enough to not be granted offspring of their own."

Then another thought popped into my head, "But what of my mother's appearance? Didn't anyone notice that she didn't appear to be in a family way?" I queried. Herman spoke now, joking with me, "No, Josie, your mother had gained weight and was kind of a rotund woman then and could easily have concealed carrying a child without suspicion otherwise. And she would likely throw something at me for saying so out loud!" We all three had to giggle some at that comment. He was right, that is how I always picture her when she comes into my thoughts. What overwhelming news this is! I am not an only child as I thought! I have a sister, and it's a twin sister. I am astounded to learn that I have even more family ties here than I ever thought possible. This is what has been persistently hovering in my thoughts taunting me to come back here, I know it. But all of it would have continued for the remainder of my lifetime if not for the letter from Arnold, if I had let it go unnoticed. Somehow, with the guidance from all above and gone before me, he located me and set me on this wondrous journey back into time. And my children will have an aunt and their children a great aunt! And they will undoubtedly be relieved that there really were significant reasons for me to return home to Riggins, Idaho. They no longer need fear for my safety here; I am enveloped in the strong Bewer family and am heartily welcomed within the community of Salvation.

Chapter Sixteen

JUSTIFICATIONS

I could hardly wait to get to the switchboard office in Marion's house to place my call home today. I have such enormous news for my family to hear! They will be delighted that my search ended so well and that my instincts proved to be correct that I had important people to find. But I would wait for them to update me on their lives over the last couple of days before I start babbling out my incredible news.

I asked, "Are you all there tonight?" "Yes, we're all here." I heard multiple voices say together and laugh as they said it. I just wanted to verify that all three children were on the line so that I could share my happiness with them. Mae said, "You sound pretty cheerful today Mother." I replied, "So do you, my dear, what's new with you and Madelyn?" I wanted to change the subject so that I wouldn't dominate the conversation just yet, and give them each a chance to speak. Mae said, "I have something wonderful to tell you, I'm adopting one of the children from the Fort." "You are? How did you decide to do that?" I inquired of her. "Well, Madelyn is always so lonely at home, and is always bringing someone home to play with. And with Jack gone now, chances are she won't have a sibling." I said, "Perhaps you will find someone to love again and marry and have more children." Mae responded, "That may be Mother, but that won't happen for a long time, I'm not ready for something like that. All Madelyn talks about is having a baby sister, so we're going to bring one of the younger girls at the Fort into our home."

"Sounds like you've already decided on a girl then, have you?" I responded. "Oh, yes, I will definitely be getting a daughter and Madelyn has already decided which side of the bed she will be sleeping on," she said. "I think that's very generous of you to adopt one of the unfortunate children, and I'm proud of you for making that decision,'" I told her. "Thank you, I think it will benefit all of us, and our little Madelyn most of all," Mae said. "And I wouldn't mind having another grandchild in my life, either! Does my new granddaughter have a name?" I asked. "Yes, of course she has a name, she is called Kar Mon, but Madelyn calls her Carmen; we aren't certain of the origin of the name or the meaning. We do not know either what tribe that she is from; she was left here as a baby and no one knows by whom. She was just found in a basket, wrapped up nice and warm though, on the porch of the nurse's cabin one morning just as so many orphans are. It has never been determined who left her there. Several women who were pregnant were questioned, but all of their babies were present in the home," Mae answered. "She is Madelyn's closest friend and she really is the most in need of a home of all the children at the Fort. Which is probably why Madelyn singled her out to be close to; she loves being a little mother to the younger children." I replied, "I am very happy for your little family, give Madelyn and Kar Mol a big hug and a kiss from their Grandmother."

Anna grabbed the phone from her younger sister;."I think it's a great idea too, and I'll get another niece out of the deal!" she chimed in. "And we could use something exciting around here right now, with all the negativity going on." I questioned, "What are those people doing to you now, still throwing things at your house and into the yard?" "Yes," she replied, "but they've taken it to a higher level, they are throwing dangerous things now; we have had two windows broken out with rocks. And our front gate was ripped off and thrown out into the street and then they were brave enough to come right into the yard. They ripped up all of my flowers beds, and cut my shrubs off down to the ground. Then they came up onto our porch and smashed the bench that Lee designed and built for that spot." she told me angrily. "I can't believe they would do such drastic things; whoever is doing this should be locked up," I said. Anna told me that the sheriff was looking into it and questioning their neighbors as possible witnesses. But the damage had been done in the middle of the night, so chances were slim that anyone saw anything while it was happening. She said, "We're afraid now to let Michael out of our sight, and we're not letting him go down to the school. He would rather be at home or at the newspaper office with us anyway." I asked her, "Is he afraid with all the threats and vandalism?" "He's terrified." she replied. "And he's worried that they're going to do something to hurt us, maybe throw rocks at us when we walk outside of the house. So, he never wants to go outside at all now, and when we do go somewhere, he is so scared, he hides behind every tree and bush all the way into town. And while that is kind of comical to watch him do, it's also a very sad thing for him to feel he has to do." I replied, "I'm so sorry that those people are being so underhanded and hiding so no one can identify the culprit. Trying to get you and Lee to shut down the presses and stop the production of printing the news of their own hometown, what traitors they are. They should be more understanding of your situation with a business that you started on your own and are entitled to keep running. And they certainly should have respect for your family. I hope none of these people turn out to be friends or neighbors of yours." I did my best to calm her down and reassured her that they were doing the right thing in keeping a tight watchful eye on Michael to keep him from danger. And there are plenty of children who do not go to school, that have to stay home and tend the livestock or the crops in the fields. I wasn't the least bit worried about him learning; both his Mother and Father are intelligent enough to instruct him properly without sending him down the road to the one room schoolhouse.

Allen got on the line now and triumphantly told me, "Mother, you won't believe it, I sold your house the day before yesterday. A man stopped by the lumber yard and saw the for sale sign for the house. I took him to see it and he said he'd buy it right on the spot. I couldn't believe it, he said he just had to go to the bank and get his money out." My mouth dropped open in shock, "Really, you sold it that quickly? That's wonderful news! Then I'll be able to move in with you, Beth and Joseph when I get home." "Yes, you certainly will, I walked to the bank with the man, and he withdrew the money from his account and paid me in CASH!" Allen said loudly. "CASH, he'll have no mortgage on the place, he must be a rich man." I commented. "I think so too." Allen said, "And now we've all got plenty of money too." I had told the children that when I sold the house and moved into the Looking Glass that I wouldn't need any money to keep up the house. I would only have to provide for my personal expenses and medical care. So, I had decided to give each family a lump sum from the sale of the house. They could all use the money now while they are young and establishing themselves, rather than hanging onto it until after I am deceased to will it to them. And then Allen said, "I want to thank you Mother, for giving us all some money. It will help us get the Inn running and give my sisters an extra boost too." I replied, "You are all very welcome, I feel that it is the right thing to do and hope it gives each of you a little head start on life." "I'm certain that it will," he replied.

"I've got a funny thing to tell you now, strange and unnerving actually. We moved all of your things from the house and into the Inn." "Already?" I asked. "Yes, Beth and I set up your furniture nice and neat in the room that you chose on the first floor yesterday. We went back in this morning to carry in some boxes with your clothes and other things and all of the furniture was gone. Empty-the room was empty." "How could that be possible?" I asked. "I don't have any idea and neither does Beth. Baby Joseph is certainly not old enough to play a prank on anyone." He answered. "We started looking around room by room then and found your furniture, all set up in perfect condition in one of the rooms in the front of the Inn overlooking the river. We don't know how it got there, but we think it's a more appropriate home for you anyway, instead of tucked into the back corner of the place." "Well, thank you, it's kind of you to give me one of the nicer rental rooms." I said humbly. Then he said, "And we can only suspect that your furniture was moved the same way the place keeps itself clean and sparkling without us doing any work on it. So, it's best to just leave that alone, in the interest of not upsetting whoever or whatever is responsible." I guess that perhaps there is some truth to the legend of the spirits of the original owners drifting around the hotel. Maybe I would even witness some of their special caretaking. I was grateful to be cared for and taken into their home, and if it came with a couple of friendly ghosts, then I would never find myself lonely.

And now it was my turn to speak and share my good fortune with them, so I just it blurted out. "I found them! I found my family, lots of them!" Mae was on the other end, probably holding the phone away from her ear as far as was possible, but I heard her say, "Really?" I said, "Yes, really and I-you-we all have cousins, an uncle and a great uncle! I found them right where my grandfather said that they had gone into hiding and they still live there. They made a whole town right there on the other side of Preacher Mountain and called it Salvation, because they felt that they were saved from extinction." Mae's voice teetered a bit as she asked me, "Who did you find Mother?" I'm sure she felt relieved that my trip had merit and happy for me that I had found my lost ones after all. Some of the names of the people that I would tell them about would be familiar to them as the cousins that I had played with and told mischievous stories of. But nothing like this story would be, this was just plain unbelievable.

I began my tale telling immediately, "I found that my Uncle Herman is still alive, the one with the farm where I did all of those naughty things while I stayed there. And his children, Roger and Mary Jane still live here too, and I went to see them at their house up in Bean Creek Saddle the other day. And I had breakfast at the Cattleman Café, and little did I know that their sister, Luanne and her husband own the place. I did not recognize her the first time that I ate there and then I found out that she had actually taken my order and delivered my food!" "Wow," they all cheered at once into the telephone. "Really, they're all still there? And you've seen them all already?" Mae inquired. "That's amazing that you found them living there and right where you thought they would be Mother." Anna extolled. "Thank you," I replied tearfully, praise from my children always made me weak and grateful; they were a conscientious family. Allen spoke up, "What was their reaction to find out that you are still alive?" "They were all in a state of shock and not sure they believed what their eyes were revealing to them." I answered. "But when they saw me they absolutely knew without a doubt that I was their Josie, back from the dead or wherever I had drifted in from.   And they gathered all the people together living in Salvation so that I could meet the generations that had been born after I left them." I'm not sure who was talking now, because I could hear them talking to each other in the background.   All chattering about my cousins thinking that the dead had risen, or the dead walking, something like that.   I think they were genuinely relieved that it had all turned out so well, but they hadn't heard the best part yet.

"There's one person I haven't told you about my reunion with yet." I began quietly. "Who is that Mother?" was the response. "I told you that I had a cousin that I rarely saw, Sharon is her name." I said.   "What happened?   Didn't she believe it was you?" they asked.   "No, no, that's not it, she was the first person that I saw and she recognized me immediately." I told them. "Then what was it?" they asked again.   I said that they should all be sitting down and holding hands for the news I was going to deliver to them.   They replied that they were sitting down and had their heads tightly together all trying to listen and that was friendly enough.   I laughed because they were quite often comical, but also from nervousness for the next portion of my speech.   It must have felt like a long pause to them, because they urged me to start, and I spoke very calmly and clearly, "Sharon is my sister, my sister, I have a sister!" I could hear the oh's and ah's and the various rumblings on the other end.   Anna said, "How could that be; you're an only child, why wouldn't anyone have told you before?   You lived with them out there for seventeen years and no one said a word?"   "No, they didn't," I quipped.   I could hear ranges of astonishment in their voices, but they stepped back from their inquiry to congratulate me on my good fortune and new family member.

I rambled on again, "It is quite an intricate story and fascinating, I learned things that happened in this family that I never would have imagined could happen to us or anyone else. Things that people only read about in the mystery novels that keep us spellbound, anticipating the ending. The details are astonishing, and I can't wait to share them all with you when I get home. There are stories of murder, and horrible acts of cruelty, and ones of ultimate compassion and love for other human beings." "What! What murder, whose murder, what cruelty? And love too? All of that happened when? Come on, Mother, tell us," they demanded. I guess they weren't going to wait, and it wouldn't be fair to leave them dangling on the other end with only a taste of my discoveries. So, I gave them a briefing of the tragedies that happened to my shattered mother and grandparents and the impact and results that it had on their lives. I shared with them what I had learned here, and the story of all of it was met with shock, speculation and happiness. I assured them that I would learn more as I spent more time with everyone here and would have more details each time that I spoke with them.

I said that we probably should end the call now, we had talked an extensive length of time, and it had been an exhausting few days and I needed to rest. I need to visit with Rose yet, and there still is more to find, and I need to put some closure to those feelings. I would not go into detail because I had never told them anything about the longings that I had kept secret. Nor any of the other things or people that I suspected were a part of my last year there, one lost and left behind thirty years past. But before I ended the conversation, I teased them further and asked them, "Did I mention that Sharon is my twin sister? Yes, you heard correct; twin sister." And then there was silence; nothing but silence; from the other end of the long telephone line home.

PART TWO

Chapter Seventeen

THE RANSACKED INTRUSION

I had taken a horse and buggy for hire and ridden out to Allison Creek to visit our old homestead. I had come up the road and there it was, just as I remember it, the driveway on the west side of the house, with the shed standing straight ahead. I recognized the house, yard and outbuildings immediately from my memories of living here as a young girl. The barn was still standing where Rose and I would play in the haymow and use the top side of the stairway as a slide. There was the unique little house that I always wanted to play in, but was never allowed. I later found out it housed a well that we could activate if our primary one ceased to produce good water. I saw the silo, where myself and my friends were allowed to play, despite the fact that we could easily have climbed up the tall silo and fallen off at some point. I got down off the wagon and tied up the horse to the hitching post by the gate. I was facing straight east, and there was the most beautiful view. I could see the large garden area, still bordered by the plum and apple trees, and the berry bushes which had always been so lush and abundant. The house was sitting on the top of a hill, facing another house on the opposite hill with a substantial valley between them.

That house was where my best friend Rose lived and where we had ridden her horses for countless hours. The creek ran through the base of the valley and was still trickling through and under the little bridge across it. Rose and I had spent many hours wading in that creek and sliding around on it in our boots when it froze over in the wintertime. I had almost forgotten how beautiful it was here, I have been away for such a very long time; it was decades ago but feels more like centuries now. But I have a feeling of home and warmth, just standing here in this yard where Rose and I would sit on the rope swing hung from a massive oak tree. The house really has changed very little since we left it behind in our hasty escape long ago. It has just turned more of a faded aqua color than it had been then and didn't look quite as large as I recalled.

I slowly approached the front porch, where my mother had scrubbed clothes, plucked chicken feathers in boiling water, and where the trap door to the basement laid in the floor. I knocked on the porch door and shakily waited awhile, but decided to venture inside when no one answered. I meekly tapped on the inner door and excitedly anticipated its opening, so that I could get a peek inside of the kitchen. I was remembering every inch of my childhood home as I stood there, getting caught up in some memories, when the door opened just a crack. An elderly woman was looking at me through a small slit, and was being as quiet and cautious as a mouse sneaking up on a piece of cheese. I introduced myself to her as Josephine LeClaire, and told her that I had lived in this house when I was a child. She said that I must be mistaken, she had lived there her whole life and the homestead had been in her family for generations. I further tried to explain to her that I had been born there and lived there for seventeen years and had numerous pictures of it in my family album. Again, she said I was mistaken, no one but the Able's had ever owned the place since it was built in the late 1800s. Who were the Ables?

Then her frail, friendly voice dropped low and she told me that she wasn't interested in what I was selling and I had better go away. And that she was onto people like me, trying to trick her into something, and she slammed the door shut hard. I stood there in shock. What had made that nice, gentle seeming woman behave so rudely? I thought that there was recognition in that woman's eyes when I told her who I was and that her home had been my home too. What made her change so drastically? It was as if she had suddenly remembered something that made her afraid of me. I turned around with tears streaming down my cheeks and left the way I had come, down the sidewalk and out the gate past beautiful flowers and shrubbery. I wonder if they could possibly be offshoots from my time when this yard was always abloom with beauty and color. I was disheartened that I was unable to enter the house where I grew up and look around a bit, so I climbed up into the wagon and just sat there. It occurred to me then that perhaps the old woman was afraid I had wanted to lay claim to the place as mine. After we left, it would have been just sitting there for anyone to occupy, not legally, but certainly our return to occupy the house again would never happen. So, a nice family had taken it over, it looked like they had cared for it very well, I would just have to be grateful for that.

I tried to regain control of my crumbling emotions and looked across the valley to Rose's house on the next hill. I could really use Rose's shoulder to cry on right now, I miss her so much, more than I ever realized that I did, now that I am back here again. A woman's voice came from behind me, "Josie, Josie, are you real? Lucille said a strange lady who lived here was at the door and I didn't ever let her finish her sentence, I knew it was you. I had chills and goose bumps up and down my arms!" I climbed out of the wagon and replied, "I remember those goose bumps of yours, you always got them when you were excited about something!" "And I'm certainly excited to see you!" she said. I ran into her arms and said, "Me too, Rose, me too!" "How did you know where I lived?" Rose asked. "I didn't know; I was just coming to visit my old house and maybe yours too over there." I responded, nodding my head in the direction of her place. "Yes," she chattered, "How convenient that I live within walking distance of my folks over there." I told her the story of the letter and then handed it to her to read. She put her hand on her heart and said, "Oh, that man of mine, what a wonderful thing to do!" "Yes, in so many ways." I said. Then we both laughed at that one, I never suspected that she might be connected to the man who wrote the letter.

"I was afraid you would be in New Meadows. My cousin Sharon-or sister Sharon-I guess, said you stayed there some nights." I told her. "Yes, I do. My husband, Fritz, that's what most people call him, is away on business often. You know about your sister now?" she squeaked in high pitched tone. "Yes, I know the whole story, she told me everything and I spent a couple of days meeting family members all over again." I answered her. "Oh Josie, I'm so glad you've returned. I was sick, physically sick when I heard about what your parents and grandparents had done to you, all of it. How horrible was it for you when you found out?" She inquired. "I was so ill and in a coma when they took me out of here, and I remained that way until just before we reached the Idaho border and my grandmother passed on." I told her. "I mean about the other stuff that uh, you know, that happened-happened to you." Rose asked. "You mean about the war and being separated from all of my family and you Rose? I do not remember anything that happened right before we left in that horrible storm. My family said I was in a coma for months and the last thing that I remember about being here is you and I riding your horses and getting into trouble all the time with you," I laughed. "You lost your memory?" Rose commented. "Yes, I think I lost close to a year, the way I went back over the months before our escape," I replied. Rose then said, "Oh, Josie, you lost more than that, sweet Josie."

And then Lucille came out of the house again, this time laughing and coming straight toward me. She was smiling and said, "Josie, I know you, you're Frederick and Isadora's daughter, they were our good friends." Rose said, "This is my mother-in-law, Arnold's mother, Lucille, and we live here in your old house now." Then Rose leaned in and whispered into my ear, "Lucille has trouble remembering things sometimes, she didn't mean to be rude when you went to the door, she just didn't know you that moment." I shook my head in understanding and sympathy, I also knew what it was like to not remember things as they really were, only mine was disease related and hers was age related. We spent the afternoon reminiscing in the spacious living room with the picture window looking out the front of the house. I never got around to asking Rose about that comment that she made about losing more than just a year of my memory. I will have to the next time we get together again, and hopefully I will be able to meet and thank Arnold for contacting me and urging me to come back here.

After my day out at the old place with Lucille and Rose, I was filled with exhilaration at being reunited with my best friend again, but I was also very exhausted. But I felt something else too; I felt uneasy and could sense that something was amiss when I reached the Riggins Motel and began walking towards my cottage. I began to have strange and cramping feelings in my stomach and they increased as I walked up the steps to my door. I put my key in the door lock, but it wasn't necessary. It was not locked; in fact, the door wasn't even on its frame. It was just leaning there, giving the impression that it was closed, and I knew that something was definitely wrong in there. I was almost doubled over with distress and stabbing pain, my instincts had proved dead on. My shelter had been thoroughly ransacked; nothing had been left unsearched and even the furniture had been overturned. The intruder or intruders searched through all of my personal items as well as destroyed every inch of the three room rental. In the bedroom, they even tore the mattress and box spring from the bed and sliced it open. What were they looking for? Who would invade my privacy like this? What secret do they hope to uncover by the destruction of the entire cottage and ravaging through my things? If I had any doubt before that I was unwelcome here, a clear statement had just been violently relayed onto me. But they certainly should know who I am by now, that I was family to the entire village of Salvation. Or perhaps that is precisely why this has happened. I clutched my still twisting stomach and sank down onto the floor and tears just began to gush from my eyes. All of this time of frustration in which I held my emotions hidden had just opened up and they came pouring out.

So should I try and scream loudly or leave to go for help elsewhere? But who was going to hear me from inside my cottage and come and help me? I could go back to Rose's for shelter; I could rely upon her for protection or help in any manner. But I'm too afraid to go back outside, and I had already returned the horse and buggy, so I have no method of escape anyway. I only came here to find my roots, but somebody wants me to leave here very badly, and I have no idea why that could possibly be. I peeked out the door of my room and saw several people standing in the driveway of the parking area. I very hesitantly and almost in a whisper called to .hem, perhaps they couldn't hear me in my shallow voice. I began to call a little louder with panic in my voice, but they just turned the other way. Suddenly, I feel all alone in an outrageous hostile situation and no had heard me, so no one uttered a word; it was as if I had not spoken at all.

I had crawled through the rubble to the doorway and out onto the threshold above the steps. At my presence there, the people scurried toward me to see me crouching there like a scared little rabbit that just spotted the big, bad fox. I screamed at them, "Why won't anyone help me? Someone has broken into my room and torn this place to shreds and everything from my suitcases too." By then my voice was cracking lightly, but I kept myself audible to ask them, "What is the matter with all of you people here? I am just an innocent visitor to your town and I am of no danger to anyone?" I cried. I kept on ranting and spewing out all of my feelings, "Is all of this carefulness and stiffness a result of the war that changed everyone's lives thirty years ago? My life, my parents' life and my grandparents' lives were affected too. We were forced to flee our home forever to hide and never see another family member until now." With that blurted out, I was completely spent of any energy and my voice had cracked and dried up.

A woman spoke to me now, "What are you talking about Josie? Yes, we know who you are now, what is wrong? What do you mean someone tore up your room and belongings?" I replied to her, "I was screaming just now for help and no one came." She answered me. "I was standing here talking with my friends and none of us heard you or knew anything was wrong until we saw you crawling out the door." Perhaps in my anxiety and fear, I just thought that I was yelling at the top of my lungs and nothing was coming out of my voice box at all. The women began to make offers now to come in and help me and I began to relax some, but I still will not leave my cluttered fortress. But I responded that yes, I would accept their nice offer to sort through the rubble and set the furniture in its rightful places. I stood up and I stumbled clumsily backwards and invited the woman and her friends inside for a look at the disheveled mess that once had been my belongings. They propped the door back up against one wall and put the mattress and my bedding right again while I just stood bewildered and watched them.

The sound of horses riding hard and fast came through the drive, and some yelling ensued between the two yet faceless riders. They swung down off of their horses and proceeded to push and shove each other and then they began to punch and pound on each other. All the while they were shouting back and forth, but I could not understand what they were saying; they were too far from the room. The women went back outside to watch what was happening between the two men, but I stood mute in my shambled mess. Finally, I could not stand the suspense any longer and stepped outside myself; I needed to see what the commotion was too. Especially if it somehow was related to what had just happened here in my room. I couldn't get a look at either one of the men fighting; they were moving too fast and they were hitting each other and knocking each other down. And then I heard them screaming at each other, and the one said, "You're not supposed to be here, not in this town, not in this parking lot, nowhere near here. When they ran your father out of this territory, he was told never to show his face around here and that pertains to you too, Johnny." Then the other man spoke up, "I just had to find out if this was really the daughter of the wench that caused my father all the trouble and got him beat up and run off. I figure it would be fitting if I had a go round with her, just like my father did with her mother." Then the first man lunged at the second man with hands clenched and landed them around the latter's neck. He began shaking the man violently in an apparent effort to choke him. And he said, "Shut up you son of a bitch, don't forget that your father killed Isadora's brother, Hubert for trying to rescue her after your father had beaten her." He kept on choking the man until some men from the crowd pulled the man upright and said, "He's not worth it, just like his old man, John wasn't worth nothing and proved it by what he did to the Blue Doves." The man they were holding back was obviously the good one and the one on the ground appeared to be the bad man. The good man spoke now, "They're right, neither one of you are or were worth fighting about; I don't care if you are my cousin, stay the hell away from Josie."

He said my name; could the handsome stranger who appears to be defending my honor and my mother's honor be the man that I hope him to be? I have never heard his voice or seen his face, but I have pictured him a hundred, no a thousand times in my head and in my dreams. I had such high expectations that I would not only find family members on this journey home, but also the love of my life whose presence I had always felt. It seemed to haunt me continually; I felt so strongly that he was real and a large part of my life. But there was still that which I grew up with, that it was all just a fever induced romance and not a life that I had been deprived of living. How I had heard that over and over and over, and consequently a part of me believed it. Why would my parents lie to me? What would have been their motive? But still, I had felt him so strongly within me since I can remember last. I have said a few words every day to our ancestors in secret hoping that someday my life would unfold and I could remember what really happened to me. Perhaps now is that time.

The heavily booted footsteps of a solid individual resounded on the top platform of the steps and was about to come face to face with me. I had ducked back inside of the room and clutched tightly onto the ruined door. I was having trouble breathing and shaking with anticipation. I peered out of a corner of the tattered curtain hanging from the window that I was hiding behind and took a deep breath. I began to feel that the palpitations of my heart could almost be heard outside the building, I was sure it was pounding that loudly. The crowd that was assembled outside had simultaneously silenced themselves since the arrival of the two men and moved closer to my cottage. I believe that they were holding their breath too, awaiting the results of the introduction of the aggressive stranger and myself. The tension and fear that I had been bombarded with were starting to evaporate now and I felt a connection to this man-a strong connection.

The knock on the door frame which I had longed for now came as a light tap, then a louder one, and then a strong knock. I gathered myself together and stepped out into the room, and a handsome, strong featured male stood before me. What I saw was a weathered cattleman with dark hair entwined with silver, and he had taken off his white cowboy hat and held it at his left side. Then he extended his right hand out to me and spoke the words that would forever mark this moment in both of our lives from this day forward. His smooth voice and even tone articulated the most crucial words to confirm my sanity and the love I had always felt in my heart. He looked into my eyes and simply said, "Hello, I'm Robert Ray Mon."

Chapter Eighteen

REVELATIONS

I was looking into the vivid brown eyes of the most distinguished face that I have ever been so fortunate to gaze upon.   He had unique defining features, coupled with the smooth lines of a sincere, gentle person and an air of confidence and intelligence.   The texture of his face revealed the undeniable coloring of a Nez Perce Native American mixed with a romantic air of a French Canadian.   He had a sort of unknowing smile on his face, as if he was not quite sure whether to hold back a little or broaden it in greeting.   When his hand rose, he offered it to me slowly and I in return began to let go of my tension and raised my hand to meet his.   We softly joined our hands together and I was overcome with a sense of comfort and elation at the same moment.   He was the person who had followed me, watched me and worried over me.   I know it.   I feel it.   And now he was here coming to my rescue from the horrible man he had just fought with.   I finally get to meet him.   Our hands dropped as we studied the expressions on each other's face and the intensity of the eyes now staring into one another's.   In the same instant we leaned forward slowly into a soft embrace that felt vaguely familiar and comfortable to me.   The softness quickly changed to a fierce need for togetherness as the hugging tightened and locked us together with all of the strength that we both possessed.   Robert and I remained entwined for what seemed like many minutes had passed, when in reality only several seconds had elapsed.

The crowd had been breathlessly and intently watching the bonding of these two individuals who had just been introduced to each other.....once again.   They did not dare breathe or move for fear of interruption of this obviously, compassionate moment between victim and rescuer. I pulled back sharply from the familiar stranger and looked at him starkly with a look on my fragile face that was not at all as one might have expected from these bonding moments. Instead, confusion, anxiety and disbelief appeared in my eyes and on my quivering lips. I began to shake, as if something had taken control of me from my insides, causing me to feel feverish and weak. I released my grip on this man and pushed him away from me, struggled around past him, ran down the steps and through our audience. I didn't know where I was running off to, I just knew I had to get away from all of this which I didn't quite comprehend yet. What was happening to me? I should be still firmly gripped in Robert's embrace, not erratically hurrying away from him-hadn't I waited my entire life for this moment?

I bolted down the lane and crossed the road from the motel and continued running erratically, my heart lurching downward into my stomach. I ran until I reached the Salmon River, maybe if I just walk into the river and cool off, things will make sense to me. Yes, that is what I need to do, and I will feel much better, this was just too much excitement for me at once. My room had been ransacked, I found out I have a sister, I've been reunited with my best friend and I have just met my guardian angel. I have realized that this is what has driven me so hard to travel back here to find my family genealogy and my own history. Will I uncover other secrets that have been hidden for decades? How many more will there be? My head began to throb and thrust flashes of memories back and forth through my mind. They spun and shot out of the dark, and I was so overwhelmed I began to feel sick to my stomach. My throat went dry, I was overcome with dizziness and my body was going limp. I tried to move, but I found that I was rooted to the bench that I had plopped myself down upon to rest from the shock of witnessing my first vision. A flash of this man's face smiling at me, not recently, but as a young man. Something had been stolen from me and buried within me, presumably to remain that way forever. Why? An entire portion of my life had been trapped in my subconscious for thirty years and my consciousness wiped clean of any events from that time. It had only left me with lies and denials of the actual occurrences of my youth and first love for what purpose? Was it because it was not suitable or convenient for everyone else, except Robert and me?

My parents and grandfather had told me that everything I remembered about the summer of my sixteenth year was all a result of the sickness. That I had been overcome with a fever that lasted for months and had left me dazed and near to death for several more months. They repeatedly told me that I had created a romantic saga to get me through the illness and a reason to hope for life and not give up and die. I recall little of the beginning of our hasty journey; my first real memory was saying goodbye to my grandmother upon her deathbed. When she contracted the fever, it consumed her severely and with her age and frailty added in, she went quickly. After a time in North Dakota, I began to regain my mind and body strength, but there were things still ever present that disturbed me greatly. I just could not accept that things were as they seemed, that didn't feel right to me and it never would.

Oh, my goodness, warm floods of feelings are taking me over, and I cannot lift my head from this bench. Tiny bits and pieces of crushing information are bombarding my delicate state of mind and physical presence. My memory is flooding back to me now that I have met the protective stranger who has been in every corner to which I turn. My whole life since the fever struck me has been a lie devised solely to keep me from the boy whom they did not want me to love. My parents maintained this story consistently, that we had left Riggins prior to the Army raid to remove the Nez Perce to reservations, and that we were a lucky household to have escaped together. We traveled furiously in spite of the fact that my grandmother and I were both near death and had only stopped running so furiously shortly after her death and burial. And that I had become so violently ill with the smallpox just before we hurried away that most of my memories of that time were false ones. They had manufactured this whole other life, which for a time I had clung to so dearly, not really knowing what to believe. Absolutely not that my parents and grandfather whom I trusted with complete certainty had devised such a devious plot to erase my past from me, as well as start life over in North Dakota. Whether it was a fever induced romance, or a crucial portion of my life that I remembered, the day has miraculously surfaced for me to find out.

Robert Ray Mon, yes, it was about Robert-Robert and I-Robert and Josie. We had an intense love for each other, yes, and it was indeed real. I had loved the boy and he had loved the girl. We had furiously and desperately planned our future together and then it was torn away from us.   Both Robert and the family I lived with had been afraid that I was in grave danger from this killing disease that had overcome me despite their diligent attempts to nurse me. And then the memory just stops abruptly, leaving my life an empty page with only feelings of guilt, despair and emptiness and no reasoning for it. And then somehow I had ended up back with my family on Allison Creek. I don't know though how that could have had happened,

I guess I will need a lot of help remembering everything accurately. But, it must have been poor Robert-oh; he must have been heartsick to be the one who had to deliver me to my parent's home. How else would I have gotten there, no one knew where we were, or did they? I do remember now that I no longer considered it my home, and I wouldn't have been happy to have woken up there.

Throughout my fever, I had short, blurry thoughts which felt incredibly real to me. During these brief, fleeting memories of what I believed must have been my past life started to appear, pieces of Robert would always be present. The first fuzzy blurb that came to me was an incident with the knocking on the door and calling out my name, which couldn't possibly have happened because we were miles away from each other. I believe it was a possible transference of Robert standing in the yard in Wenatchee screaming for me because I was missing. And that would have been the last thing that had happened to our incredible love, so it makes sense that it would be the first history to appear, even if it was somewhat clouded in my misjudgments of the events.

I imagined that someone was knocking on the door and yelling for me, and I remember two instances of this while lying in the wagon during my hallucinogenic state of mind. The caller said, "Josie, please answer me, I need to know if you are all right." And the next time, "Please Josie, please come out and talk to me." "I could have done neither of these things in my bedridden condition. I was far into a state of hysteria and confusion from the raging temperature in my body, and I had no clear judgment as I was being controlled by my illness and its effects. In one second of feverish insanity, I thought there was an intruder, and in the next second, I believed it was Robert, and then again my father. When I believed it was my father playing a cruel trick on me to see if I would be loyal to him or not, I began to scream hysterically. I barked at the knocker to go away, and never bother me again, and I heard no voice from the person outside of the house. I do not know if any additional words were spoken because I was hurling a tirade of vicious words towards the outsider that I believed to be there and more than likely I made no coherent sense at all. I lost all sense of reasoning and reacted as a wild animal growling and snarling at the individual hammering on the door. I thought that is what my father wanted to hear from me because I was trying to convince him that I no longer had any feelings for Robert. But what if it had been Robert? And I had driven him away with my delirious ranting or terrible words which would be most hurtful to the man that I loved more than my existence. Had I given up my chance at real happiness, at real love, at unconditional acceptance? Perhaps he had come to plead with my father for my return and the blessing of our love and future marriage?

I also, had the twisted idea that my father was maybe enticing me into revealing a plot that Robert and I had made to run away together or perhaps reveal a secret meeting location. My fear was so intense of hurting Robert, whom in the time that I had with him, had become the most important person in my world. We had made so many plans for our future lives together, and if my father found out they would now be unfulfilled dreams and passions. The discussions of going underground with the Blue Dove tribe had devastated us, and we swore to remain together and had planned to hastily leave, then we would head for the Oregon coastline. But now, under duress of the pox, I was being manipulated into giving up my love for this boy and being forced into a deep, black void that my mother and father had laid out for me.

When I awoke, it was Robert who was there cradling me in his arms like a precious infant. He was quietly pleading and whispering, "Please be all right, please be all right." I opened my eyes and really looked at him now, pausing to focus on every line of his handsome face. I know every inch of this incredible man's head, even though thirty years have passed since we had been separated. I spoke in a low tone and simply said to him, "My Robert." The tears slowly dripped from his eyes directly onto my cheeks and I then uttered, "My Appaloosa." He knew instantly that I was fully aware of who he was and hoarsely whispered, "My Josie's back. I so was afraid that you would never recognize me and remember what we had together. My life has been so empty without you, Josie." Robert began to sob harder and let his emotions pour from him and held me gently, yet fiercely.

His heart hadn't slowed down from the pummeling sensation he had been experiencing since the day he first saw me in Riggins. And the crying had partially relieved him of the tension and heartbreak he had been harboring inside of him from the loss of the years we had designed for ourselves. Robert lifted my frail looking body upright, positioning me as carefully as if I was a gentle flower who might be crushed if handled too roughly. And we turned toward one another so we might look into each other's eyes, but not letting go of either of our shaking hands. And then he started to tell me the story of our love and our life together from the very beginning.

"Josie, the sun shone each day that I was with you, but the days have all been dark since you left me."

Chapter Nineteen

JOSIE'S FIRST LOVE

There was a monumental celebration on the first day of May, 1904, at Short's Bar, just east of Riggins about two miles, on the south side of the Salmon River. The bar was famous for the placer gold mined there, and became a recreational area for the miners and their families. The people would be traveling from all the surrounding communities to attend this annual festival. Each spring right before planting time this gathering would be held, because throughout the summer and into the fall harvest there would be no time for socializing. But this year's celebration would be an extra special day, filled with some happiness to see old friends again, and sadness that it would be the last get together of any sort. In the near future, all of the Nez Perce peoples were being ripped from this land that had been home to their families for generations and generations.

To give it an air of authenticity and remembrance of the heritage of most of the residents here, it was held in the only architectural structure remaining of our Nez Perce tribe. These winter sleeping quarters were called the "Fortress," as the people would hibernate much as the bear did during the cold winter months. It was a long building constructed with logs, mud, soft bark and the sweat and toil of those designated to build it. It was designed with bunk beds three high on each long wall as sleeping quarters. The end walls each had a fireplace in front of it; one was open for general heating and conversing around and the other was of a larger nature and was round with a partial roof over it for hanging pots to cook. A very generous share of flat stones had to be handpicked; they were necessary for the ledge on the inside of the fire pit, for the baking of bread and drying of herbs. All stones were held together with clay which continually cured itself each time the heat reached it. The overhead covering was built from antlers to withstand the hot temperatures without worry of a fire to the pit itself. In the very center of the antlers was a stone chimney that went up and out through the roof. The roof over the entire structure had removable areas for ventilation, which were faithfully opened each day to clear the air. This disallowed the smoke to fill up the dormitory where the people had to live all winter to escape the harsh, northern Idaho winters.

We were seated next to each other at a long table in the Fortress, each enjoying a glass of a special punch only allowed on such occasions. This punch as it was so named was made by blending together the last of the fruits that had been dried for winter. The strawberries, huckleberries and lemon mixture made a delicious and refreshing drink. The young people were given the pretty red liquid alone, but the adults were allowed the extra ingredient of a homemade fermented beverage mixed into their glasses. Each family had prepared their specialty dish, sometimes with recipes handed down for generations, to be kept alive through them. My mother loved baking sweet treats, and her favorite among many, many recipes were her fruit breads, with nuts and grains in them. She also had made a tomato soup with all kinds of chunky cut up vegetables in it, another family tradition. My friend Rose's mother had prepared Sweet Camas Pie; that had a 'secret ingredient' which we learned was three tablespoons of whisky.

It was a moment like I had never experienced before and certainly never would again, these first moments when you recognize the soul mate that you were fated to love. When we saw each other for that incredible second in time, we were frozen awestruck and unable to move or speak. I do not remember who spoke first, but we exchanged greetings and introduced ourselves. He said, "Hello, my name is Robert Ray Mon," and I replied, "Hi, I'm Josie LeClaire, my mother is from the Blue Dove family." We shook hands and experienced an intense connection that was so tight that an instantaneous friendship began right there-no, it was more than friendship, it was love, I was sure of that. It was so exciting that I had an aching in the pit of my stomach and began to shake lightly while talking to him. We spent the entire afternoon sharing stories of our childhood and of our dreams. He aspired to expand their ranching operation beyond their current one to include more than tending horses to training and breaking the wild ones that were brought in. He was devising a plan with his father where they, along with seasoned ranch hands, would hire out as guides for travelers, hunters and fisherman. So he was a young man developing skills in several fields, as well as being groomed to take over the ranch someday and homestead it with his own family.

I believe he was telling me that he would be a good provider to the young woman that he would choose to marry and have a family with. My heart immediately reacted by pounding so loudly that I do not know what he said next. I hope it wasn't terribly important because I did not hear one word of it. Even though we had just met, I was certain that I would be that woman who would be fortunate enough to marry Mr. Robert Ray Mon. Mr. and Mrs. Robert Ray Mon, Mrs. Robert Ray Mon, Mrs. Josie Ray Mon, that was the sound of every girl's dream. This man made me feel like I would always be the happiest wife here in Idaho, and I would be treated always with love and respect. I just knew that from that moment that Robert and I had entered into a bond that would not be broken by either of us.

I reciprocated in the conversation by telling Robert that I had also been taught many skills by my mother and father. I relayed to him that I had been taught to keep house and that I had been learning how to prepare meals for many years already. I spoke of the variety of dishes that I had learned for both everyday life and also specialty recipes reserved only for events and occasions of celebration. I told him that my mother and grandmother had made sure that I was skilled in the crafts of our ancestors. I had promised them that no matter how our world progressed, I would never forget that these things must be preserved for our heritage. I would always be able to instruct the next generation in these precious arts that should not be discarded in lieu of new innovations. I was dressed in native clothing for the celebration and I mentioned that I had sewn the garments that I was wearing and had hand beaded it myself. I could see that I had impressed him and that he was as sure as I was that we would be each other's perfect mate. And from that moment I believe that each of us had plans running through our minds for a future together.

The entire afternoon was spent getting to know each other with no conscious acknowledgement that there were any other people present at all. We made plans to meet the following Sunday in Florence, the old mining town just a few miles from my house, that would become our special meeting place for just the two of us. We could always be alone there and have total privacy, because its buildings were empty and it was not used for anything except for the occasional sightseers. We declared that this would also provide us with a solitary meeting space to meet if some kind of upset had occurred in the family circle or village. We would always know where to find each other if one could not be found elsewhere. Robert and I will keep this between us and not allow anyone else to know, except for my best friend Rose, of course.

If you take the road up Allison Creek from my home, you will arrive at "Fabulous Florence," one of the earliest boomtowns resulting from the gold rush in the 1860's. It was just a little farther up the road from the area in which I had always gone to pick the leafy plants that were crucial in cooking and healing. I had spent many hours alone there or with Rose, pretending that it was our town and creating wonderful fantasies as young children do. We would play house, get married and have children and live deliriously happy lives until it was time to go home for the day, and then we would come back as soon as we could to our make-believe world. This would be the perfect place for Robert and I to have privacy; I had already had many, many happy times there. Only the time spent with him would not be pretending, it would be the beginning of our life together.

The day had come to a close and I faintly heard my mother call for me. I wonder how many times she called my name before she broke the absolute concentration with which we held our conversation. Robert politely and somewhat jokingly stood up and looked at me, and said "It was wonderful to make your acquaintance today, my dear." I replied with a "Thank you, kind sir, I enjoyed your company as well."

When we started the walk home, my mother wasted little time in asking me whose company I had been enthralled in all day. She had a smile on her face while I was giving her the details of meeting Robert. She understood completely that I was experiencing the delightful stage of having my first crush on a boy. I chattered all the way home about all that I had learned and told her that I was sure he would be the man that I would marry. At which, her grin widened, no doubt remembering her first infatuation as a young lady with her lips turned up to a smile, which she didn't do very often. My mother's curiosity increased as she asked, "What is Robert's last name?" I replied giggling, "Oh, Mother, I have forgotten it." She nodded and laughed, no doubt remembering how she met my father and how that felt as a young woman. Even though I could recount much of the afternoon's conversation in detail, I honestly did not remember his last name. It would turn out in a very short time that Robert's last name would be the very source of trouble that would rip apart our relationship. It would have been to our advantage if I had mispronounced it or misspelled it when I did tell her what it was.

Next Sunday had come and I hurriedly finished my chores for the morning and ate a bowl of venison stew, which I had helped my mother to prepare. I was in such a state of anticipation that it was difficult to eat much though. I just wanted to rush out of there and off to meet Robert. When I had finished as much as I could, I swiftly prepared for my trek along the banks of our beautiful stream. I took enough time to fill my water pouch, which my grandmother had sewn together with elk hide for the lining and rabbit fur on the outside. The elk hide provides insulation and keeps the water cool and clean and the fur offers softness against my skin as I wore it tucked inside my shirt. My mother and grandmother both possessed the ability to make something out of anything or practically nothing. I was driven with anticipation for my rendezvous with Robert; this would be our first time alone together. My mother gave me a hug, a pat on the back and said, "Have a nice day with your new friend." I turned and waved as I went through the door and said, "I will, Mother, thank you." I hurried down our path to the creek west of our farm, and I wanted to run as fast as I could to get there. I was surprised I did not see my father working in the fields as I crossed our property. He raised beef cattle and did some crop farming, in addition to his job at the lumber mill.

When I reached Allison Creek, I continued along the east side going north until I reached the little bridge that we had built across it to the other side. I had actually been present and helped drag wood when the original bridge of a fallen tree had been replaced with planking and rope. It was not a great distance across, perhaps twenty-five feet, so it did not require a great deal of support. It was accomplished with sturdy construction on each bank and swayed somewhat, but not enough to make anyone feel uneasy about crossing over on it. I was so excited that I was being quite careless crashing through the tall grass, rocks and huckleberry bushes. As a result I tripped over a large rock, and caught my carefully combed hair on a bramble bush, which upon untangling it, whipped across my face. I did not know how deep the gash was, but it produced enough blood that I could feel it in my left eye. I patted it with the inside of my skirt, along with the water from my pouch, as I had nothing else available to me. Now I would certainly not make the good impression that I had hoped on a first date, and I was nervous enough already. I was disheveled and bloody and now added tears to my facial disarray, he will think at the very least that I am clumsy and careless. I cleaned up the best that I could with the rest of my water and hoped the blood would not surface through the outer side of my skirt.

I continued on through the wooded area to where the ghost town was neatly tucked into the middle for protection from all type of weathers elements. I sat down to collect myself on a neatly crafted pine log bench alongside of the railing leading into the general store. I was imagining what this day would hold for Robert and me, and was extremely grateful that I arrived first to calm myself from the rough trail that led me here. When I regained my breath, I moved to sit under a very old gnarled weeping willow tree in the shade to cool myself. It was just beginning to bud out and the spring foliage was bursting to come alive again after its cold winter hibernation. Looking at this beautiful site and peaceful place of refuge, I was able to still my anxieties and see nature re-awakening all around me. I believe now that I am ready to see my first love come strolling up the path to meet me.

It was at that moment that I heard the sound of horse hooves upon the dirt and the crackling of brush. They were of a slow, even step and I was not the least bit worried that it might be someone else. Robert had ridden into the small, grassy area and approached very timidly, eyes searching for me as if he was not certain that he would find me there at all. Did he have even a fleeting thought that I would not come here today? I was partially hidden from his view by the magnificent branches of the willow tree, but still out in the open enough for him to find me quickly. When he located me seated on the bench, his expectant eyes stopped straight in from of him, and a wide smile beamed across his handsome face. Robert was riding atop a black and white Appaloosa stallion, upon which he sat comfortable and gracefully. The horse appeared to be of excellent demeanor and had clearly been well trained. There was a white flicker in the middle of each deep brown eye, perhaps it was a glint of fire, or a hummingbird fluttering its tiny wings within the centers. This could very well have been a portrait depicting a youthful lad proudly striding his battle steed awaiting his command to rush into battle. The young brave yet with an enthusiastic lighthearted look to his face, representing the fact that he had not yet been burdened by the horrors of war. Hopefully, he would never be forced to kill other human beings, to save the lives of his family and tribe, as well as himself. Robert was as I was, half French Canadian, half Nez Perce, but had almost all Native features and very few French traces. While I was more of a lighter balance of the two, and my reddish brown hair did not show traces of Indian genealogy.

Robert had reached me now and swung lightly down with all the seasoned grace of a true animal lover and trainer. He would never cause fright to this magnificent creature that trusted him to be given gentle care. At first he approached slowly, until he could see me more clearly. His pace then quickened as he saw me in my moderate disheveled state. He knelt down before me to view my condition closer and said, "My God, what has happened to you?" Judging from his reaction, I had underestimated the extent of my appearance. He asked, "Your forehead is wide open, what has done this much damage to you?" I replied that it had been a huckleberry briar and relayed the rest of the story of the trip to Florence. Once again, I was fully engulfed in tears, more from embarrassment and humiliation than from anything that had befallen my physical nature.

Robert with his caring persona comforted me and whispered to me, "Don't cry anymore Josie, I will repair the cut for you, I've done it many, many times." He continued, "Usually, though it's an injury to a horse or another animal, but they usually heal proper witho;t a scar!" It may have soundly slightly like he was cracking a joke, but he was perfectly serious in his declaration.

I blubbered embarrassed, "Yes, help me, please." With that, he went back to his horse and retrieved a pack that he always carried for such emergency treatments. I clearly was a lucky girl, that, my new friend was a person prepared for trouble of this sort. He began by washing out the cut, which he commented was quite jagged, but he assured me that with some healing herbs, it would be as if I had never met with that nasty bush with thorns. That was a very confident statement for someone so young to promise to a young gal at this point in her life who was terribly self conscious of how attractive she was or was not. I wondered aloud, "How does a berry that tastes so sweet and is so beautiful, grow on such wicked, thorny vines?" He smiled at me and said, "Sometimes sweetness comes with danger." Then he applied a piece of softened bark over the herbs with a little sticky pine pitch on the edges to hold it in place and told me that it should heal just fine. I was to treat it the same way that he had each day until the torn skin had fused itself back together. And no scar would remain to remember the unfortunate mishap of this day. This was a method carried through from an older time, but those methods served so well that there was no need to discard them.

Robert said he was sorry that he was unable to repair my bloody skirt and began to untangle my hair. I was so upset that I had completely forgotten that my neatly combed and pinned hair had become snarled and torn from its clip. This made me feel both terrible and wonderful at the same time, he was so kind and caring with his touch, but I was still undeniably mortified. I had sufficiently relaxed again now after his doctoring that the tears began to flood back in to my eyes and quietly drizzled down onto my cheeks. He silently said, "Don't cry my Josie, you're beautiful to me." Such sweet sentiment from such a young lad, how did I become so lucky as to find him and for him to be interested in me. He had called me, "my Josie!" Does this mean that he already considers me to be his girlfriend? My giggly, boy crazy, teenage thoughts began to make my heart beat faster and awake the napping butterflies again. This is how I had felt a short time ago on my stumbling walk up through the woods to meet Robert with such exciting feelings running through me. Our afternoon continued to be a very pleasant one; we each talked about our lives up to this point, and I told him about my best friend Rose, and he spoke of his best friend Fritz. We told each other childhood stories and laughing at the silly things that children do.

Robert said that he would not allow me to venture up here on foot ever again. I retorted by telling him that I had been coming here since I was old enough to leave the house. He mounted his horse and pulled me up behind him, and said he would pick me up at my house and bring another horse along for me to ride, if that suited me. I replied, "Yes, Robert that suits me well." Even though I'm not so sure that I would prefer riding alone to the comfort of being seated behind him with my arms twirled around his waist. We wound our way through the south end of town and returned to the trail that I had taken up to meet him. Now, we laughed and joked about the evils of the sharp, knifelike thorn bushes I had encountered on the way up. We rode his horse at a snail's pace just chatting as new loves do in beginning a relationship. I believed that he would prove to be as romantic and pleasurable to be with as he was kind and gentle. And that this friendship would escalate into a sweet romance filled with respect for each other and an undeniable intense attraction. It had been an incredible day, mixed with pleasure and pain, and I had found an amazingly compassionate boy.

We made plans to meet again next Sunday, but decided that I would stay home where I would be safe until he arrived for me with a horse in tow. We slowly wound our way down to Allison Creek and Robert dropped me off at our modest two story home on the outskirts of Riggins to the east.

Robert needed to be back at the ranch northwest of Riggins in the town of Lucile off of Cow Creek. Robert had never desired to be anywhere else or with anyone else; the horses and people on the ranch were sufficient company for him. Until now, they had always been his first love, but that had all changed last Sunday at the spring celebration. The only love for other human beings he had felt was for his mother and father; he knew no other such love existed. He was sure now what love between a man and a woman was, and wouldn't be able to wait very long to tell Josie that he loved her. He knew that she was someone very special and that it was she that he wanted to spend the rest of his life with.

Robert would be going away for some time to further his horse training skills, and he had decided that when he was finished with his first grueling weeks of orientation, that he would send for her. To develop a plan of sacred secrecy would be the only way that this could play out; this wasn't something that either family would approve of and permit unless they were married. They were both too young to be on an overnight together, so they would need to create another excuse for them to be in that area at the same time. Perhaps he would find someone in need of the help of a young lady in their home or some other tasks appropriate for a teenage girl. Robert never would have possibly fathomed that he would indeed be seeking a refuge for her rather than a happy place for them to see each other every day.

Chapter Twenty

THE BITTERNESS OF LOVE

When I returned home from my afternoon with Robert, my Mother could visibly witness the undeniable elation on my face. I told my Mother that I knew that Robert was the man that I would marry someday. It is every Mother's profound wish that her daughter find someone that she truly loves to marry. Not to just have a marriage of convenience as so many of the girls of her day were dealt, with marriages that were sometimes arranged for family gain, status or monetary exchanges. I babbled on about our wonderful afternoon spent with questions and answers of each other's lives, and sharing stories of our childhoods.

She was not at all panicked by the bandage on my face, because she could see that it had been quite skillfully prepared and placed over my wound. I excitedly told her of my entanglement with the briar bushes and subsequent cut to my forehead and that Robert had treated it with special herbs and made a covering for it from soft, pounded bark. I explained that he works on a large horse ranch, and that Robert has learned skills to deal with every aspect of raising horses including those of doctoring the injuries and even acting as mid-wife for the easier births, which didn't require the veterinarian to visit the ranch. My mother nodded as I told her of all of the good qualities that I thought Robert possessed and that he was now my boyfriend.

She grinned slyly and inquired once again as to Robert's last name or if I had been too embarrassed to ask him again or too excited to remember it. I answered her with a giggle and a beaming grin, "Its Ray Mon." I think my Mother's heart stopped beating for a full minute before she opened her mouth wide in disbelief. And then there was an immediate transformation in her character, it took only a second from time to change her from radiating sunshine to blinding lightning. Her face had taken on a dreadfully serious look and the color of a red hot chili pepper that began to shoot brilliant hot flames with her speech. She quite poignantly screamed, "No, you shall never see that boy again, or speak of him, or even think about him." In that one sentence, it was if our house was made of glass and had burst forth with sharp slivers that drove into my body. And each and every shard causing unimaginable pain, heartbreak and scars; scars that would remain deep well into my future, while the cut from the brambles would be unnoticeable very shortly. The memories of that day would be forever emblazoned with this heart wrenching moment. My world had had a beginning and an end in the span of just a few short hours; the elation that I had felt earlier had now been clouded with turmoil.

She could not grasp that of all the boys I could possibly choose to fall in love with, it would be Robert Ray Mon. But still, she would not enlighten me as to why she could so overwhelmingly hate someone whom she had never even met. What was this? I am completely baffled as to why this had all taken place and what I could do to straighten this mess out. If she would just calm herself, I was certain that I could convince her to let Robert come for supper and she would surely change this unreasonable attitude toward him. I pleaded with her, "But, Mother, if you would just meet Robert, you would see that he is a nice boy. You said yourself that he took good care of me and properly treated my wound on my forehead. Please let him come over, please Mother, please." She just screamed at me again, "No, Josie, no Ray Mon will ever set foot in this house or see my daughter, never, I forbid it!"

It was revealing that it was Robert's last name of Ray Mon that had sent my mother spinning out of control. My answer lies there and it was wretchedly apparent that she was not going to reveal the hideousness behind her tantrum and her echoing words. "No, you shall never see that boy again, or speak of him, or even think about him." That sentence had been emblazoned in my mind and would remain there for the rest of my existence on this earth. I would get nowhere speaking with my mother at this time with her in this state of crazed anger. I just need to distance myself from her now. I am so heartsick that I have found that one special love in someone only to have my mother disapprove and try to prevent it from happening. Without any valid reason, that's what upsets me so. I retreated to my room and threw myself down on the bed and violently and loudly sobbed myself to sleep. I heard my father come home from work and my mother still in her agitated mood, erratically told him of the horridness of the afternoon. My father did not raise his voice, but rather whispered his comments to my mother, none of which I was able to hear. But the very fact that he did not come into my room to check on me, proved he must be siding with my mother on this. I had always been his special little girl; would that be lost to me on this day too?

I had been allowed a free rein and had spent many hours each day either in the woods or down at the creek. I enjoyed the solitude and had become quite efficient in the gathering of herbs, roots and berries and helped my family with the sale of them. But now, I would never again be able to venture forth anywhere without the careful scrutiny of my mother. And should I be able to escape her diligent watch, I would have to endure her hot temper and assuming accusations.

Robert had planned to swing by and pick me up next Sunday afternoon, and we would ride our horses upstream on Allison Creek toward Old Florence again. He was going to help me to gather fresh herbs that had finally been relieved of their crypt of snow and frost and were showing themselves now to greet the sun and a new spring. Just like a budding new love being born into the world, with all of its newness and the excitement of discovery. How can I get word to Robert of this horrible argument? He lives on a ranch in Lucile, it is too far to walk, and I will have to borrow or steal a horse if necessary. I will get up early tomorrow morning, before my parents and grandparents do and quietly leave the house through my window. This is not how I have dreamed so many, many times of how my first love would be and be reacted to by my family. But things won't always be in this much turmoil, will they? Sunday afternoon at the spring gathering was the perfect beginning that I had always envisioned. And at the cold winter fortress today on our very first date, I had spent the afternoon with truly the perfect boy of those dreams of mine. And then it had been destroyed in just a matter of minutes.

I arose before dawn and dressed in the riding breaches that my mother had sewn for me from the elk hides my father had tanned last winter. I took only one change of clothing, as I wanted nothing from that room that my parents had given to me right now. After a very scattered night of sleep, I had decided that I would ask my best friend Rose to help me. I have no doubt that she will; I must gently tap on her window as not to alert her family that I am there. Rose's family is more fortunate than mine and owns two fine mares for the sole purpose of riding and buggy travels. Rose's chores each morning include feeding, brushing, exercising the horses and making sure that they remain healthy. She alone would know that I had borrowed Buttercup and ridden her to Lucile to seek out Robert at the ranch.

It was much a much easier task than I had anticipated. Rose was already in the barn when I arrived, and I could hear her humming while she worked. I blurted out hysterically my sad tale before I told her of the wondrousness of my rendezvous with my now more-precious-than-ever Robert. Being my very closest friend, she empathized with me and did what she was able to console me. And we both agreed that I must make plans to live elsewhere and only return to gather my few modest belongings and clothing. I must make my way to somewhere that I would not be treated so poorly and with such outrage merely for my choice of sweetheart.

Rose had already treated Buttercup to a good brushing and her breakfast and was now ready to be taken out for her morning exercise. I had ridden her many times, so we weren't strangers to each other and suited each other comfortably. With a few words of encouragement and a comforting hug from Rose, I rode off north on the east banks of the Salmon River. I would ride there until I came to the town of Lucile and crossed over Cow Creek, west to the ranch. Robert had described the area in which he had grown up, so I was confident that I would easily locate the ranch, and anyone living in the area would know where the Ray Mon ranch was. But I didn't need any assistance; I was able to see the gate bearing their sign. It said, 'Ray Mon Ranch – Breeding & Breaking.' I silently pleaded under my breath, "Please let Robert be here, please let Robert be here today." Not wanting him to be away from the ranch delivering a horse that has been trained or out rounding up a new one to be tamed, I hadn't thought ahead to what I would do if he was not there, I'd tackle that problem if it arose.

I rode unhurriedly down the road as not to attract any attention to us and not to spook any of their horses in the corral or Buttercup. I did not see any one outside as I rode in, so I tied up my horse on a hitching post by the barn away from the corral. My hope was that in doing so, all would remain quiet and wouldn't cause a noisy disturbance between the horses. I entered the first barn and found no one there, so I went out the back and through another barn with still no activity. As I moved into the next one I saw a group of men loading hay bales onto a wagon. As I moved closer, I was able to distinguish Robert's back facing me. They all paused and turned to look at me, and when Robert saw me, he threw down his pitchfork and started toward me. If I hadn't appeared so forlorn standing there, I'm sure the boys would have whistled, laughed and teased Robert for having a girl come looking for him in the barn.

Robert strode quickly toward me, and when he reached me, he stood very close to me and looked me directly in the eye. "Something's wrong, isn't it?" he asked. I had shed all of my tears throughout the night, so I exhaustingly announced, "Yes, it's all wrong, this life is all wrong." He replied with, "What do you mean, life's all wrong?" Then he put his arm around me and steered me toward the empty barn that I had just passed through. I began to spill forth the details of my return home the day before from our wonderful picnic and of the confrontation with my Mother. Here again I stand with Robert, looking pitiful and helpless, and had no opportunity to fix myself up and look nice for seeing him again. I saw a true sadness in Robert's eyes and he said, "How could they hurt you this way?" "They barely had a glimpse of me last week at the spring celebration, and we haven't even been introduced yet." I was able to mutter with my voice strained, "It doesn't matter Robert, I'm leaving them to be with you." My friend Rose, from whom I borrowed the horse to get here, will help me too."

We would need to find a place to harbor me with someone that my family did not know, at least until the anger and bitterness subsided. But I would not go back to live with them now; it was no longer home to me, it was their house and I had no desire to cross that threshold ever again. Rose will go sneak my things out for me, out the window from which I had taken flight to sever the ties between parents and child. Rose would no doubt be the first person questioned in this awful ordeal and that would be very soon, I would expect. But the bond that she and I had developed since our childhood would not be betrayed. It was stronger than any allegiance that either of us had to our parents. And now I had Robert, a very kind and caring person whom I felt I could trust and rely on completely.

Robert said that he knew the perfect place for me to stay and no one would have the slightest clue to look for me there. On the edge of the ranch, was a weathered, old home that was just a few miles away, but in complete seclusion and out of sight from the ranch. It was occupied by a woman and a child who worked as a maid in his home in the main house where he and his parents lived. He was sure, that she would love the company and some help with her little granddaughter, as she was a widow. She and the little girl made their way to the main house on an old retired horse every morning, regardless of the weather. But the Ray Mons were not demanding people and she didn't work long days, even though she worked every day except Sundays. Robert said the woman's name was Evelyn, her granddaughter's name was Alice, and her husband's name had been George. He had worked for the ranch also, but he had been deceased right after little Alice had come to live with them. And poor Alice was orphaned as an infant and would never remember her parents; they had left her through an unfortunate accident. They had been traveling to the house of a friend and their wagon had overturned, failing to negotiate a sharp curve on a mountain trail. So, Evelyn and George had taken on the responsibility of caring for their only grandchild and considered it a privilege to do so.

Both Evelyn and George had gentle, generous natures and would raise Alice in that manner as well. And then George had left them just a few short months after the tragic accident that took their son and his wife.

Evelyn preferred to spend what little free time she had teaching Alice various things, so she had no social life and her only contact with other adults were the Ray Mon's and their visitors. Evelyn had been by Mrs. Ray Mons side since the day she had been born on the homestead. Robert's grandmother had been present at the birth and helped her burst forth into the world. Evelyn was of the third generation of her family that had worked as ranch hands and housemaids, but despite that, she and Lucy Ray Mon were as close as sisters. So there was no question that she would remain exactly where she was after George passed away. She was as much part of their family as biological members were.

It had been a long day already and the fatigue and stress were reflected in my eyes and across my face. Robert thought it would be a good idea for me to try to rest some before going to

Evelyn's in the afternoon. He said that this could be a wonderful time for us, because we would be living just a short distance from each other and could see each other every day. At that, I brightened some; those were comforting words to hear from the boy I had chosen above everyone else. Robert had grown from my suitor to also my lifeline in this short time that we had been acquainted with each other. This is where I belonged now, and no one would come between us now. I slept in the barn on a makeshift bed of straw and feed bags. I was so exhausted that it mattered little where I laid my aching body and confused mind. Robert needed to get back to his ranching duties for a couple hours, but he said he would check in on me. When he did, I was resting comfortably, and he returned to the corral with work with the horses.

When I awoke, I began again to focus on the situation that has developed since I told my mother who I believed my true love to be. I tried to smooth my hair and clothing and wipe the sleep from my eyes in an effort to prepare for Robert's return. He has only seen me looking presentable once at the spring gathering; yesterday and today I have been an unlucky mess. I felt perfectly safe and at ease here and made no attempt to venture from the barn to look for Robert. He came shortly thereafter with water, a cloth and the bandage kit from his saddlebag that I recognized from the other day. He gently removed the old bandage from my forehead and said that it was healing well. Then he cleaned it with the cloth and water, put fresh herbs on the wound and placed a clean bandage over that. Robert asked me how I felt now and I replied that I had rested well and was very happy to be here and for him to be the first person to see upon waking. The only thing that could have made it better than this would be to wake up in Robert's arms. But I could not tell him this; he quite possibly could misconstrue my meaning and thus lose respect for me.

Robert said, "Josie, I can see that you are worried about how your face looks. Don't, you are beautiful to me." Those were the exact words he had used as I was bleeding all over him in Florence. There has never been such tender treatment or true compassion known to me that Robert had shown yesterday. Nearly my entire family; close and extended, are very stern, unsmiling people. Possibly life is just so hard on them that they have never experienced many happy times. But last week, my mother had genuinely been excited to hear that I had found this incredible boy, whom I was sure would be my partner for life. But then after the briefest of conversations, the slate had flipped from utter joy and genuine interest, to disdain and mistrust. My mother had turned on me and spoke of Robert as if he were a rattlesnake about to eat her young.

No, I would not think of this now. I was being mended by the most important person in my life. One whom I know will always treat me fairly and lovingly and not with the coldness I have grown up with. His parents had taught him how to love and that love alone was the most crucial element in our life on earth; without it you are nothing and will have nothing. You will have no desire to live, challenge and embrace life to every possible extent, to not miss out on one minute of a wondrous future. Anything less would be an immense waste of life, to merely trudge through each day pretending to be alive and have a fruitful existence. Even a stranger would be able to see through this façade, if one should try to bluff their way into making people believe it. We were fated to find each other and fall in love and to become each other's reason for living. Our circumstances have been very bizarre and a complete mystery with this outrageous discrimination to the surname of Ray Mon.

Chapter Twenty-One

THE SEARCH FOR JOSIE

The sound of hard, hammering hooves approaching was accompanied by a shrill, hysterical girl's voice. It was Rose shouting, "Where's Robert, does anyone know where Robert is?" Rose blurted out. "Please help me find him; I need to talk to him and Josie." Robert and I flew out of the barn and Robert caught Rose as she leapt off of her horse and pulled her out of sight into the barn. "Josie's parents are frantically searching for her and came to me, but I did not say a word. I promise to you on all of our years of friendship and sisterhood. When your mother went into your room this morning and you were gone, she alerted your father. They said they immediately knew that you had slipped out during the night. And since you never do anything or go anywhere without telling me, they assumed I was either with you or that I knew where you were. You know me better than anyone, Josie, and you know that when I tell a lie it shows all over my face. So, even though I told them that I didn't know what was happening, I'm sure that they knew I was not telling the truth."

I spoke through my tears, "I believe you Rose, and I know that you would protect me, no matter what the situation." I gave Rose a huge hug and muttered, "You had better take Buttercup and get her home before your father notices that she's missing. When my parents talk to yours, they may put the missing horse together with my absence. Then they'll know you've been collaborating with me for sure, and you won't be able to lie your way out of it." Rose nodded her head in agreement.

It wouldn't be long now before the LeClaire's would be paying a visit to the Ray Mons, now that they were aware who Robert was. Robert immediately called on one of the boys that I had seen in the barn, and quickly told him to take Rose and me to Evelyn's house, through the woods east of the ranch. Robert said that we would be unnoticed there, and his friend could show Rose the way home from there. He would explain the circumstances to his family's most endeared friend, Evelyn, who was back at his house working. He said that Evelyn was like a second mother to him, and wouldn't hesitate to help us out. Robert did his best to give me all this information in a hurry. H'e wanted me to get away quickly, but clearly wanted to tell me some details about where I was going also.

The trail was a couple of miles to the house and a very pleasant trail to follow. A gentle, well trodden path had been ground down through the pasture along a fence line. Either side of the road was lined with elegant, budding maple trees awaiting their flowers and wild blooms already surfacing on the trails borders, making it seem somewhat like one was going down a road to heaven. It wasn't hard to realize why Evelyn valued this time traveling down this lane; even a few moments spent here would lift one's spirits and chase away any bad happenings of the day. Robert's friend told us that Mrs. Ray Mon had offered Evelyn and Alice a room in the house, but she had only agreed to stay in the winter months, when the weather made the trip rough. It was her alone time with Alice, while sauntering along on old Peanuts, who was never in a hurry to get anywhere.

The boy leading the way told us his name was Fritz , and he also had spent most of his young years at the ranch. His father had worked there before he was married, and now Fritz had been old enough to be given a job there along with him. Fritz proudly told us that Robert was his best friend, and he had heard all about me and was glad that I made Robert so happy. I had to wonder what Robert had told him, because twice now there had hardly been anything special about me, I was just injured and an emotional mess. But he must see something in me worth the trouble that he went to patching my face and calming my shame over my torn and tattered state. And now, what he was willing to go through for me from this point forward.

Would he be able to hide me at Evelyn's for very long? Would Evelyn or Alice tell the Ray Mons that I was staying at her house with them? Despite the closeness of Evelyn and Robert, she still had an allegiance to her employer and lifelong friends. And Alice was a little girl, and wouldn't understand what a secret was; she most likely will say something to give it away. She may say that a girl sleeps at our house, or eats supper with us or just plain announce that Josie is there. There could only be one possibility of someone named Josie at her house, and all would be given away. Then Evelyn, who had not been in any trouble or the cause of any in her entire life, would be in a substantial amount of conflict with the Ray Mons.

We reached Evelyn and Alice's house; it was an old house with asphalt siding of rose and gray. This was the original house when the Ray Mon farm was first established, while it was still a small milking operation. When the Ray Mon brothers decided to phase out milking and concentrate on horse breaking and training, and increase the crops as well, the move was made to the new location. The main house was then built to accommodate several families if necessary, and two barns were started, which had now grown to six.

The steps were on the side of the house, next to the driveway, the door swung open into the summer kitchen, with a wooden door on a squeaking spring hinge. It was pretty typical in large farm homes where all the preparations for canning and storing of the food surplus to be used in the winter months took place. This kept the original kitchen free for the cooking and serving of the regular three meals a day required for a hard working farm family. And it kept that part of the home cooler without the hot steam coming off the kettles and canners. The summer kitchen usually was breezier due to extra ventilation for the stove that was simmering vegetables all day. Corn alone took four hours in a large iron kettle to process in the jars with salt to ensure that there would not be any spoilage. Very little food was attainable in the frozen, snowy conditions other than an unfortunate deer, rabbit or squirrel that popped out for a stroll on the fields of ice.

Fritz led us through the summer kitchen into the main kitchen, painted a warm shade of pale yellow. Beyond that was the living room; this house had a very welcoming feeling with its modest, cozy furniture. There was a wood stove on one side of the room and a drying rack for clothes on the other. Off to the left was a bedroom turned playroom for little Alice and a sewing room for Evelyn. To the right, you could access the front porch and go out into the front yard.

I thanked Fritz and Rose for rescuing me and aiding me in hiding from my family. Fritz spoke up and said, "Robert is my best friend, and I would do anything for him. He told me that he knew immediately when he met you that he wanted to be with you forever." Rose and I were both close to tears now, but she managed to speak softly, "Me too, Josie, I'll keep helping you if I can." I hugged her tightly and told her, "You have risked enough for me already; I don't want you to get into any trouble. I won't be able to see you for awhile, so come ask Robert where I am when things settle down a bit. I'm not going home again, not until my parents accept Robert, and if they don't, I'm not going back, ever." Both of us were in full blown sobbing, but managing to understand each other just the same. Even our new friend Fritz's eyes had welled up with water, watching the two of us say our goodbyes. I told them that I would be fine now, and that they had better speed back to where they were expected to be at this time of the day.

After they left, I felt the sensation of fatigue setting in quickly; I went out onto the front porch and slumped down into a big wooden chair. Strangely, I should feel out of place or uncomfortable in the house of someone I have never met, but I felt oddly at home. It didn't take long before the full effects of this day and previous ones hit me like a wrecking ball. I laid my head on the side table and tears soon engulfed me, I was so exhausted, but I thought little more. Sleep finally took over and my real life began to interact with my subconscious, to make everything worse than it had been with my eyes open. The demons of yours dreams feel like reality, and can be so horrible that it is amazing that people do not succumb to them and die of shock. Or maybe that is what happens sometimes instead of passing away quietly as is mostly commonly believed. I was fortunate to awake at the sound of a dog barking, and remained frozen to not attract attention if there was someone outside. But I did not see anyone or even the dog; I crawled onto the floor behind my chair, to hide in the event that something was about to happen. I had been awakened so abruptly that now my dream thoughts were beginning to surface. There had been horses, the sounds of lots of horses thundering down the lane towards the house. I felt a panicky feeling, and I knew that they were coming for me. The closer they rode up, the more my heart began to race and sweat beads began to form on my forehead. There was my father and grandfather along with the Sheriff and his deputy, they had found me.

My fears were alleviated when my nightmare remembrance was interrupted by the pleasant sound of one horse's hooves approaching the house. I peeked around the corner from the chair and saw that it was an old chubby horse, with a woman and child for its passengers. Although we hadn't met each other yet, I had an instant warm feeling just upon seeing her, I knew that I would grow to love these two people. I stepped out of the front porch when they came down the driveway and waved to them and they smiled and waved in return. When they rode up right next to me I extended my arms to pull Alice off of the horse. Evelyn dismounted also and said, "Hi, Josie, it's nice to meet you." I replied, "It's nice to meet you too, Evelyn, I hope that it's alright that I am here." As she took the saddle and blanket off of Peanuts, she said, "Yes, it is, Robert explained everything to me. And he told me all about how you met and again that night after you had gone on your first date." We walked over to the barn and put the tired old horse inside the corral and gave her food and water. Evelyn took my hand and said, "Come now, let's sit and talk for awhile." We sat down on the large, wooden yard chairs and Alice jumped up on my lap, she was a very outgoing child and wasn't intimidated in the least by my presence.

Evelyn, Alice and I chatted like old friends, the other not wanting to spoil the moment by bringing up the matter that I had run away and was hiding out at her house. But, finally, Evelyn asked me, "What happened between you and your parents that you ran away?" I had a feeling just then, that she really didn't need many explanations. I just felt it in the way she positioned her mouth, she knew the whole story, the one that I did not know. But I spoke of everything I remembered in the haze of Sunday evening and this morning's escape from home. She said that I could stay there for awhile, but someone would think to search here for me eventually. I knew that she was right, but for the moment, I was safe in the company of a friend.

A single rider slowly entered through the ranch gates, seemingly reluctant to reach the circle in front of the house. My father had never dared to venture onto these premises before now; had my mother found out, my father would be miserable from that point on. Or quite possibly he may not have lived another day to be miserable at all. The senseless, outrageous tragedy that had occurred here about two decades ago had resulted in a hateful rift between the two families.

Frederick gingerly got off his horse and tied it up loosely on the hitching post and walked up onto the porch. Robert's mother opened the door and could hardly believe who she saw standing there. Frederick politely said, "Good morning Lucy." She was in a partial state of shock but replied a feeble "Hello, Frederick." He nodded his head in acknowledgement and she offered him a chair on the front porch and they sat down. He asked her if his daughter had been there this morning, and the look that he received in return told the truth that Mrs. Ray Mon had not seen Josie. He told Lucy what had transpired the day before between Isadora and Josie when Josie had told her mother what Robert's last name was. Isadora's hatred for the Ray Mons flooded to the surface, and she blew up at Josie in a rage of abhorrent words. Lucy said that Robert had told them all about her and his feelings for her and that he had found his special someone. She was genuinely happy for him, but wondered if this might be a devastating relationship ending in bitter disappointment for both of them. Frederick told Lucy everything that had occurred after Robert had met Josie last weekend. All of Isadora's reactions and tantrums, which he said didn't really surprise him at all under the circumstances. But Frederick said they shouldn't have withheld certain truths concerning the two families, he felt it wrong to conceal them. And now as a result of it all, Josie was gone, had run fast away from them because of her mother's disapproval of Robert and for lack of honesty all of these years.

Robert conveniently disappeared so he would not have to lie to my father and his mother. Since he had not had the opportunity to speak to his parents about today's events, they would be telling the truth when asked about Josie's whereabouts also. He would be summoned eventually to clarify all the details when his father returned home tonight. Lucy's face portrayed an obvious strain as Frederick painfully relayed the events as they had been described by Isadora to him. Lucy said, "I guess we were all thinking pretty shortsightedly that our children would never meet and that we would never again have the past brought to the current to deal with all over again." Frederick replied, "Yes, it was an unrealistic wish that we could hide this forever, I have never agreed with Isadora and her father in this. We should have just let history stand as it is and not try and bury it as if it had never happened." Lucy answered, "I think we've been living under a time bomb; such a tragic occurrence is bound to surface at some time. And I agree with you, if we had openly shared the hatred of the LeClaire's for the Ray Mons, we would not be facing this today." Frederick nodded his head in agreement, he had always felt that it was a sad, devastating part of all of them, but should have definitely been included in the story of their lives. To totally dismiss the existence of the people involved was probably a bigger travesty than revealing the sins of those involved.

Lucy spoke again now, "James will be saddened by the happenings of the last twenty-four hours, but also relieved that he will no longer have to hide this shame from Robert. I hope that James will open up to him and reveal all the things that have been hidden from him for so long." She also said she was sorry that our children had gotten together under these circumstances, but if they felt this strongly about one another, then there would be nothing anyone could to do keep them apart. Frederick wearily shook his head, "Isadora and Ignatious will never accept Robert as even an acquaintance and certainly revolt against any attempt by them to pursue a life together. Josie's Grandmother Annahah, never approved of withholding the incident surrounding this tragic ruination of so many lives, but had agreed to remain quiet to honor her husband and daughter's wishes." Frederick painfully told Lucy that in light of what was about to happen in the eradication of the village this year, it was even more imperative that they find her immediately. If she should be lost in the shuffle somehow, they may never see her again. She needs to be running away with her family right now, not Robert.

Frederick left Lucy Ray Mon waving to him from the porch as he mounted his horse and started down the long road out through the gates of the ranch. He was pretty sure that Isadora would react badly to the news that he found no knowledge of Josie's whereabouts and therefore was unable to bring her home. She was livid as he had predicted and immediately screamed at him for not finding her and dragging her back home, kicking and screaming if necessary. She strongly suggested that he had not searched the Ray Mon ranch thoroughly enough, because now that she was mixed up with "that boy," he certainly would be hiding her there somewhere. But it was not a lie that she was not at the ranch; she was after all, at Evelyn's home, and no one ever thought to refer to her small plot of land as being a part of the ranch. Even though there was no legal deed naming Evelyn or her family as title to the property, it was still considered theirs as far as anyone was concerned.

Isadora uttered shakily, "If not with the Ray Mon boy, then where could she be?" Frederick replied, "I don't know, Isa, but I spoke with Lucy, and I believe she was telling the truth when she said she had not seen Josie." Frederick added, "Lucy said that she and James had not met Josie, but Robert had told her that he had met the girl he wanted to spend the rest of his life with." He further relayed to Isadora everything that Lucy had said about Robert's excitement about his first love to them. He had said that her last name was LeClaire, which they didn't need to be told; they knew exactly whose daughter she was, she looked so much like Isadora. They had seen them together at the social last week laughing and talking, appearing to have a genuine interest in each other. They hoped that the two wouldn't become too close and begin to inquire as to why their families had never crossed paths or at least met at a social gathering this past sixteen years. Lucy said that she hoped that Robert had not noticed the furrowed, almost fearful expressions on their faces when he was honestly sharing an important portion of his life with them. James and Lucy had decided against telling Robert everything just now and listened to the boy tell of his exciting first love. They would discuss how and when to break the details of the LeClaire-Ray Mon feud to him when James was back and would not be leaving again. This kind of news shared with Robert would require his presence as a father, not to be gone doing business, but here helping his son to cope with this.

James Ray Mon had returned to the ranch after a long stretch of bidding for horse training clients. Every couple of months a meeting was held and attended by prospective trainers and owners to line up the horses to the ranches that would be breaking and boarding them for the summer. It had been successful, and the Ray Mon ranch would be home to ten beautiful animals in need of some significant calming down and to be taught the manners of being ridden. And ten was about all they could successfully and properly handle in the course of the summer months. It would be an excellent year profit-wise for them and Robert's first real encounter one-on-one with the animals. Robert was seventeen now, and his father felt he was ready to experience more than just helping out and watching the other trainers. This was his time to become an adult in the working world of ranching and business.

When James put his hand on the doorknob to enter the kitchen, he could sense that something didn't feel right. The house was very, very quiet-alarmingly quiet. Lucy and Robert were sitting in the living room, not speaking, just waiting for him to come home. James stood and looked at the pair of them before asking, "What's the matter here, has something happened?" "Yes," Lucy replied. "Well, what, tell me," James worriedly responded. "Frederick LeClaire visited us here today," Lucy answered. James hung his head, "I'm not surprised, and I wish I had been home to talk to him too. It's been a long time since we've spoken to one another." Lucy sat up straight and whispered, "Josie has run away. When she told her mother who Robert was, she lost her temper and told her she couldn't see him, ever." James shook his head in partial disbelief of the situation. If the LeClaire's wanted to keep the children apart, there would be many confrontations between the families. Again, all the guilt and anguish from so many years ago were right here at the surface again. He would have to choose his words carefully to not bring it into the conversation. James turned to Robert and sharply asked him, "Do you know where Josie is?" Robert felt trapped, he just wasn't sure if he could trust them to not reveal her, and he would not jeopardize Josie or her life if he thought it meant that it would lead to her going back home. Would they understand his feelings of protection for her? But he felt that his good relationship with his parents would stand behind him in the end. He had no reason to ever have any secrets from them; this was the first dilemma in his sixteen years. Other than skinned knees and broken toes from the horses stepping on them, his growing up years had been nothing but pleasurable for both parents and child.

Robert spoke up, "Josie told me everything that happened last night, we had a wonderful day together, and then she got home and her mother blew up when she heard my last name. What would cause her to do that? What's the difference what my name is, I want to be with Josie and she wants to be with me," he demanded. "I've never even gotten into the simplest amount of trouble, and our family has a good reputation and hasn't committed any crimes to shame our good name." Poor Robert, he didn't know that he had indirectly hit upon the exact reason for all the discomfort surrounding this heartache with Josie and him. But James and Lucy knew exactly what the LeClaire's objection to their last name was and stood in silence while Robert questioned it. While the horrific scandal surrounding them had deadly consequences and destroyed both families, the burden of the ordeal still weighed heaviest on the LeClaires.

Chapter Twenty-Two

WILDHORSE BUTTE

I have been living with Evelyn and Alice in their comfortable home for two weeks now and each day I cry and comfort myself that I will not be discovered hiding here. It's been fairly simple though challenging to keep me well hidden within the house from outsiders. It will be heartbreaking and be a harsh adjustment to leave here, as I have grown extremely close to Evelyn and Alice and will always cherish them as a part of my family. And it's somewhat sad that these newcomers into my life have come to mean more to me than my actual family members at this moment in time, simply because of the unfairness of this entire situation.

Although, I have never left my refuge in the little farmhouse, Evelyn and Robert have kept me apprised of the happenings outside of my sequestered location. I will always feel indebted to Evelyn for her hospitality and the heavy stress that I was putting her through. Clearly, I must be a tremendous burden to her along with worrying about little Alice spilling the news one day to James and Lucy that I live in their attic. Evelyn was too staunch of character to betray Robert and me; Robert was the son she never had, and she would protect him as if he was her birth child.

It is becoming too dangerous for all of us to have me remain here. This usually quiet home and outbuildings have been searched and searched and searched again trying to locate me. My family stands firmly that Robert is aware of my location and repeatedly have told him that they want him to return me home immediately. Soon the Army will be sending personnel to each and every homestead for the purpose of taking a census of every person living in this and the surrounding areas. There are rumors of an evacuation of all the Nez Perce in the area, a rumor that is fast approaching reality I am told. They will all be taken from their lands, homes, families, giving up each and every thing and be transferred to a reservation in the near future. And that coupled with the fear of a hateful confrontation with my parents, I am not willing to risk being discovered. Either way, I will become strictly detached from my life as it has been. I'm quite confident that my family would contrive a way to lock me down so tightly that there will be no hope of escape. And the Army talking about relocation will accomplish that also, and either way there will be no hope of ever seeing my Robert again and my life will be over.

My family is determined that Robert and Rose played a part in my disappearance, and have not ceased questioning them about it. They have repeatedly told my parents that I said goodbye to them in an erratic and hurtful state and would not be talked out of running away from everyone, including Rose, my best friend, and Robert, the boy whom I fell deeply in love with the first time our eyes met at the picnic. They did not find it hard to put on a convincing act each time they were questioned; they each would burst into tears and sob. The entire scenario was very stressful for them, and there was always the immense fear of being caught in this careful lie concerning my whereabouts. For their sake as well as mine, it was inevitably time that I am relocated to another, safer hiding place, one that is not so close by to them. I had truly been blessed with the friendship of my best friend and the love of a great man, and I would be able to depend upon him, regardless of the issue that was facing us. I sincerely hope that someday I will be able to be the same person to him and be out in the open and stand by his side for whatever reason he should need me to.

As I was begging my subconscious to remain calm, that this nightmare really would end, Robert was making arrangements for me to stay with someone else. A man that lived on the Columbia River over in Washington State who needed someone to help with his children would gladly take me into his home. The ranch had been contracted to break some horses over in Wildhorse Butte, which lay to the east of Pittsburgh Landing on the Idaho and Oregon border. He had been contracted to spend at least four weeks training a group of horses on a large cattle ranch. There was another man working there also, who said his name was Edward. Edward told him that he had a small ranch and in addition to his cattle and crop duties, he did odd jobs for some additional income. He had been there repairing a couple pieces of farm machinery, and they had gotten acquainted during meal time and in the evening while sleeping in the same bunkhouse. Robert had learned that he lived in about the middle of the state on the east side of the river in a tiny village called Wenatchee where he lived with his two small children. Edward was a widower raising a boy of four and a girl of two years of age, who had lost their mother very early in their young lives. When Robert mentioned that his ranch was located in Lucile, he told Robert that he and his wife had once had close friends from the Lucile area. They were a young couple who were both deceased now and had left behind a little girl. He had lost track of her but he thought that he remembered that she lived with her grandmother on a large ranch where she was a housekeeper.

Robert said that his mouth fell wide open when Edward told him this. So he asked the man, "You wouldn't be talking about a child named Alice, would you?" "Yes," was the reply he received; "I believe that was her name." "And her grandmother," Robert asked, "Could she possibly be Evelyn?" Edward shook his head in agreement, "You know, I think Evelyn is the mother to the lady I knew." Robert laughed and excitedly replied, "People talk about it being a small world, and it certainly is true." "Evelyn and Alice live on our ranch, and Evelyn takes good care of all of us. In fact, she helped bring me into this world. She is much more than a housekeeper to us; Evelyn and little Alice are an important part of the Ray Mon family." Edward shook his head and said, "I guess we all have a connection somewhere don't we?" Robert grinned and nodded, knowing that a tremendous opportunity had just opened up for us to have absolute seclusion and privacy. His place was many days ride from Lucile, thus enabling us to be void of the continual pressures of Robert having to sneak into Evelyn's house to visit me without severe repercussions every minute. And I am hoping to be able to see the sun again and embrace the daylight hours, not spending my endless hours and days in a windowless room.

Robert did not hesitate to present our situation to Edward, he felt this man to be an answer to our plight, since he had been delivered to us at this precise time. He also told Edward that he would have Evelyn write a letter to him, verifying that he was speaking the truth in our tragic, overwhelming story. Robert said, "We would be forever grateful to you for your generosity, and I will repay you by taking on some of your load with the planting and harvesting, and I know that Josie would love watching your children." Edward extended his hand to Robert and the two men shook hands firmly in agreement. A deal had been struck and would benefit every one of the five people involved. It was a practical, beneficial arrangement for all. Robert said he thought he could see a somewhat lighter expression on Edward's face, where there had been so much despair when he had first met him. Edward said that his children definitely needed the influence of a woman again. They had a maternal grandmother for guidance, but she was an older woman and they did not see her very often. The children were with a neighbor now, but they lived alone on the ranch with Edward. Robert continued, "It will cost you nothing to house Josie, I will provide for her. I earn a nice salary and I will provide a portion of that for food and supplies and anything she wants or needs." Edward replied that he did not have to include food in that bargain, he would be glad to feed both of us for helping out. He was raised to make sure that you treat people well that are kind enough to help lessen your workload.

And this connection between Robert and Edward had begun by simple chance, their jobs putting them together in the same place at the same time. A new friendship, such as this could enrich both of their lives and the lives of those held in reverence by each of them. And further, finding out that they had both been fortunate to know Evelyn and her family, whom each held in high regard. They were of solid character and loved by all who knew them, and no one, regardless of situation would ever be turned away from their door.

Robert returned home a day or so later from Wildhorse Butte and rode straight to Evelyn's little farm without stopping at the main house first. I heard him ride up and quickly went through my well practiced ritual of going into hiding up in the attic crawlspace. The room that accessed the small opening into the rafters had only a door for entry and no window. I could not see out and no one was able to see in. I was reasonably safe moving around in that room. But upon even hearing the slightest sound or even the sensing that someone or some animal was approaching sent me swiftly back up into my cubbyhole under the sometimes leaky roof. I would remain motionless, with my breath held tight and my eyes closed, with the only sound being made was that of my heart, thumping so fiercely that I was sure it would be heard outside the house.

Robert knew that I would be laying there so frightened in fear for my very soul being ripped from me, that he must sound the signal for all clear the second he rode into the yard. He had found an old dinner bell that the cooks on a cattle drive used to call in the herders to let me know it was he who had ridden into the yard. He kept it down inside the drinking well and would hoist it up and ring it five times, pausing in between each gong sound in exactly the same manner each time. As soon as I heard that, my body relaxed and the tension was released some. But I would remain frozen to my spot until Robert actually peeked through the storage door in the wall and up into my tiny prison cell. It was entirely possible that someone had been witness to this ritual and would imitate it to see what results would stem from its use. I had been locked away here at Evelyn's, and it was beginning to affect me physically as well as mentally. Two weeks probably doesn't sound like a long time, but it felt like a jail cell to me until Evelyn and Alice came home every evening. I was becoming pale, to almost a graying color; the lack of sunlight was doing damage to my skin color, as well as being locked up was damaging to my mind's function. It was time to be relocated to a better hideaway, one that was free from darkness and the minute amount of space I have been resigned to waiting out my days. There had been a steady stream of people dropping in to inquire if I had visited here, and each time that they were questioned, Evelyn and Alice held to their story that I had not. But no one had forced their way in to search or ransack the farm in an effort to locate me. Evelyn was of undisputable character and truly liked by everyone who had ever met her. Evelyn and Robert were very close, so it was natural for her to be a suspect in my disappearance, and my faithful friend Rose was being followed everywhere also. I had only been able to see her twice since this nightmare had begun, and that had been a risky ordeal to arrange the meetings for all concerned. I don't know how extensive the search was for me elsewhere, but I would expect that they were keeping an eye on everyone involved in Robert's and my life. But I had not been discovered here, so it made me a little sad to think that my family wasn't diligently overturning people's lives to find me.

Robert came crawling through the closet now and he was humming as he opened the door to see me lying there tearfully waiting for his rescue. Smiling at him the best that I could from the twisted, angled position that I was in I gasped, "Oh, Robert, it has been such a long wait for your return; you've been gone for days." He pulled me out into the room and clutched me tightly when I was completely immersed into his arms. He hurriedly blurted out, "We won't have to do this anymore Josie! I've found a place for you to stay where you don't have to spend all of your time in a dark hole." Robert was crying now, it wrenched and stabbed at his gut each and every time he had to see me hiding this way just so that we could be together. "Where are we going?" I sobbed, "Will there be windows?" "Yes, Josie there will be windows and trees and flowers and the freedom to see all of them, all of the time," he told me with a wide grin and while laughing.

Then Robert began to tell the whole story of the random meeting of a man named Edward and the mutual plans that they had made between them. Robert's arms were wrapped around me; my body sagged with relief and the tears began and they would not end, the news was so overwhelmingly exciting. Could it be a possibility that Robert and I were destined after all to have a future together? I shook my head in approval of these plans; it would not be necessary to live in total seclusion with so many restrictions. This was more than I had hoped for in my thoughts while hiding in Evelyn's house! Robert will still have to pretend to be ignorant concerning my whereabouts, and appear to be saddened that I have left him behind as well. He was fairly confident that his parents would remain tight lipped if he were to tell them the truth about us, but he wasn't ready to take that step and that risk just yet. If they had any hint that Robert was lying to them, they were not showing it on their faces when they spoke with Robert. Probably at the very least, they had deduced that he was visiting her on his trips to other ranches to train horses. That was partially true, he would usually incorporate an extra day onto those trips to sneak back just to spend a few hours with me. Or sometimes he would just say that he was going out to visit Evelyn and Alice, he quite frequently stayed with them, so there was no suspicion there. He would help her around the place and spend some time with his favorite little girl. We looked forward to and hoped for a time that a better situation would come into play for us and now it finally has. I will spend my last night here tonight with Evelyn and Alice, and Robert will come for me tomorrow morning a couple hours before dawn. Robert knows every inch of every road surrounding this area and beyond and was positive that we could sneak out of here well before daylight.

When Evelyn and Alice arrived home that night, I trembled with excitement as I heard little Alice open her music box in her bedroom below me. That was their signal to me, just as was the dinner bell Robert's identifying chime. They were surprised when they came upstairs that I was not tucked away on my slat bed in the attic. I was out into the room in full view when they entered and I ran to embrace both of them. They could see that I was a very happy girl, as I pulled Alice onto my lap and began to giggle and tickle my little friend. I mumbled out the news Robert had brought to me this afternoon; it was unexpected good news but mingled with heartbreaking feelings. My heart was twisting hard as I continued to tell them the story of the odd meeting that Robert had had with Edward and that I would be leaving them in a few short hours. This would be an evening of mixed emotions, the elation of knowing that something better is happening for Robert and I, and of much sadness, having to leave these two wonderful people who have become so tremendously important to me. And that would darken the path to moving on to something more secure, less restraining and much better for my health. I've learned a lot about family and relationships from these girls, in a different manner than that with parents and grandparents.

There would be no sleep here tonight, we did not want to waste the last precious minutes that we would be in this house together with our eyes closed. We all remained in my windowless haven, not risking chances out in the open on the eve of my last day here with my surrogate family. But this room was hardly a confinement chamber to me; it had held many special moments and activities most nights of my fortunate placement within these walls. It was time spent of sheer enjoyment and we had created our own little family each evening when they returned home from their ranch duties. We had bonded together in strength of a love that would remain an integral part of each of us for the rest of our lives. What comforted us that evening was in knowing that we would see each other again, this was not a permanent goodbye. Just a separation of sorts. I would only be far enough away to be able to relish life again and only hide when there was an extreme suspicion of intrusion.

The three of us girls turned to one of our favorite pastimes of satisfying our sweet tooth urges to mark this evening as a memorable one. We had taught each other much in our hours of comfortable, soothing conversation and activities. I had learned very many cooking, baking and candy recipes from Evelyn; no one that I know has the knack for creating delectable treats as she does. And I had taught her the beading and needlework that my limited sixteen years of experience could possibly give her that my mother had taught to me. I had helped her begin to create many beautiful dresses and skirts for herself and our beautiful princess girl based on what I had learned in my former life. And while I had spent a significant amount of kitchen time growing up, I had never learned as many things about baking as I had in the short amount of time that I had been here. So, cookies it was, rolled balls of peanut butter dough, sneaking a taste pretty often and Alice with her face and all fingers full of delicious stickiness. Although, I wasn't able to actually witness them baking in the oven downstairs, I could certainly smell them from my room. That smell always lifted the heaviness of my heart and eased the pain of another day spent in seclusion. This house has been the warmest and most welcoming home that I have ever had the fortunate opportunity to be allowed to partake of its wonders of love.

Robert arrived wide awake and eager to retrieve me to make the trip cross country to Edwards's ranch house. It was about three a.m. and he found us all huddled together, with Alice bundled in her favorite pink blanket, asleep in my lap. We had fallen asleep after our feast of peanut butter cookies and milk wrapped in each other's arms. We had been talking until we had begun speaking in whispers and finally could speak no more. It was best not to wake the sleeping child cuddling against me. We had explained it all to her last night, and reassured her that I would not be very far away from her. We had told her that visits would be possible as soon as we were settled in our new location; we would not tell her too much, she was after all, still a small child. A child who had been put under extreme pressure to keep such an elaborate secret as the fact that I was living in their house for such a long time. She had held her tongue and never betrayed me to anyone at the ranch or to those coming to continually inquire about me; but we won't burden the young one this time.

Robert had quietly snuck into our dark, silent fortress, with only our lantern still lighting up the room with no windows. He stood there gazing at us for some time he later told me, the three of us looking so natural together, and he knew that this would be earth shattering to our emotions. Gradually, Evelyn and I returned to consciousness and knew that the moment for separation had come. We remained as we were, unmoving for a bit, we did not want to rush our last precious moments together, moments that would remain with us forever. As I stood up to transfer Alice to her grandmother's arms, I looked directly into Evelyn's eyes and she into mine. The look that was exchanged between us was understood by each of us, we were a part of each other now and nothing could take that from us.

Once Robert had removed my things that I had packed and set by the door, he came back and extended his hand to me. If it were not for the leading hand, I would have remained frozen in my gaze with Evelyn, unable to move on my own power. He led me from the house, and once outside the door, he stopped and curled me up in his strong arms and hugged me hard. He said, "Josie, we're beginning the next chapter in our lives today, and I'm so glad that it's a chapter that we will be spending together." I dug my head into his shoulder and began to shift my thoughts to what lay ahead for us. He hoisted me up and onto a horse that gave me a feeling of reassurance the second that I was seated upon its warm, sturdy, unwavering back. I felt as confident trusting the animals that Robert had trained just as well as the trainer, his caring nature had transferred to them. It was very dark and I could not see my steed, but I believe that she had to be smiling, being given such a special duty.

Robert said it would be a long ride, and that we would cover the journey in about four days, but that when he was coming to see me, he could do it in two. In the month that I had known him, this would be the first time that we would be alone together since all of this horror had happened. We had spent one wonderfully exciting afternoon together, but by the time that day had ended that was all wiped away from us on the surface, but we would always remember and treasure it. It had created the basis for us to endure this hell that we had been thrown into due to some tragedy or scandal that had happened long ago. We were being chastised for something that occurred in another generation and no one would due us the courtesy of informing us what that life altering issue was. Something that was so powerful, so horrific, that it was to define the lives of two young people before they even had a chance to discover life for themselves.

He wanted to spend the extra time riding along slowly, allowing me to enjoy the outdoors, which I had been deprived of for so long. He was taking me somewhere in the state of Washington, far enough away from Lucile and Riggins where the chance of recognition would be slight. We wouldn't be tempting fate by attending any social events or going into any of the surrounding towns, but we didn't need that anyway. We were young, in love, had found a place to be together; that was all we needed out of life right now. And time-time to figure out what it was that had happened to our young lives that we had no control over. And time to plan our future, one that we planned on spending together, no matter what the consequences may be and what opposition we may face because of it.

We rode slowly out into the dark morning hours and headed straight west. We had no other option but to ride through the ranch lands. We would gratefully be clear of Ray Mon property when we reached the Snake River and it would guide us upstream until we reached Lower Pittsburgh Landing. At that junction, we would cross over the Snake and step into Oregon and for me that would be for the first time in another state. Robert had timed it so that we would cross the river at dawn, dark enough to be under cover, but light enough to guide us across safely. I had no worries that Robert would deliver me to the little family that was waiting for me to join them and form some new beginnings for all of us. For a young man of seventeen, he was educated in the ways of the weather, traveling conditions and all landmarks around us. And in addition to that, he wasn't only an expert on the Appaloosa, he read people correctly as well as any seasoned adult. His first impression of Edward was of a trustworthy, hard working man who had suffered the misfortune to lose his wife to illness and struggle to balance his children and his ranch. And that feeling that Robert had when he had shaken Edward's hand had confirmed that judgment of the man.

Robert and I stopped just after daylight. We had entered the Wallowa Valley now, and we were pleased with our traveled distance. We required some breakfast as did the horses. Robert had planned for our nourishment, of course, just as he planned everything to the detail. We made a small campfire and brewed coffee, bacon and biscuits, which we gobbled down as if we'd not eaten in days. All of the stress in planning and preparation for this escape as well as the morning's ride had left us famished. We didn't talk while we ate, just smiled at each other; we were there together and that was our focus right then. We had taken an extreme chance in all that we had undertaken in this past thirty days and the outcome was in our favor. We had successfully completed something no teenagers should even have to attempt. When we had finished feasting and the last sips of coffee taken, we gently set down our cups and stood up. It was then that we came together in our first embrace that was free of fear, not hurried, and not stressed. Our feelings for each other took hold and the arms wrapped around each other spoke words that we did not have to say. We took one another's hand and silently took a stroll to enjoy the early morning sunrise and appreciate some of the beauty of this breathtaking country that we were standing in.

We were overwhelmed with its brilliant greenery and hillside curvature. The area was vast and open, providing us with a spectacular view all around us. The exercise did us well, and our horses did the opposite of us and laid down for a break for their tired legs, while we leisurely walked around the area for a little while. Then we decided that the pressure and the travel had tired and weakened us, and we should also get in some rest before we went any farther today. Robert pulled the bedroll from his horse and laid it down in front of a stump, out in the open skies, so that I could feel the warmth of the sun while we napped. When we had allowed ourselves a brief respite, we could begin to make preparations for the next steps in our lives.

As I lay there waiting quietly and calmly next to my rescuer, my consciousness drifted back to the never ending days prior to this one. It was hard for me to believe that it was over; and even perhaps that it had happened at all. And while it had been wonderful in so many ways at Evelyn's, when I was hiding it was a horrible experience for me. My pitch black sliver of space in the attic filled my nostrils with soot and often trickled into my eyes, making the time pass even more horribly. It had felt like years that I was burrowed into Evelyn's house, and quite often I was sure that I would never make it out of there safely. It became so smothering to me that I felt I would die from the taste and feel of the black clouds hanging in my throat, I had only water for relief and a bucket to spit into. I dared not to cough or choke; noise would be my undoing, and I would be hauled from my hiding space.

But this evening I will sleep free out into the night, with fresh air and a moonlit sky and under a magnitude of bright stars. And everything would be different, I would not be alone, but rather I would be holding onto the man that I loved. What a relief to be where there would be nothing or no one to hinder our thoughts or stop our voices, and we could slumber for the first time in many, many days peacefully. An animal daring to wander into our campsite would be driven back by our enthusiasm for life and survival instincts, which couldn't possibly be any stronger than they have been recently. We could survive anything now that we were in the open space of the world and would no longer have to cower and hide each time a noise was heard and a presence suspected.

Robert and I rested for a couple of hours, and it was about high noon when we awoke refreshed and ready to ride out again. We allowed the horses some water again before we mounted them. Hopefully, a fresh stream would be close by the next time that we stopped, enabling us to replenish our supply. He had packed enough onto the horses for a full day, and I still had with me the water pouch that I had taken on the day of our first meeting for my hike up the mountainside to meet him. Slowly, we continued along the Snake River, which had turned now to the northwest, and we were now positioned on the south side of the river. Robert told me that we had been in the state of Washington now for an hour or so and had progressed really well today. We felt that we were well beyond any reason to rush, so we kept a nice steady pace, laughing and talking as we rode and appreciating the absence of any other people.

We traveled until the sun was just beginning to dip down into the landscape, probably three or four hours, with just a few short breaks off of the horses. It was time to set up camp for the evening's layover and Robert had spotted a nice little cliff overhang into the side of the Snake River Canyon walls. With trees on either side of the mouth of the cave like shelter, it made a picturesque little haven for us to spend our first night alone together. I would soon realize that he had thought of everything possible that he could to ensure that this would be the perfect evening for us. First, he dusted out the opening into the little rock formation with a handy branch from a pine tree nearby. I kept asking him to let me help him do something, anything to ready our sleeping quarters for the night; he declined my offer each and every time. He repeatedly told me that I had been through a horrendous ordeal just to be with him, so I would be doing nothing at all on this trip. Next, he neatly laid our bed rolls inside; we would sleep with our fee,t out and our heads inside the cave. The feeling of safety is about the only way to getting a minimum of sleep while out in the wilderness. And feet are much less vulnerable and even less valuable than your head and upper torso areas are to you. Then he went off on a search for dry firewood and he said he would stay well within earshot of me. Hopefully, nothing would, but if something should occur that would require that I scream for help, he'd be there like lightning to the rescue.

I always grinned widely when he said things like that, because he had actually rescued me just like the knight in shining armor on the white steed rescues the princess and saves her from everlasting doom. And ride in and sweep me away he did, and here we were on our gallant steeds and off to find a castle, or at least a lodging of some kind! He would pick up on my grin sometimes and say, "T'was my pleasure, my lady." And I, always proudly replied with a "me too, my knight." And that was cause for a gentle but very meaningful embrace that spelled out our love for each other clearly. We would pull apart and look into each other's eyes before releasing each other and separating so that Robert could go off where he needed to. Although, I didn't have anywhere to go when I was living at Evelyn's except back into hiding, his hugs were enough to keep me living in the attic room these past weeks. Robert told me quite frequently that I was his lady love from his first glance my way, and I would become tingly and blush, somewhat embarrassed but elated to have found him.

When he returned with the wood, he built us a nice fire for our very first supper together. He put on the coffee pot and some camas roots to cook for us, to accompany the dried meat and bread that he had stolen from the family larder in the wee hours this morning before coming to get me. When we had finished eating that delicious, well prepared meal, I produced my cookies that Evelyn and Alice had made with me last night. Robert had forgotten to bring some precious candy, and he apologized for that, knowing how very much I loved the delicious sweet flavors of it. I then told him the story of my last wonderful evening in the room with no windows, savoring the precious moments that I had left with those two females that had become family to my heart.

We huddled into our little cubbyhole, which was close enough to the glowing fire to keep us warm for the night and served as a deterrent for any animals that may consider wandering in. Robert assured me that he would keep it burning brightly throughout the night. He had spent numerous nights out in the open ranges traveling here and there and had told me he sleeps with one eye shut and the other is on the fire. He said, "Josie, do you think I'm going to let you down by letting anything happen to you now? I will always treat you like a porcelain doll, very pretty and fragile. Just like I did the first time you hiked up the mountain to meet me and your face was bleeding from the huckleberry briars." "And what you did for my forehead healed without even the slightest mark that I had been gashed whatsoever," I remembered. "But I'm not that fragile, I think that I'm pretty tough, I've just spent a couple of weeks hiding in an old house in a cramped little space." "Ok, I guess you only look like you could shatter like fine china, but inside you're pretty strong willed." Robert retorted.

My mother had never told me anything about the male species or what it was like to grow up and fall in love. And certainly the topic of what happens between and men and women any sexual nature was absolutely a forbidden subject. I never had a chance to beg for guidance on a part of life that is natural to every human being. So, I would have to learn everything on my own, and let my instincts judge what was right and wrong and when it would be right or wrong. After our first afternoon on the mountain, I was forced to leave my home for him to remain in my life. The time spent in the farm house, we had talked about our lives as they were before and would be; now we would begin to speak about things as they are. I was completely enveloped by him and we were holding each other as tightly as we could grasp onto one another. And from there, we slipped into slumber and dreamland in each other's arms, which was the most reassuring, loving feeling I had ever experienced in my young years.

And soon it was daybreak, the night had disappeared and now the faded colors of pink and orange were coming to us out of the earth to give light to another day. Neither of us had moved from our original positions of last night, we were still safely cradled against one another and did not want to move. We would have remained there forever, if such a thing was possible to do. And Robert had mentioned that maybe we should be thinking of the two of us breaking off completely from all who knew us and just heading for Canada where we could be together freely. But he said he wasn't quite ready to split from his family yet; he would to need save some money to start off on our own. Yes, money was a necessity to start a life together, without it we would soon be miserable and regretting our decision. We could go anywhere that we pleased and feel confident that we could make it in the big world alone, if we had the security of not being penniless to get set up someplace.

ALONE TOGETHER AT LAST

When the sun came up over the mountains, it was truly the most wondrous sight my youthful eyes had ever seen, it had been so long since I had viewed a sunrise. The way the colors just peeked through in vivid streaks intertwined with each other, shining out to create light. I was awake before Robert was, and I carefully sat up to fully enjoy the beauty of the sunrise. I was chilled now. The fire, though still burning, had gotten low, with glowing coals, giving off a minimum of heat. I didn't want to disturb Robert by removing any of the covers, so I would just bear the coolness of dawn while watching the glow from the sky. But it wasn't long and without making any sound at all, Robert lifted the blanket up onto my shoulders and tucked it all the way around me and then wrapped himself around me. I was feeling very cozy and was warming up quickly, with the strong, loving arms of the man I love tied around me radiating the love he felt for me.

We uttered not one word to each other, just basking in the wonder of being with each other and not wanting these precious moments to ever end. Robert and I were alone with the world out here, with nature all around us and nobody or nothing to take control over us. It was the most free, uncomplicated time that either of us had ever experienced, why did life with our families have to be so controlling? Always thinking that they know what is best for us, just because they are our parents, and even though it is their job to guide us along, they aren't always right. We can't always live our lives based on the experiences of others. Each person has to go through their various trials and learn from their own mistakes in order to truly know right from wrong.   Robert and I knew that we would need to relish each second of possible joy from this time together, any time alone was irreplaceable.   We knew what our future held, we were destined to be together forever, and fate had kept secret my recent whereabouts and Robert's visits to me.   It was the present we were unsure of, how often will we see each other now that I would be so many miles from his ranch in Lucile?   Robert as always, reassured me that it is only a temporary solution, and he did keep his word that I would only hide at Evelyn's until he found somewhere better.   Now living with Edward is just until he can save some money and maybe make a connection to work somewhere long term.   I put my complete heart and faith in Robert and it will happen; we will live happily ever after someday, someday very soon, I hope.

Today, we decided we wouldn't ride very far, but rather we would lollygag now the rest of the way to Wenatchee. Robert had warned Edward not to expect us any particular day.   And certainly we were not eager to share one another with the outside world, or have any interference on our private time.   So, we galloped along for a couple of hours and then Robert stopped his horse and standing up declared, "This is it! We're staying here tonight! What a beauty of a creek!" It was a pretty little stream; again, he had chosen another place to camp that we would be unforgettable.   We dismounted and stood by our horses, just savoring the quiet, solitude of yet another wonder that was created for us by Mother Nature.   Robert took the reins from my hand and led both of the horses to a nearby cluster of bushes and tied them up.   When he returned he quietly looked into my eyes and then he took my hand and pulled me gently over to a mound of huge rocks. He looked nervous and mischievous all at the same time, with that crooked grin on his face but with tears in his eyes. I wasn't sure what was going to happen next, but it was going to be something serious, that much I could read on his handsome face. I could also see the effects of the sun that had further reddened his complexion and the beginning of worry lines around his eyes. He is such a young man to have started to show signs of a man who is aging yet, when he is only a boy of seventeen. But I guess that I hardly feel like a gal of sixteen years old myself, with all of the agony that has transpired for Robert and I after discovering that there is a Ray Mon and Blue Dove feud. Robert and I each carry one half Nez Perce blood within our veins and our stubborn determination will carry us through this mysterious ordeal concerning our families.

Robert took both of my hands in his and lightly shook each of them, and it was apparent that he was preparing to say something very important. His lips opened slightly and then closed again; he looked at me and then down at our entwined hands. Finally, the corners of his mouth curved up into a warm smile and the soft spoken words slowly came out. "Josie, my Josie, I love you very much." I wanted to speak but he raised his hand to stop me. "You and I are intent on spending our lifetimes together. And I don't want us to have to wait any further. I want our future to begin this very minute." I gazed at him with eyes full of warm, heavy tears and a blazing heat filled my throbbing heart while he made me feel as if I were the only person in his world. I had not heard such words of incredible sentiment before from anyone, and I would cherish each word he spoke to me forever and ever. "Will you marry me, Josie? Please say you will." I was fully engulfed in tears now, I know I expected Robert and I would marry someday, but I didn't think it would happen until this was all over. But then again, when would this all be over? I guess Robert didn't have an answer to our quandary either, or he wouldn't be moving ahead so quickly. With quivering lips and every inch of my body vibrating with nervousness, I breathed out a whispered, "Yes, Robert, yes, of course I will marry you." He said, "Tonight, I want it to be tonight." "But there is no one here to marry us Robert," I squeaked. "It doesn't matter if it is only the two of us, we'll marry each other under the stars and our ancestors. They will watch us vow ourselves to one another and make the stars shiner brighter with their approval," he answered. I didn't even need a moment to ponder on his rationalization, for Robert and me to pledge our love for each other is all that we needed.

My heart was twisting and turning with unspeakable, delightful pain; this was a moment that every young girl wants to experience. When the man she is hopelessly in love with, declares his love for her and asks her to spend the rest of her life in his heart. I couldn't speak, but I managed to make my head move in an up and down motion, so that he would know that I was agreeing with him. Robert picked me up and began twirling me around in a circle and when we finally stopped, we were both dizzy and fell to the ground. We watched each other for a few moments before sharing a brief, soft, kiss and then Robert rolled us over and over we just laid there and giggled.

"C'mon," he said, "let's go swimming." And into the creek we went and swished our feet in the cool, refreshing water, and waded down to where it was waist deep. He grabbed my hand as he threw himself in and pulled me along with him; we splashed and laughed and threw water at each other. It was perfect-perfect courting time, I guess you could say. We were falling in love with each other fast, and tonight we would take a huge step forward into our lives as young, married adults. When the sun started to go down, we sauntered back upstream to where we had left our horses. We each had preparations to make for the most important evening in our lives, that on which we would seal our love for each other by pledging it to one another in our marriage vows.

Our resting place for tonight would be pretty much out in the open, we were hopeful that tonight's weather would hold as beautifully as the daytime hours did. The sprawling oak tree up a small hill from the creek would have to serve for our protection tonight, and the carpet of fallen leaves would cushion our slumber. Robert told me to go and get ready for our wedding under our tree that would serve as our wedding chamber this evening. And then he told me not to look back down to the creek for any reason, and I nodded my head in agreement, making him promise not to sneak a peek up the hill either. We would both do the best that we could in these surroundings to prepare something special for our ceremony.

I had found some beautiful yellow and orange flowers of the late fall to carry as I had seen so many times on a day such as this. I combed and smoothed down my hair and carefully placed one brilliantly colored bloom into the twist of hair that I had wound together on top of my head. I had few items of clothing with me, and among them was a beautifully, handcrafted dress which my Mother had spent countless hours stitching in the dim light of evening. The dress was white with pink threading throughout it in a fancy pattern with rows and rows of zigzagging threads that almost looked like a picket fence going around the bottom of the skirt. She called the fabric of the dress, "hucktooth." It had additional threads on top of the actual fabric, which were used to weave decorative

268

stitches throughout. She had designed it herself; she had an amazing talent for creating her own patterns, and I always had the fanciest needlework on my dresses of all the young gals. My mother would approve of the dress that I have chosen for my nuptials, but my grandmother would not. She would have preferred traditional tribal costume to a white man's version of proper attire. It made me a little sad that neither of them could be here tonight, but their lack of approval made that quite impossible. And it would not matter if we took our places as husband and wife here or anywhere else, they would never be present due to something that happened long ago and obviously caused an unforgiving hatred.

Around my wrist I wrapped the exquisitely detailed headband that my grandmother and I had hand-beaded in accordance with tribal custom and symbols. This was the bride's gift to the groom, which I would give to my young brave on the day of my intended wedding. All young Nez Perce girls were instructed to make one at the age of twelve to fourteen. Once a girl moved into her teen years, she could be married at any time and on short notice. We had beaded a likeness of Kokopelli directly in the center of the headband; he was quite certainly present as witness to any nuptials being recited anywhere. Kokopelli is the god of mischief, fertility and abundance. On each side of Kokopelli were symbols pertinent to the couple; to the left I had placed a colorful teepee which represented a happy and fruitful home, and his side was represented with an Appaloosa horse. The right side was left bare until you knew which tribe or nationality your intended was, or in our case, both being the same; I chose the Appaloosa because it represented him individually. I finished mine while I was at hiding in Evelyn's house. I was now certain that Robert was to be my destiny. It was one of my most prized possessions and could hardly be left behind when I had left my family home to make one with Robert.

I was completely ready to become Mrs. Robert Ray Mon and found that I was not the least bit nervous. I had carefully pressed the wrinkles from my dress with my hands the best that I could. It had been wadded up in a saddle bag for a couple of days. Only one thing was missing and that was my shoes, I only had dirty old riding boots with me, so I would be a barefoot bride. But I was sure that Robert would pay no attention, he loved me no matter if I was tattered and torn or crying with a tear stained face.

When I began to slowly and carefully descend the hill, I saw Robert standing there beside the bubbling creek. There was a beautiful circle of flowers encompassing him that he had picked and arranged for the site of our wedding vows. He was wearing a clean set of riding clothes in black and white with a spotless black cowboy hat. Robert was an amazingly handsome man, with each of his features blending perfectly together. He carried the mixture of Nez Perce and French Canadian as elegantly as the horses that he trained and taught to stand proud.

I walked to the left of him, stopped and turned so that we were directly facing each other. Robert was standing there with his hands behind his back, holding something that I could see was white. He smiled broadly and said, "You are the most beautiful bride on this earth, and I am so very proud that you are mine. And I have something that I would like to give to you in honor of this special day." He extended his hand and in it he held his great, great grandmother's delicate, hand crocheted, lace mantilla which he had been told many times that she wore on her wedding day. It had belonged on his mother's side of the family who was of Spanish descent, and it had been handed down and as traditional headdress to be worn by Spaniard brides. He held a corner of it in each hand and gently laid it on top of my hair and covered my face with it. It was also a tradition for the bride's face to remain covered until the vows had been spoken and it was time for the first kiss sealing the marriage. In a Native American ceremony it would be quite different, there would no kissing or touching until in the privacy of the teepee. We were trying to be respectful of all of the family traditions that we were aware of; we by no means wanted to forget our lineages that created us. And we were also creating a tradition of our own here today that we would hand down to our children and hopefully to their children—our grandchildren.

When he had finished placing the square of lace at just the right angle, he took a step back and said, "Thank you for wearing this veil in thought of my grandmothers who were so precious to me." I replied, "Robert, I am ever so pleased that you would want me to wear something that belonged to your grandmothers, I know how much you loved them." "Yes, I did," he replied choking back his tears briefly remembering the loss of them in his life. When he had regained his composure, I said, "Robert, I have something to give to you also, that I made with the help of my grandmother. It was just finished while I was staying with Evelyn and Alice, and they helped me to transform my idea into a work of art." And then I explained the entire concept of this tradition between two members of the Nez Perce, even though his mother was of the same tribe as I, perhaps he wasn't aware of this ritual.

And then we both ceased to speak and just adoringly admired each other in our wedding attire. He was the first to break the silence; he sweetly looked into my softly crying eyes, and said, "Josie, my love for you will be everlasting; I will respect you and honor our marriage vows to each other. When we are fortunate enough to be in good health, we shall share our great love. When you are ill, I will relentlessly care for you until you are well again. Never will there be a time when I am not completely yours. I marry you Josephine Anna LeClaire in the name of our forefathers and ancestors that we both hold sacred." I didn't know what I was going to say to Robert while I was getting ready, I tried to think of unforgettable words that would tell him how much I loved him and what this evening meant to me. But, I could think of nothing that would suffice in relaying my complicated feelings to him. But I was confident that when the moment arrived, I would be able to open my heart and speak words only reserved for him. And that is what happened; after I regained my voice, I softly, lovingly said, "Robert, I am ready to begin the next phase of my life by joining with you in marriage. I never dreamed such a man as you would exist for me, and I will have no other in my lifetime. I pledge to return all respect and honor shown to me by you and my love felt for you will never fail to be the deepest love shared by two people. I believe that we shall never speak an unkind word between us and there will be no time of bitterness in our life." Nothing more need to be said, we had both expressed the same feelings to each other, though in different words, we had bound ourselves together as one being tonight.

The resounding presence of our ancestors was astoundingly apparent to us, because when we looked up, we viewed the largest star in the universe fall from the sky in our honor tonight. Our marriage had been witnessed and commented on by sending that illuminating burst of fire shooting down immediately after pronouncing our words of declaration.

Robert and I delicately moved forward, locked in one another's sight to share our first kiss as husband and wife. We truly believed that this commitment was blessed by those above us and would be recognized as a solemn union between us. We clung together, with the slightest sound of tears, rejoicing in what we had shared tonight and relieved that we had found a way to become a part of each other. The kiss that we shared was so passionate, so forceful that the inside of my cheeks began to tingle. This wasn't a kiss that imagination or day dreaming that would have ever occurred to a young girl. It was overwhelming with intensity, and I was extremely unprepared for the effects that it would bring to me. This incredible kiss seemed to last for hours, the tingling feeling deepening into the rest of my body.

When we unlocked ourselves from that magnificent first meeting of our young lips, we were unable to speak. We clasped our hands together and smiled shyly at one another, each knowing what was to follow. We slowly started up the little path to our evening chamber awaiting us under the sprawling branches of the oak tree. There was no reason for us to rush, we were sharing the ultimate love for each other for the first time and would soon become a part of one another. We sat down on our marital bed and Robert took my face into his hands, and quietly said, "I love you, Josie Ray Mon." I shook my head filled with so many emotions in agreement with him, unable to even whisper the words in return.

Chapter Twenty-Four ≈

A NEW LIFE IN WENATCHEE

It is fitting that a new portion of my life begins now at summer's end. This is my favorite season that nature shares with us. The warm picturesque beauty of the fall cannot be compared to any other time of the year. Our trip had resulted in a very pleasant one with the autumn colors engulfing us even though we had been riding through some pretty lonely territory. This area was without a lot of homesteads, and we had seen only a few signs of little villages in this part of the state. And the little dot on the road which was Wenatchee was home to only of a handful of families. In any sparsely populated location, if you were lucky enough to be accepted into that community, you would be rewarded by being closely guarded by them. No doubt, they would be wondering about my arrival into their little burgh. I'm not sure what Edward has told them, maybe nothing yet. I was relatively sure that he would simply tell the villagers that he had found a young gal who was able to come and live with them to take care of the children. We would just have to clearly establish where I came from for the sake of remaining secretive as to who I really am. If I would just keep to myself and not get too acquainted with anyone, it should be a relatively simple task for me to accomplish. Our lives would once again be unraveled and thrown into chaos if I was discovered living here. We would need to take precautions so that situation would never arise. I would need to pick a new name to go by in Wenatchee so that the children don't give me away if asked their babysitter's name. Robert and I had joked around with all kinds of strange names that would give no clue as to who I really was, but agreed on nothing. Finally, a name I had always liked came to me, Lucinda. I doubted that anyone would think to link me with that name. And the middle name derived from the first part of Robert's last name, though spelled different. And the new last name we just made up, not chancing any element of distinction. So, I would be introduced to the kids under the fictitious name of Lucinda Rae Lee.

Edward had given Robert good directions that led us right to his small ranch, and as we rode onto the man's property we heard a dog barking. When we could clearly see the house itself, we saw two little faces peeking through the curtains out the window at us. We waved and smiled, and they giggled, turned away and let the curtains drop. The porch door opened onto two crooked little steps, and down them came the two toddlers out to greet us. Edward had apparently prepared them for our arrival, and they were excited to have some company. Edward smiled graciously at me as his children came right to me laughing and hugging me, which I welcomed and reciprocated. Now he knew he had correctly judged his new friend Robert and the advice of his mother's friend Evelyn and had made a wise choice. His heart felt lighter and his anxiety eased immediately, and he began to form tears which never left the corners of his eyes, but nonetheless were there. They would be alright, his kids would be alright now, and the two of them would have a surrogate mother to care for them. And I was good with children, and life is always much more enjoyable when in the company of children. Their innocence precludes any serious issues, and allows us to take a few steps backward and see life very simply as they do. Edward could sense the peaceful manner in which his children would be instructed and was pleased with my appearance. He thought I looked like a very sincere person who would genuinely help him to care for his family. Anyone could see by the lines just starting to wrinkle on his face that he had been under an extreme amount of duress recently. But underneath that rugged, sun leathered face you could see a gentle man trying to emerge again. Maybe with the addition of me to his household, he could once again be the light hearted man that he was when his wife was still with them. Edward only asked one thing of me and that was to keep the details of the children's mother's death very simple. He did not want to frighten his small son and daughter into thinking that each time someone had a fever or became ill that they would pass away and out of their lives.

The house was an old house, a very old, impoverished farm homestead that had always been in Edward's family. It did not feel like there had been a presence of happiness there for quite some time. It was dark, with the windows closed up and curtains down and the worn and fading wood both inside and outside of the house. The steps leading onto the porch were well worn and sagging slightly downhill as was the porch itself. The porch was clearly used for storing wood and was where the clothes washing took place. The door into the kitchen was ill fitting and gave the impression of a cold, drafty, old shack. But when you opened that door, straight ahead of you was the wood stove, which was filling the room with warmth. And in addition to heating the home, the stove was also spilling forth the pleasing aroma of baking bread. Edward was trying hard to give these little ones a sense of togetherness with just the three of them, he just didn't know how in some respects; he was a father, not a mother. Parts of every day, with no exception, the children played alone and ran around the yard and barn, while Edward did his chores. The oldest looking after the youngest, the best that he could be expected to, being only four years old himself.

When the children were pried from my legs by their father, protesting all the while, he looked up and spoke to me. He said as he scooped up the little girl, "Hello, Lucinda and welcome to our home." I nodded in reply and said, "Thank you, Edward, I'm happy to meet you and your children." And I continued, "What are their names, Sir?" That brought a laugh from him as he told me, "I've never been Sir to anybody, so please, just call me Edward." Happily, I replied, "Ok, I will." I was happy to know that I could be casual and at ease with him, it would make it easier to create a family atmosphere for everyone concerned. Edward pushed the children in front of him and began to introduce them, "This guy here is Paul and this sweet little thing is Mary."

Both of the kids had fair skin and sandy brown hair, Mary carrying some freckles on her small face. They each had chestnut brown eyes, the color of acorns dropped from a tree in the fall. I could clearly see characteristics of Edward in Paul, with his round shaped face and the curvature of his chin, but not at all in the girl, she must resemble her mother, I thought. And what a beautiful lady she will grow up to be, her features were already very distinctive. Her face was oval with high cheek bones and her face was so fair, it was almost pink, with those subtle freckles. Edward had a receding hair line and although his hair was dark brown now, I could picture him losing most of it before he turned forty years old. And his face displayed the rugged, leathery skin so common with ranchers who are outside in all of the weathers elements.

Right away the girl tried to say my name, but what came out was, "Hey, Cinda, will you play babies with me?" "Yes, Mary, I would love to play babies with you." I replied. "C'mon, let's go, I show you." Mary said as she grabbed my hand and began to pull me into the house. I looked over my shoulder as I was being led away, and said, "See you in a bit, I guess I'm off to play with Mary." Edward and Robert shook their heads and laughed, happy to see that it was going to be an easy transition for all of us. The kids seemed to be very well adjusted children despite the sad circumstances of the lack of maternal influence in the household. After we had played pretend with her dolls for awhile, I suggested we go and see what everyone else was doing. I did not want Paul to feel left out, that I had chosen Mary over him because I was a girl too. I wanted to establish from the very beginning that I would give each of them the same amount of attention. Hopefully, I would be able to bond with Paul as instantly as I had with his younger sister. Paul was shyly peeking out at me from between the two men as they sat outside on the bench talking. I couldn't tell if he would be the quiet one or the mischievous one, I guess I would see soon enough. His dad was trying to get him to hop off of the bench and come see what we were doing, but I sensed that he would need some persuasion. I smiled and said, "Paul, do you have a dog? I see a bowl of food and water on the porch, or do you have a cat?" He giggled and beaming widely and said, "I've got me a dog, cats are for girls!" And he took off running, looking back hollered, "C'mon lady, I'll show you!" That's all that it took and we went off down the hill to the barn, so he could proudly introduce me to his dog. It wasn't long before the two young ones were following me everywhere and begging to sit on my lap whenever I would sit down.

The rest of the afternoon went that smoothly too. Edward had taken the fresh bread from the oven when it was ready and had put a pot with a chicken, potatoes and vegetables in its place. That was an excellent way to start out my stay with them, all of us having a family meal together. And Robert and I had eaten well on the journey, but certainly nothing like what we feasted on here tonight. When supper was finished and each person had carried their plates and utensils to the sink and the food was put away, it was time for nightly reading. Edward had been fortunate that he had been allowed to learn to read so many people did not, and he was grateful to share this skill with his loved ones. The kids were allowed to each select one book to be read in front of the fireplace, where they sat in an oversized rocking chair with their father. It was a tender, touching, sight to witness. He had done a very good job with them, despite juggling his ranching duties, the house, meals and the needs of these young children. Paul and Mary quietly skipped off to bed after being read to without a single complaint or excuse to get out of their beds again. Their father tucked them in tightly, kissed them on the forehead, and whispered, "I'll be here to see you when the sun wakes up, my little chickadees."

I contemplated whether or not to press the man to talk about the death of his spouse so soon after my arrival, but still felt this was the right time to bring it up. I wanted to dispel any awkwardness at the beginning of our friendship., I felt that we should be honest and tell each other the tales of our lives. Thus, the better the understanding of what he and the children had gone through up to this point and a clearer view of what had transpired for Robert and I in the last couple of weeks. And what had the children been told? The truth? The partial truth? Or because of their young ages, were they only given a gilded version? Was ;heir mother dead to them or just gone from them for an extended period of time?

Edward, the children and I blended well together and actually made a nice little family, except that I wasn't really their mother and I wasn't Edward's wife either. But Paul and Mary knew that, and were adjusting well to the newcomer into their home and made me feel as if it was my own home, too. We spent several months together and had what could be considered a normal life together. Edward was able to spend more hours on the ranch, repairing his aging farm equipment, bringing it back to full operation. He still did some repairs off of the ranch for some quick cash, which he put into the ranch to enable it to function more profitably as well. Each day he would come in and have supper with the children and I and he would read to them in the evening before their bedtime. He wasn't so stressed about the financial aspect of life nor the constant worry of who would watch Paul and Mary while he struggled to make enough money to keep going. It was in no way a hardship to me either, I enjoyed every minute of my days spent and certainly never regarded it as a job to be here. I spent every minute with them, and we taught each other many things; it does not matter what age you are, there is always room for more learning. We worked in the garden and fed the dog and cats, cleaned the house and made meals and baked cookies together. And each day, we would build towers from wooden blocks that Edward had cut out and painted for them. We played babies and house with the two pretty little dolls that were Mary's world and used the clothes basket for their bed. Some days, Mary herself would wrap up in a blanket and put a bonnet on her head, and pretend to be a baby too. Paul and I drew roads in a pile of sand out in the yard and our imaginations created a town, adding houses, stores and of course, a sheriff's office, with the same wooden blocks we had built the towers with. Our lives and hearts had been enriched by this experience and agreed that Robert's discovery of Edward that day working in Wildhorse Butte had been an exceptional blessing for all of us.

I had a wonderful life there with them and learned a lot about caring for children and hoped that I would be lucky enough to have some with Robert one day. Robert and I had often broached the subject of what would happen next for us and the decision was a quick, logical one. We would stay right here in Wenatchee of course, I could never leave Edward and the children now after bonding so closely with them all. It would be difficult for Robert to manage the horse ranch from here though, and we weren't sure how to handle that hurdle just yet. It would mean that I would see Robert only once a week, just as I did now, and I suppose that kind of a marriage wouldn't work for a long term arrangement for most people. But he assured me that something would happen at just the right time for us. We had come this far and it had turned out beautifully; we had no reason to think that it would end.

Almost immediately, I made a dear friend down the road a ways in a tiny little house, so tiny there was barely room for the three of them. Edward had told me about this nice little family, and said that the wife had helped him out a few times by taking care of Paul and Mary. But only in an extreme emergency could she be called upon; she had been taking care of her sickly mother, who was close to death. She passed away before I had an opportunity to meet them, but was there to attend the funeral with Edward and the children. Upon meeting the woman that day and shaking her hand, we both sensed that this was the beginning of a never ending friendship. Her name was Nari, her husband Ned, and their little boy's name was Bonner. I learned that living in the house that was no bigger than a hunting shanty was through a stroke of horrible misfortune.

They had lived across the field a couple of acres in a brick house that was so large that it housed several families within the same family. It was never determined how the fire started, but it became intense almost immediately. Nari, Ned and Bonner were awakened by Nari's father; the fire was in his wing of the house and would not reach their sleeping quarters for awhile. They were able to evacuate safely into the yard, while Nari's father went back into his side of the house to get his wife out. By that time the flames were fierce and the smoke was billowing around him and his wife lay upon the bed nearly unconscious. He dragged her from their bedroom and through three adjoining rooms before arriving on the front porch. Ned was waiting out there after having placed Nari and Bonner into a shed for safety from the black smoke encircling the yard. The door to the porch opened and Nari's mother was tossed out the door at the same time as her father collapsed onto the floor. Ned dragged the woman out into the yard some distance from the house and went into the porch to see why his father in law had not also jumped out of the door with his wife. He crawled into the porch as low to the floor as he possibly could and felt around for him and finally got hold of an arm. He knew it would do neither of them any good if he tried to call to the man, so he just began to pull him along with him as he backed out of the porch. He managed to drag him out to where he had left his wife laying, and by that time Nari had ran across the yard to tend to her mother, who was unresponsive. Sadly, her father was already gone; he had gotten the four of them out of the burning house, but had succumbed to the long draws of smoke and it took his life. Then they had moved into the tiny abode by Edward's house out of need for shelter, and because it was sitting there unoccupied by the owner.

Nari and I spent a good deal of time together after that, the children played together while we gardened and canned food for the winter season. We enjoyed each other's company and friendship and we recognized the fact that we had been drawn together during tragic times for both of us and that further strengthened our bond. We shared the stories of our last moments with our parents, hers because they were both deceased and mine because they had given up looking for me in little more than a month's time.

As I was holding closely onto Robert's arm, remembering, relating my accounting of the ordeals and wonderment that we had gone through to fall in love and run away together, I smiled. Even when I thought of the situations that had been unpleasant parts of our story, I still smiled, because they were factors in solidifying our deep, undying love. I asked Robert if either Edward's or Nari's families were still living over in Wenatchee. He told me that he hadn't seen any of them lately, but something in his voice, led me to think otherwise. He just didn't sound quite sincere about what he was saying, and seemed to be straying from what needed to be said. Something was distracting him and he seemed to be concentrating hard, very hard.

I took the conversation from him and blurted out, "And then I woke up in a cabin in the mountains of Idaho on our way to an unknown destination to be free of captivity. That's what my parents and grandparents told me. Right, Robert, isn't that what happened? How did that happen? How did my parents find me? I was happy, so extremely happy, married to you and living with Edward and the children, how did they take me away from you? Did they just discover me after what, a year or so? And just step in and grab me and rip me loose from your arms?" I had asked so many question, that I could hardly breathe, but kept on going. "I know that I had contracted a lingering fever, something that must have begun before I left here. When I awakened in that cold, dank, shack and saw my mother's face, I knew I was where I did not belong, but also too ill to remember where my heart felt that I should be. My body felt broken and ravaged and I was immobile and was barely audible. But I make no error in remembering a deep, stabbing, grief stricken pain, like a jagged, piercing sword passing through my heart," I finished in tears.

Robert's face went pale, even more colorless than pale; it was gray, as when the blood is completely drained from the body. "No, Josie, that's not," stuttering with quivering lips trying desperately to continue, "not the…not the way it happened." "My sweet, sweet Josie, you've lost so much these past thirty years, I don't know how to begin to tell you about your life with me before you left." His mind began to spin and dizzy his thoughts. It started pounding and communicating with his stomach, which started churning, cramping and feeling about to purge. He was physically sickened that he was going to have to tell her the truth, so many, many truths about many, many things. My god, how can life be so bittersweet? He was ecstatic to have Josie back in his arms once again. It is astonishingly the most amazing miracle that he could have ever hoped and prayed for. And contrarily, it was a moment in time that he had dreaded, should it ever materialize. How am I going to prepare her for the shocks that I am about to impose upon her delicate state of mind? There are so many missing pieces for her, I'm not sure how I will be able to do this to her. Her version of life will forever be altered and shaken upside down when she learns of her secret life with me. There were devastating details involved in this nightmare that for him had lasted thirty years and for her that were just coming to the surface. And the horrendous guilt- he had never been able deal with the mountainous guilt-he had ruined their lives. The burden was all his; his fault, and his alone, a devastating decision that had cost so many their lives and subsequent ruination. And consequently he had never been able to let go of Josie. Each day was daunted in memory of her and what should have been.

Chapter Twenty-Five ≈

THE STORM HAS PASSED

It was a measure of five days before anyone attempted to go into town, because there was still a need for caution. It was an unnerving period of time when one's mind imagined all sorts of horrible things, waiting for the tornado-like weather to end, and anticipating that the Army had completely pulled out of Riggins. And even then, one couldn't be sure that they hadn't left some soldiers behind to nab any stragglers that they felt should be moved out. It was particularly harsh for Robert. He did not sleep, he paced, and he worried, and started over again. And he had cried, many, many times over; the sheer thought of his poor sick Josie in the midst of this entire crisis had him overwrought with an intense fear for her. His mother Lucy stayed by Robert's side offering her support to him during this unknowing and unsettling time in her son's life. Everybody was aware of his feelings for Josie and sympathized with him tenderly, and gently tried to assure him that he would find her. And they knew he would never give up until he did or had exhausted every possible lead. And then what would happen to him if he did not succeed in finding his Josie again?

None of them could fathom what was happening within the confines of the village turned prison. Were the people being treated kindly as promised by the government? So many questions were weighing heavily on their minds, and they also had tremendous feelings of guilt, being more or less safe on the Ray Mon Ranch. James had insisted that everyone stay at the ranch, and being the generous folks that James and Lucy were, they encouraged all of the people that worked there and their families to stay there with them. There had been no attempted raid, as they had anticipated that there might possibly be, and they had waited out the storm in uninterrupted agony. There would be no relief from this anxiety, no pleasant thoughts of anything, no thinking of one's self, only the feeling of concern for anyone involved. When the time had finally arrived, James would not allow his son to face what he may find in town alone, so he accompanied him along with his friend Fritz. They would soon discover the details surrounding the Army evacuation, and most crucial to Robert, what had happened to his precious Josie and the rest of the LeClaire and Blue Dove families.

The windstorm that had come ripping through the valley stirred up the entire area and left immense amounts of damage. Trees were uprooted and entire homesteads had been torn into pieces. In speaking with some of the people remaining in Riggins, they learned that in the midst of the horrific storm that they had endured just five days ago, some good had indeed come from it. Its timing had come as a blessing to some of the people that had been seized and were being held captive by the Army. The storm had transformed the Captain's orderly plan into perfect chaos and the situation fell out of his control when a whole group of people waiting to be transported to the reservation had escaped. And in the inclement weather, they had deemed it useless to even attempt to track them down. They had not actually discovered them missing until the storm had completely passed through the area. Although there had not been a great deal of lead time for the escapees, the captain determined that he didn't have enough personnel to spare to chase after them. The weather had been so severe that it was quite possible that some of them died in their escape attempt, and the amount they would recapture wouldn't be worth the effort. He would take the remaining people and do what he had been ordered to do, despite the lack of a full roster of Nez Perce.

Robert, his father and Fritz carefully skirted the edge of town and rode as fast as they could to the east out to Allison Creek to check on Josie's family at their house. He suddenly became cold, as if a bucket of ice had suddenly been dumped over him, he had pains in his chest, his ears were ringing and it all intensified as they got closer to the homestead. And his worst fears were observed; the place was clearly abandoned, they searched the house and the barn. They called out their names and meticulously looked through the place, and checked every floor board in every room, hoping to find a trap door. But they found nothing, there was nobody crouching in the dark waiting for them to free them, it was not as simple as that. The search was futile here. It was clear that Josie and her family were gone, but gone where? Robert and Josie had been ripped apart again, and this time they may never be reunited.

The only people remaining in the area were the white couples and their families that were in no danger of being yanked out of their homes and lives. And at that, there were very few people in the little town; most of them had gone to stay with relatives or friends outside the chaos. Anyone with a hint of Native American on their skin or in their blood could easily be mistaken for the ones that were scheduled to be moved onto the reservation. Just because their name would not be on the Army's list, didn't mean that mistakes couldn't be made and the wrong people taken out. Even Rose was gone, and he didn't know enough about Josie's best friend to possibly guess where she and her family had gone to wait out the invasion by the Army.

Robert had no interest in anything other than finding his Josie ,and he was so downhearted over not being able to find a trace of her, that he wasn't listening very well when his Father and Fritz were speaking with friends. These people had witnessed the parade of proud Native Americans being ripped from their homes and their beloved state of Idaho. James asked them if anyone had any knowledge of what happened to Frederick and Isadora LeClaire and their daughter, Josie or the grandparents. All in the circle shook their heads negatively, no one had actually seen them in the train of prisoners, and sadly they had watched them march off, one by one. They had looked into the eyes of each and every one taking that last walk through Riggins and away from everything they had achieved and loved. Robert could do nothing but hunch over in agony, completely frozen, with his heart hammering out of control. He was now deaf to any more of the words being spoken by the others, even though they were standing right next to him. He felt as if his stomach was being ripped out of him; he became empty, hollow inside, and knew at that moment, that he would feel this way for the remainder of his life. His future had been stolen from him. His physical love for Josie may have been destroyed, but his heart and memories would forever hold her close to him.

James helped Robert get up from the steps he had sunk down onto, and they mounted their horses. They rode slowly back to the ranch without speaking, taking in the storm damage along the way. There was no reason to be in a hurry, there wasn't anything to be happy about today. They all felt great sadness for all of the townsfolk who had been forcibly removed almost a week ago now and would more than likely never return. Robert lagged behind the other two, letting his horse follow the other horses, not caring about the trail home; his trusty horse knew the way. When they reached the ranch, Fritz had stopped to wait for him outside the horse barn, and grabbed the reins when he slid off of his horse. Robert was in an obvious state of shock and confusion from it all, and he said nothing, just looked at Fritz pitifully and shook his head back and forth, sadly at him. Fritz understood his facial expressions; they had found no trace of Josie and her family, no lead as to what had happened to them. Robert would need to be left alone awhile and he would need a period of silence to deal with these unimaginable circumstances that had been placed before him. He walked slowly with shoulders hung low into the horse barn, where he could think clearer, away from the crowd of people waiting in the house. His father could enlighten his mother and everyone else nervously anticipating the news from town; he could not.

Robert needed a brief respite from all of them to plan how he would begin to search for her. He would not give up this easily, he would not. He spent much time assessing the tremendous guilt he was now carrying. If only he wouldn't have allowed her ill, feverish body to be abducted by her parents, he would not be without her by his side. If the fever had left her in Wenatchee, he wouldn't have given up on bringing her back to good health and delivered her into the hands of her family. He would never be able to forgive himself; he would live with the weight of a thousand stones worth of regret each and every day, forever. This was his entire life falling apart right here, right now and he needed to do everything he could possibly imagine to save it. Robert would not resign himself to spending the rest of his life without her, not without risking that same life to rescue her too. That evening when the house was dark and everyone had gone to bed, he finally emerged from the barn. He had made his decision, he was going after her, he didn't know where he was going, but he had to try and find her. The townspeople had said that they definitely were not among the string of downtrodden Nez Perce being led out east out of town. Had they been hiding and discovered at the farm at the last minute? Allison Creek was right on their way to cross through Idaho and into Montana, and if the Army had detected the slightest movement at their place they would surely have checked it out.

Robert went into the parlor and sat down at the desk. He painstakingly wrote his parents a long, compassionate and apologetic letter for leaving them in this way. He told them he had left to find his Josie and passed on some of his feelings of guilt that he had thought about while in the barn. He told them that he would only look a couple of weeks in one direction and if he found no leads, he would come home, to see if there had been any news of her. And if not, he would strike out in another direction, he didn't care how cold the trail would be. He had to keep trying. Someone may contact them to tell them something, anything of their family, and if he didn't check in, he may miss an opportunity to get to her. He said that he couldn't lose Josie, he had to try and find her and he would keep trying until he did. He didn't want his parents to worry about his absence or his safety, and knew that they would be concerned that he had taken off alone. He loved both of his parents. They were just as important to him as Josie was, and he didn't want to upset them or break their hearts. They had supported his love for her and would understand he needed to do this to deal with the delicate loss of the love of a lifetime.

Robert continued writing his plan to search for Josie and her family. He told them that he could travel faster and farther than they could with a sick girl and two elderly grandparents and probably a wagon.   He felt that he could catch up to them. They would be moving slowly, and certainly he would find signs of which direction they had headed.   With the storm making their travel difficult and the day that the remaining residents of Riggins had said that the Army left with the train of people, he guessed the lead time to be probably six to eight days. That depending on if they left straight from Wenatchee after they kidnapped their daughter.   He was trying to justify his reasons for going after them, but he really didn't need to convince them that he was doing the right thing; his father would have done the same thing if his mother was missing.   He closed his letter by saying that he loved them both and would return safely, hopefully with Josie and her family.   He put it in an envelope and propped it up on the writing desk where they would find it in the morning.

One thing terrified him: the thought that they might have taken Josie out in the rain and the wind when she was so sick with the fever.   They wouldn't have left in the midst of the treacherous storm, would they?   Would they have risked her health that way?   But still, if they wanted to avoid being discovered, they may have left the day that the rain began pummeling down on the area.   So many worries swirling around in his head, he had get out of here and start looking for them.   He would ride hard and rest little.   He quietly went into the kitchen and packed some food staples for his journey, he would get water from the well on the way to the barn. Then he went up to his room and grabbed a change of clothes and a picture of Josie and himself that had been taken during the summer. Even though he would never forget one single feature on his lady love's delicate face or the way her hair flowed down her back, the picture would give him comfort.   He had remembered to take her prayer stones from underneath the pillow that Josie had been resting her lovely head on before he left Edward's house. She would be devastated to learn eventually that they had been left behind in the haste of snatching her away from the family in Wenatchee.

Next, he opened up the locked room where they kept the guns and ammunition. He grabbed his rifle, a bunch of shells and a hunting knife. He would need all of these, not so much to protect himself but also to kill wild game for food. His bedroll and the camping pack containing pans, plates, a coffee pot and eating utensils was out in the barn with the saddles, those items were always ready to go in a hurry. He saddled up his horse Thunder and loaded all of his supplies onto him, and finally he was ready to go. He walked his horse slowly out of the barn and took a last glance at the house that he was leaving. He felt terrible sneaking off like this, but he knew they wouldn't let him go alone, and this was something he needed to do alone. And even if they approved and wished him well in his effort to find Josie, he would have to wait until morning to speak with them, and he wasn't willing to wait one more minute.

Robert had reasoned that if they indeed had struck out on their own and were not discovered by the Army, that they would have taken a northeastern route. They were aware that the caravan of people would be traveling almost straight east to cross the Rocky Mountains ironically enough, at the Nez Perce Pass. And it would make no logistical sense to travel in a southerly direction; the desert area would offer them nothing, no food, no cover and definitely no place to hide. The best place for him to begin his search was at their ranch on Allison Creek, hopefully to find some sign of the trail that they took that he could follow. He could easily get over there, check the house and barn out and be gone by daylight. So, he came down from Lucile and stayed on the east side of Riggins, thus avoiding any possible disturbance that he could cause riding through town. He didn't want to take the chance of waking up any light sleepers or setting off any animals to make a ruckus either.

When he arrived at the ranch, he could see that it was going to be tough to find any leads for him to follow, everything had washed out. There were ripped up rows of dirt and sand where the water had run in every imaginable direction, it must have changed course a dozen times. Nothing that appeared to be definite tracks that a wagon's four wheels could have made, and again, he was sure they could not have all been on horseback. His sweet Josie was near to death and her aged grandmother had been small, feeble and sickly looking for quite some time. It made him feel weak and sick to think of them taking his Josie with them in the blinding rain, raging thunder and deadly lightning present. What were they thinking? Were they just in that desperate a state of mind to risk her very life to separate them? They should have left her behind if they had cared for her as unconditionally as he did. She would surely die on the way, so why not just leave her there in town somewhere, and then she may or may not survive. But she wouldn't be exposed to the horrors of the primitive traveling in her condition.

Robert was frantically looking about him for any possible leads to where to go, but everything was either washed out or dried into caked ruts, and nothing looked like a path to follow. It would make no sense for the LeClaires to follow the Salmon River to the east, that was the route well known that the Army would be taking to reach the Rocky Mountains. He would just have to go on a hunch then, so he rode through the ranch and headed on northeast to the little burgh of Florence. Without any signs whatsoever to guide him, he was about to travel over the exact same trail that Josie and her family had just recently trudged through in the mud. He followed the banks of Allison Creek all the way to its end and Florence lay dead east of the dried up northern bank of the creek. He had been thinking about what he would do, if it was he who was trying to escape with three women and one more man. He would take on the most impassible territory that he could manage to travel, and try to remain hidden with a comatose girl in a wagon on his way to his destination. But did they have an actual destination in mind? Had this escape been a possibility all this time? Had they secretly planned on pursuing a carefully orchestrated means of getting away from everyone and keeping it completely quiet from anyone other than themselves? Perhaps this was the case, but he secretly hoped that even in her fragile condition, maybe Josie had told them of their plan to seek out the peaceful lands of Oregon and he would find her there. His mind thought it, but his heart knew they would never go anywhere that involved Josie and him being together.

As he rode, he pursued his search on every route he could fathom, even the irrational areas that might be used to evade pursuers. But he found nothing at all. These places provided him with no hints that anyone had recently traveled through them, every turn he took led him no closer to finding Josie and her family. Before he realized it two weeks had passed and he had followed all creeks along his path and looked behind every hill, rock and tree for clues in his pursuit of them. He crossed the South Fork of the Clearwater River and then what he believed was first the Loscha River and then the Middle Fork of the Clearwater River, and now he was staring at the foot of a mountain. He knew his geography quite well, he would bet money that he was about to go up through Lookout Peak, which had an elevation of 6,840 feet. He wasn't sure he wanted to attempt to do this, but on the other hand, how could he forgive himself if they were up there and he hadn't looked, then again, he couldn't look everywhere. How much was too much? How much was enough?

Robert decided to camp here for the night, it was nearly dark now, and he was in a nice little grove of trees for shelter. It would be foolish to keep going without thinking it through now, he had kept pretty much on the course he had chosen from the beginning. Now, he had to decide how much farther north he should go. He had to think logically for a minute, would they tackle a peak of this size with their small caravan? No, they would not, he reasoned, they wouldn't possibly attempt something of this magnitude, with two elderly people and a sick young girl, would they? He thought about it as he awaited sleep to take him over, and before his eyes closed for the night, he planned that he would head for home at first light. He would ride until he found himself at the next major river bed, and that would be the North Fork of the Clearwater River. Then he would turn and follow it southwest until it turned northward again, at which point he would continue southwest across the land. He should be able to pick up a road and that would put him close to the Town of Pierce, and from there he could get home easily.

This was what he needed to do now, he was going home. His searches had been unprofitable and he needed to check in and see if anyone had heard anything of the LeClaires. He made it home without any trouble, no more searching under rock or crevice, just pushing himself and his horse until he entered the gates of the Ray Mon Ranch once again. He was certainly not in any way prepared for the kind of homecoming that awaited him there; he had been sure there would be good news waiting. The blank, solemn expressions on James and Lucy's faces told the story as he walked up the steps to the porch to greet them. They had gotten word from a ranch hand that Robert was seen coming across the field and were waiting for him when he rode in. In his father's outstretched hand was a letter that they had received while Robert was traveling Idaho desperately trying to locate the only woman he knew that he would ever love. The shock hit him like falling into a well, without a bottom, he kept falling and falling, deeper and deeper into darkness, spinning him around in circles like a windmill's blades turning in a high wind. Until finally he stopped spinning and flattened out and smacked the freezing sheet of water, sending cold waves of shivers throughout him. And that brought him out of his shock and back to his senses, but this was a vivid nightmare that would repeat itself each night for the rest of his life.

Robert could not bear to read the letter which his parents said they had received from my father, which was postmarked from Canada and contained no return address. My father wrote that I had died of the fever that I had contracted before we vacated our home on Allison Creek and fled the state of Idaho. He also wrote that Grandma Annahah had been buried with Josie and that she had contracted a dysentery sickness that had enveloped her fast and furiously. In an attempt to save their family, they had lost two very important members of it, they had moved swiftly, zig zagging throughout the country in no logical order to reach Canada to elude the Army. He apologized for kidnapping Josie from Robert and taking her from her new home and family that they had built together in Wenatchee. My father wished Robert and the others well and closed the letter simply with the word, "Regretfully", before his signature. Had Frederick finally acknowledged his presence in his daughter's life by informing him of that same daughter's death? Robert said he had felt further saddened that it had taken something that tragic for my father to admit to himself that he had existed? But the letter had been an excellent hoax; we were living proof of that, he had wanted to prevent Robert from coming to look for us. But, at least the letter did lead them to assume that they were not among the prisoners taken and had indeed escaped to Canada, which of course was another falsehood.

Now it was my turn to tell Robert the story of the events as I remembered them and as they were remembered for me. We eventually dropped our surname of LeClaire and began using the fictitious name of Curtis instead. I was told the name change and the relocation would make it impossible for the Army to locate us, which was partially the truth behind it and believable under the circumstances. At the time, I did not realize there was a dual purpose to their kind of truth, a truth that would in essence brainwash me my entire life. Thirty years of damaging lies which were meant to spare me from something that happened in someone else's life or mine? I had carried all of these feelings of guilt deep within me for some unexplainable reason, and had not the slightest idea why. But I knew that my life had not happened the way I was told that it had, that I had always known. Things were a bit shady sometimes, because I didn't know what had really occurred and what was fabricated out of my illness. My mother and father told me that anything I thought I remembered preceding our trip across the United States was all just my sickness taking over my mind. And that some pretty outlandish hallucinations can occur when a person has been afflicted with such a high fever for an extended period of time. My parents maintained this scenario my entire life and repeated it over and over without the slightest variation. They always put me off and said that we needed to concentrate on the lives that we all had now and take care of Grandpa.

It is all returning rapidly now that we are here and have confirmed that my inner thoughts and intuitions of all of these years are indeed fact. Not the fantasies my mother would tell me that they were when I used to try and speak with her about them. Here I am now, in the arms of the man of my dreams, this dark stranger who has been haunting the back of my mind for thirty years. All of my life has been built on lies contrived to keep me from the man they did not want me to love. My heart had told me positively that there had been someone whom I loved deeply. How could they make that choice for me? Yes, I was a young girl, but that does not mean that I was incapable of making the right decision concerning my future and a marriage filled with love.

Eventually, I stopped telling my parents what I thought and what I felt. Those arguments drained me, ended with me feeling like I was going insane. If I suppressed these feelings, keeping them locked up within me, I could believe anything that I wanted to. I still had dreams and moments of dim flashes that perhaps were or were not real, but I kept them to myself. Whether it was a fever induced romance, or a very real one, I carried it in a part of my heart all of these years. I knew that my life contained empty pages, but there was no possible place for me to begin to fill them. I also realized that there was really no point in hanging onto something that would never be, no matter how real it felt to me. I pushed it all deep into my subconscious and began to live my life as it was in my early twenties. And that is when I met my husband and fell in love with him and concentrated on the life in front of me, not behind me.

But that has all changed once again, I am lying comfortably and safe across Robert's lap once again; my first love has just been reborn.

Chapter Twenty-Six

THE AGONY IN TRUTH

Robert let his body go limp, and slumped down onto my shoulder, while clutching so tightly around my waist that it was hurting me. I wasn't sure if it was because he wanted to ensure that I would not be able to move after he professed to me what had happened, or for his own safety and security in knowing that I was really there. But my instinct and heart told me that he needed to bear his soul to me and unload a secret as old as thirty years, something so severe occurred that he had felt it haunted his entire life thereafter. He is having great difficulty opening his heart or his voice to me, and I am nervously trembling and sweating waiting to hear this confession. I am petrified of learning what I had left behind when I was dragged to North Dakota to live with only my parents and grandparents. They raised me with so much spiritual guidance gained as members of the Blue Dove tribe, that I wholly believed that my life was just what is was. That I had simply been whisked away from harm by those who loved me and wanted a better life for me than the other families that had chosen the reservation lands for their children. All that I was ever able to remember of my younger years before I was relocated were just childhood things with my best friend Rose and cousins and neighbors. I was not aware of any event or events that had ever happened which were horrible in nature that had severely affected our lives, none at least that were ever mentioned in my presence. But I had repeatedly been told many stories of the Nez Perce versus the Army, who wanted to take over our lives and treat us like prisoners on our home lands. I heard that over and over throughout my lifetime in North Dakota, and the story of the escape was told numerous times to close personal friends who my family felt could be trusted. And the scenario I was told made perfect, logical sense in every detail, in every manner in which it was related on to me over and over again.

Did my parents know this horrific secret which Robert is about to reveal? Of course they did; now it makes sense to me, the pieces of the puzzle that was my life are starting to fall together now. That's why we took off in the middle of the night and left without telling anyone. Apparently, not one relative or neighbor knew what we were doing or what direction we were heading, only Ellsworth and Barta who had helped us with supplies. Somehow, they had ripped me away from Robert, Edward and the children, oh, those poor children, I hope nothing was done in their presence. What monsters they would have thought my parents and grandparents were. They would have been traumatized to see such a sight as me being forcibly removed from them and their home. Just like their mother had been taken in death from them, and then I had been deleted from their little lives too. I had taken on the responsibility of guiding them as a mother would do and I had promised to never leave them and would be there for them always. Oh, I'm feeling as if my heart has dropped from its normal lodging and fallen into my stomach, it aches with so much grief for them. Now, I remember loving the two of them as if they were my own children and that I had given birth to them, and they reciprocated those feelings wholeheartedly. What had happened to Paul and Mary because of this catastrophe?

Robert simply could not have been present; he would have died before he would have permitted anyone to do harm to me or steal me away from him. They had to have kidnapped me when he was out working, that's the only explanation for it, it couldn't have happened any other way. He has already told me that he never found anyone to love after I left; no one could fill the void which I had left in his heart and soul. His love for me ran so deep within him that he did not really accept my death and never gave up the hope that one day we would be reunited again.

Please Robert, please control your grief and sobbing and speak of this haunting enigma which you have been forced to live with. I can't take this confusion and anxiety any longer, I am trembling with terror and being physically drained waiting to hear. What was I, who am I, what did I do, or what happened to me? Did I do something to someone else? My god, I beg that I was not cause of the ruination of anyone else's life or harm in any conceivable direction. Or was Robert to blame for something that resulted in us being severed from each other and that's why he feels so guilty? No, I do not believe that Robert could have ever knowingly inflicted anything negative upon me and positively was not capable of bodily harm. He was a loving gentle man, and he treated all people and even the horses he trained with respect and patience. What is this hidden fact that is already tearing out our hearts and scrambling out minds before it even has a chance to come out?

And my children, my innocent children, does their mother have something in her past that will destroy their perception of me? I have selflessly dedicated myself to my husband, my three children and their families my entire life. I learned early that family is the most important thing that you can devote yourself to, and it was truly the most fulfilling part of my life. But now, I am faced with the most enormous choice of my entire life; do I tell them about it or keep it between Robert and myself? If that is even a possibility, it may have such a huge magnitude that there will be no choice in the matter. I was only seventeen years old; could it be that life altering for any of us? Or would it render such devastation onto me that the deception of trying to conceal it would be impossible, and they could read it on my face?

Anna with her career being one of gathering information and writing it in her newspaper would not be able to let any suspicion go uncovered. She would question me and coerce the information out of me, telling me that my children had a birth right to know there would be no doubt about that. And Allen has always been my protective young man and has always guarded me from the potential for anything to be harmful to his mother. He will not react well to the news that some unspeakable tragedy has happened to me. He will feel the need to fix it for me regardless of what the circumstances are or how long ago the situation occurred. My youngest daughter Mae is the sensitive one who feels pain for others and will be crushed if she finds out that her mother in her youth was a victim of any wrongdoing. Hopefully, it won't involve a situation whereby their mother is portrayed as less of a moral person than they believe me to be. Perhaps I am worrying needlessly and the story won't be as bad as my heart and stomach tell me it will be: please let that be the case.

Finally, Robert found his composure and began, "While we were living with Edward and the children you became ill, very, very ill. So ill that it became life threatening; somehow, you had contracted smallpox and were in grave danger for what seemed like an eternity to us. But miraculously, we thought that you had recovered from it after being isolated in a sterilized environment under the constant supervision of a nurse that we brought in for you. When the doctor approved your release from quarantine, you came back to live with us at the house and you appeared to be recovering quite nicely. And then the fever hit you again; it escalated and your condition worsened until we lost you to a coma," he paused to try and breathe. "It was the second most frightening time in my life. I thought I had you back and then you were gone again," he said, unable to stop choking on his tears now. "And you never, ever came back to me, until now thirty years into the future after we had found each other and then lost each other," Robert said. And then he broke down and cried for awhile, scaring me further and I finally said, "Robert, please start telling me the story now, I need to know what happened." He inhaled a deep breath and spoke, "Alright, Josie I'll tell you now about your disappearance from Edward's house." And Robert's heart weighed heavy, knowing that this would undeniably change her perception, and her feelings toward her parents and grandparents.

Robert burst in through the back porch of the house, hardly able to breathe; he had been running so fast. He had flung himself down off of his horse down by the barn and hastily let her go. He had run the distance uphill from the barn to the house. His news was so horribly astounding that his heart was beating three times its normal rate. He stopped in the kitchen to try and calm himself down before he saw Josie, to tell her what James; had finally told him. "Josie, Josie, I know what happened between our families, I know why your parents hate the Ray Mons so blatantly." Robert shrieked on his way down the hall to the bedroom where he knew that Josie was lying. She had been ill with a fever and smallpox for weeks now and could no longer be out of her bed. Josie didn't answer him, and as he approached the door to the room, Edward stepped into the doorway. He could see around Edwards's shoulders and the children were up on the bed with Josie and they were softly weeping.

Then he saw Josie lying next to them, motionless, lifeless. "No, no, she can't be dead." Edward grabbed Robert by the shoulders from behind and said, "Oh, no, Robert, my God, she's not dead." Robert's face went white with shock mixed with relief, and he started to weave and collapse. Edward spoke softly, "But she has slipped into a deep sleep, the fever has hold of her now, but she'll come back to us after it peaks." Edward felt that he should remain quiet about the many, many people who had been lost to the potent rage of the feverish diseases such as this one. Robert was sobbing uncontrollably now, as if she was already gone forever. He knelt down beside her and took her hand into his, it felt clammy and hot. He kissed her on her delicate forehead and it was positively steaming with fever and she was alarmingly still. He remained there and held his face to hers, praying that this was a nightmare and they would wake up smiling at each other as they had every morning when she was well.

Sensibility hit him now and he realized she would not get better on her own; he would need to bring her back to him. Edward had come back now with fresh, cold washcloths and handed them to Robert to administer to Josie. He spoke to Robert quietly, "We need to keep her as cooled down as possible to ride out this deep fever. I will go to town to the ice house and bring some back now that you are home with her." And Robert whispered, "I'm so sorry I wasn't here to help you take care of her." Crying now, he said, "Edward, you are a good and honorable man to have taken Josie in and now take care of her like this." Edward touched Robert on the shoulder, looked over at Josie pitifully lying there and stammered, "She's a part of this family now, too. We've been fortunate to have had her come into our house and into our hearts. Josie brought me back to the present to see that my children needed a real father." Robert managed to look up at Edward and say, "I'm sorry to talk so selfishly, you must miss your wife terribly." "Yes," Edward replied, "We certainly do miss her and she cannot be replaced, but Josie taught us about family again. And we've laughed, cried and learned how to put out lives back together and move into our futures because of her."

Robert raised his head now and looked straight into my eyes. He had gotten his emotions under control to continue with his accounting of that time. He was still holding tight to me, and I realized I was being prepared for a major blow to my heart, mind and soul. He drew in a heavy breath and began, "Josie, we started a life that we were never allowed to live, we fell in love and fought to be together and it was wonderful. We made a home for ourselves with Edward, Paul and Mary and we couldn't have felt any closer to them than if we were blood relatives. And some of the things that you are starting to remember from that time are accurate, but there are extremely important things that you don't appear to know. You were quite ill with the fever when you vanished; do you remember becoming ill Josie?" He asked me. I nodded that I did. I could picture myself now that I was beginning to remember my life back then. I closed my eyes now and saw myself lying in a bedroom unable to focus, and I believe that I was immobile. "I can feel wet, cool cloths not just on my forehead but all about my body and then just blackness and stillness," I replied breathlessly. Robert continued, "When you came down with a fever we could do nothing medically or emotionally to bring you back to us. The children even tried to beg you back to them," he said. "Your friend Nari, Edward and I took shifts around the clock, you were never alone, we tried to keep you cool, but your fever just would not subside," he continued. "We were losing you Josie, or I never would have betrayed you, betrayed us and our marriage and our everlasting love for one another." Robert was reduced to sobbing once again, but knew he had to continue to get the truth out now.

"It is my fault you ended up back with your parents escaping to North Dakota with them," he said. I was rather startled by that admission and said, "How could you possibly be responsible for my parents ripping me away from you and fleeing our homeland? I know you would never allow them to take me away from you, away from Wenatchee." "You are right, Josie," he nodded. "If I had been home, it would never have happened that way. But I was gone, I broke my promise to stay by your side, I went to go and train some horses, Edward and I were taking turns working so that one of us was always with you," he squeaked, his voice becoming strained. "They must have been watching the ranch, waiting for an opportunity to snatch you, and with me away it was the perfect time. They just moved in on an unsuspecting Edward, he was taken by total surprise at gunpoint, and they removed you from your bed. But it is I who opened...opened up the door for them to discover where we had been living for the last year and locate us," his voice barely understandable at this point. "A year, we were staying with Edward for a whole year?" I inquired. My throat was drying up now, it seems I was meant to just listen to Robert and let all of these details he was telling me sink in.

Robert went on with his recount of the events now, "We had been caring for you every minute for several weeks, and you just continued to spiral downhill. Even the children realized how serious your condition was and never left your side, sleeping with you most of the time. You had become as important to them as if you were their real mother, neither of them did really know her. It was very unfortunate, they were just too little to remember her, so when you came into our home, you really did replace her in their hearts and lives." He continued with his tone a little more in control now. "I told Edward that we needed to find Josie's stones that she used for healing the ailing when they were sick. Those special stones, where are they? She is never far from them and even takes them when she leaves home, they must be in this room somewhere. After rifling through all of the drawers, I found them in their little brown hide bag underneath your pillow. Of course, where else would you keep them but close to your person to protect yourself from the path of harm?" Then I told Edward, "We need to try and save her with them; we don't have any of her healing powers, but they are her stones, shouldn't they work on her as well as others?" Edward nodded in swift agreement. "The sacred prayer stones were placed forming a circle around your body and over your head each night after being heated on the hearth with a fire comprised of red oak branches. Red oak smoke was said to be for cleansing the body from toxins and anything foreign to the body. The red oak was rather scarce to find, and it only grew in certain regions, but Nari's husband Ned had been able to obtain some for a small price from an acquaintance. Each person present silently talked to whomever they believed in that could heal your dying body and soul. We were counting on Kokopelli to be present again too, to work one of his mysterious, magical miracles on you. And that he would be able to eradicate this escalating horror that was pulling you, our sweet Josie, closer to death," he said frowning.

That night Robert said he suggested that they hold their hands up and over me while the prayer stones were in place. But nothing, nothing they did was working to save me. He had even remembered something else to try and retrieve a memory; he pulled from our special keepsake box the tanned leather headband which I had given to him during our wedding ceremony. He entwined it around my fingers, hoping that the slightest flash of memory might bring me back to them. Or even perhaps a glint of my grandmother Annahah, who had helped me to make it for my husband of the future. He spoke as a broken and grieving man when he asked them, "Why is it impossible for her powers to heal herself? I do not believe that we are not performing these rituals right; but I do believe now that Josie's healing powers only succeed when administered to ill and injured other then herself. Her gift of healing rises up from deep within her when she commands it to for purposes of healing the sick, but her gift fails her when she herself is in eminent danger of death," he sobbed.

They all felt that I was rapidly slipping into a place where I would never return from now, and that the precious Josie that I had been to all of them had already perished. For quite awhile now there had been no need to pretend that Josie was Lucinda any longer, it was pretty clear that she had been abandoned by her family. There had been nothing, no inquiries to Robert's parents or Robert or even Rose, they just stopped looking for her. But, still, Robert felt a certain degree of remorse in taking her away from them, those she had loved and respected for her first sixteen years. He spoke to Edward and the children and said, "Our sweet Josie has been away from her parents and grandparents for a year now, certainly they know that we are here together. It's unconceivable to me that the hatred for my family is so deep that they would disown their only child for falling in love and marrying a Ray Mon. But, I feel now Josie is so close to death that they should be allowed to say their goodbyes to her. They forbid us to be together because of our family history of an appalling incident which resulted in an unfortunate division of the families from any further contact. But the situation has changed now and I am going to contact them to come to her, I feel that they should be allowed at least that courtesy," I told Edward. "So, you see Josie, it was my grave error in judgment of them that caused your expulsion from your death bed, with no apparent regard for your safety or even your life," Robert sadly admitted.

"I will try to explain everything to you," he began, "please be patient with me, these details are very difficult for me to remember and painful to speak about." I nodded my head in mute agreement; I could no longer find my voice to reply to him. "I had to be away from the ranch for a couple of days working," and added almost in apology, "But, it was the only time I wasn't home each night." And then he continued, "When I returned to you, you were gone, gone from your sick bed, how could this be?" I screamed out. "Where is she? Where's my Josie?" Edward came rushing into the house panting and the strain clear on his worn face. "They took her Robert, her parents and grandparents-they came and they just took her," he said.

"They had carefully planned this and laid in wait for me to be absent from the ranch and then moved in on Edward. He was taken by total surprise and held at gunpoint while you were removed from the house. And with no way for Edward to contact me, they had a couple of day's head start already. I headed back towards Riggins and made it almost to Lucile and then the blinding storms began. I couldn't continue, I had to stop at the ranch and then I was forced by the weather to stay there and it was days before we got out. That's the worst mistake I've ever made in my life, I should have plowed on out into the storm to find you, but my family kept insisting I would never make it and I would never find you again if I was dead. I was foolish to listen, if they could escape with a sick girl in those unrelenting sheets of wind and rain, I could have done better on my horse. I've regretted it and rethought it in my mind over and over, and it has consumed me with grief and regret," he told me.

Robert had even resorted to rituals to bring me back to him. He said that each Sunday that he was at home in Lucile, without fail he had ridden to our mountain. The memorable place where we had spent that glorious first afternoon together and had instantaneously fallen deeply in love and had begun living for each other. Otherwise, he would conduct his ceremony wherever he happened to be located while he was working; he was that dedicated to worshiping his ancestors and begging them to send me home. Robert was honored to wear the full regalia of the Nez Perce tribe that his mother had given to him that had belonged to her father, and he wore it when he could to perform his ceremony in my honor. He then laid prayer rocks in a circle around himself, the same prayer rocks that had been laid around me in my bed after I slipped into a coma. But nothing had brought me home to him-until now.

I was stunned by this devastating act performed by the people whom I had held in such high esteem, who had given me my life and my heritage with such devotion. They had just flat out forbidden me to get involved with anyone in the Ray Mon family with no spoken excuse. There had been no logical reasoning from them, just evasive speeches and screaming words of the unsuitability of a person born into that family. Then they cut me from our family when my choice was made clear to them that I would be with Robert and fled their clutches to be with the love of my life. And apparently they had no desire to reconnect with me and try to accept Robert for who he was, not what his last name happened to be. Robert said we were living in Wenatchee for about a year, and they had never contacted us. Robert was conscientious enough to inform them that I was apparently dying, and they decided to remove me from my family where I was happy, happier than I had ever believed was a possibility in any one's lifetime on this earth. We had been blessed with happiness, health and good fortune by our ancestors and spirits as we married and shared our lives with Edward and the children.

I had simply been a pawn, used to seek further revenge on Robert's family. They dragged their dying daughter out into the rain and the mud in the storm of the century. Their only daughter, their only granddaughter, she who had already been eradicated from their lives and all but declared dead to them for more than a year. Their only possible motive for this inexcusable action had to be to reap the final revenge of punishing a Ray Mon as a Ray Mon had punished them.

Chapter Twenty-Seven   ≈

<u>THE RAY MON RANCH</u>

We drove through miles and miles of crops on either side of us and Robert told me that they were all part of the ranch.   I looked at Robert and said, "Your ranch, the Ray Mon Ranch, it's right around the corner isn't it?" "Yes, it's right through there," he replied, pointing at the woods in front of us to the northwest. I could recall the details of the ranch now, the house with the never ending porch that wrapped around it and the impressive lane leading up to it. Even the outbuildings stood out vividly in my mind's eye now, and as we turned the corner, there it was, exactly as I had pictured it. The entrance still had the same grand arch proclaiming it as "The Ray Mon Ranch" over the driveway. But we did not drive in, we just stopped to look at it from the road, his parents were still living and he said that he would never have me to himself if we went up to the ranch house now. He wanted us to be alone for awhile to rekindle our history together and talk further about the memories we had made when we were young and deeply in love with each other.

We backed up and entered into one of the farm lanes around to the back side of the barns where the horses were corralled. As I sat there staring into the arena filled with horses, I smiled and I began to daydream fondly of how I gave Robert his nickname. I had bestowed "Appaloosa" onto him because I was sure that he carried the blood of horses in his veins. Robert could communicate with them with just a special look and control the highest spirited of horses that were brought in from their wild habitat. His gentle nature melted the stallions unruliness and brought them down to a suitable level for breaking and training.

At seventeen years old, he could establish an understanding with the horse simply with eye contact and the stern stare it produced. We had been told that the Appaloosa meant horse with the spotted coat, and that they originally came to America from China. We used to laugh and invent stories of how the Appaloosa got to Idaho from China; it seemed such a long way away from us. Did they perhaps take that slow boat from China that people were always joking about? Or perhaps there was truth to the story that there had been a tiny strip of land connecting the continents and the horses were actually transported here over land. We had a lot of fun together that first summer, Robert and I, even amidst all of the turmoil surrounding our friendship and the love that followed. When we were alone together, we forgot about everyone else and everything else even just for a little while. It was just us and our love for each other that was present then.

Robert whispered that he had a surprise to show me, a very special one. We walked arm and arm to the largest of the barns, one with the horse corral surrounding it on three sides. As we entered the barn, he steered me off to the left where I could see individual horse stalls, built from beautiful knotted pine slats. He led me to the farthest stall and opened the door; there standing before me was the horse that Robert had chosen for me thirty years ago. When I recovered from my shock, I realized that she couldn't possibly be the same mare; a horse's life span isn't that long! She was a beautiful mare, her coat was light auburn and her mane was the color of creamy, milk chocolate pudding with just a spattering of Appaloosa spots. These are the traits which guided Robert to choose this specific horse for me. Even in his youth he was insightful that she resembled me slightly. He opened the door inside of the stall to an adjoining one with solid walls, hiding its contents from view. What I saw there was a precious young colt, not more than a few weeks old at the most. He told me then, "Her name is Josie's Hope; her mother was Josie's Pride. She is the granddaughter to the horse that I gave to you and you named Josie's Girl." He explained. "Josie's Hope was born just before you arrived here in Idaho, so when I found out a female stranger was asking about her former life here, I had a gut feeling that it had a connection to you." Robert continued, "I only had to watch the colt steady herself for a few days and I knew and I felt that she represented something important between you and I and that something extraordinary was about to take place. And it did, her birth was the rebirth of us, Robert and Josie Ray Mon." Then I interrupted him, "While I had no inclination of anything specific about to happen, I was just consumed with fact finding, any and all facts. I guess I'm finding plenty of them too!" I exclaimed.

After I disappeared, Robert moved back to their ranch on Cow Creek all of his life and was proud of the fact that he was the third generation of Ray Mons to occupy and operate the ranch. He would live no place else now, he had remained living in the sprawling ranch house, but had also built a cabin hideaway on Kirkwood Creek. We continued driving on the same road until we reached the area where he had chosen to locate his hideaway. It was like a picture postcard with the river running only about a hundred yards behind the rustic cabin. With two waterfalls, one taller than the other, and they both ran over shallow rock into the beautiful Snake River with the towering Seven Devils Mountain as a backdrop. The scenery was a shimmering, bubbly water display, and the rain had provided the foliage with relief from the dry season and produced greenery like I had never witnessed in the Dakotas.

We walked along the picturesque river for awhile and sat down on its lush, green bank to rest.　He whispered slowly and almost tearfully that he had overwhelming and astonishing details to share with me.　He pulled me over to lean against him and gripped me like I could slip away yet again at any time.

"There is more, much, much more to our story, Josie," he whispered.　"You will be swept away when I reveal to you a devastating shock but it is the most wonderful miracle that happened between us.　You know now that you lost about a year of your memories, everything that took place here, near your home, in Lucile, in Wenatchee, all of it."　I had been safely in the comfort of his arms, but now he pushed me back upright and knelt down on the grass before me.　He knelt down before me and took both of my hands in his and looked up at me very seriously.　His eyes welled up, his lips and his hands were shaking and sweaty as he was preparing to articulate the speech he had hoped and prayed he would get to deliver for all of these years past.

"I've always been hopeful to be able to share this with you Josie; it will be a shock for you, but a very happy, amazing one."　Robert very softly, very lovingly, quietly whispered to me, "There is nothing I could possibly do that would ready you for what I am about to tell you.　You have so many questions about our life together and you have remembered some precious details and not others. This is incredible!"　He paused and gently said, "Josie, we, you and I, we had a daughter."　He began slowly, "Our love created a child, a precious baby girl who was born as beautiful as her mother."　Robert said I turned white and gazed outward with a blind stare similar to the one he saw thirty years ago when I was in my catatonic state and unresponsive. "Josie.... Josie, can you hear me? Are you alright?"

I was blatantly mystified; how is it humanly possible to forget something miraculous as the birth of one's child? One that was created out of the tremendous love that Robert and I felt for one another. Why had nine months of being in a family way and sharing the birthing process of a baby daughter with my husband been blocked from my mind? We had fought so violently hard to be together at last, and then the memory of it just vanished as though it were a dream. Wait, he said, "was" as beautiful as her mother. Terror struck me then---- "Robert did, did, the baby, did she die? Was she stillborn or didn't make it once outside of my womb? Is that the reason that she is absent from my thoughts?"

"No, no, oh, Josie, I didn't mean to scare you, she is alive and a happy, energetic woman with a zest for life, just like her mother! But she has carried with her one wish of a lifetime with her always-to know her mother. I am grateful to all above for answering her and bestowing onto her the great honor of bringing you home." Robert said. He was speaking calmly now, relieved from the mental stress of unburdening himself of the secrets of our past. "What did we name our little one, Robert?" I inquired. He replied with a smile, "Her name is Lucinda Lee Ray Mon." I smiled and shook my head, yes, we had named her very appropriately.

"When I look at her exquisite beauty, I see that she is a perfect reproduction of us, carrying half of each of us within her," Robert softly said. "Both of us being one half Nez Perce, one half French Canadian by birth created a delightful mixture." He said that he remembers that as a girl I had faded out reddish skin that was silky and smooth and my hair was a slightly wavy, red brown shade.   And he had carried more of the Native American features of his mother, and very little trace of his father; his skin was dark and his hair was dark brown, almost black.   He said that Lucinda's flesh tones resemble that of a rusty, bittersweet berry, and her face is clear and creamy like mine and her hair is straight, but thick and an interesting mix of deep reddish brown hair.   "She is truly a stunningly beautiful woman, Josie I can't wait for the two of you to meet one other."

Then my thoughts turned in a different direction. I started thinking about being taken away from her and Robert. I have a daughter who is thirty years old and have not spent one moment with her after she was born. How could they do this to me? All four of them knew of the circumstances surrounding my life and just destroyed all of it for me. Why? Why would they do such a thing to me?   They just decided that it would be better to take off for a land far away and leave my world behind? And myself being so ill, I had no say in what was happening whatsoever, I could not protest or insist that I be left here. Good or bad, bad for me, good for them, they ripped me from my family with Robert and Lucinda. And even Edward and his children, how traumatic for them to watch what took place in their home. There could be no changing the situation now, no reversal of the facts of our lives, but why did they do it? What justification did they have to do such an unthinkable thing to me and my family? My family, I had a family with Robert and Lucinda, my child, they abandoned my child, their grandchild, what insane people would do this?   The hatred for the Ray Mon family had gone way too far and I was the one who had suffered and lost the precious gift of a child.

"No, do not think of them and ruin this reunion for us and our daughter," Robert demanded very softly as if reading my thoughts. "You are right to feel horrified and furious because they forced you to live a life they wanted and not the one that you chose for yourself. But that's over now, and we must go past it. If we dwell on it we lose what we have right now in front of us, the chance to be rejoined as a family." "You're right, Robert, I have a daughter waiting for me, we have a daughter, I have a daughter named Lucinda, our child, oh, Robert, this is so overwhelming," I stuttered tearfully. The tears of happiness came quickly now, and resulted in producing droplets of tears onto our joined hands. We held ourselves frozen in time, just quietly now, relishing in this spectacular miracle before us today.

Then Robert said, "This has been a whirlwind for us, getting you to learn and accept everything that happened to us. And now, we can be a family again, you and I and Lucinda and her family. Josie, you have grandchildren too!" He was so elated now, he was crying and laughing and his voice was so loud he was almost yelling out the news. "Lucinda will be eager for you to meet her husband and their two children. Remember our good friends Nari and Ned who lived across the road from Edward? Their son Bonner, is who she married and they have a boy and a girl. They named them Josephine Nari and Ned Robert after all of their grandparents." He said, still so excited about the news he was telling me he was shaking. I started to cry again and said, "How delightful and honoring to all of us, what conscientious children to continue our legacies."

I was irreversibly touched by all of these tremendous facts that I had just learned, it was a fairy tale come true with a very happy ending. One that no princess would want to turn away from; and just leave the handsome prince standing there alone and bewildered. But I must.

I gathered all of my courage with my heart shattering into tiny pieces and prepared to break Robert's fragile heart too. I exhaled and stuttered out the words that Robert would not want to hear, "No, Robert, I cannot live here on this grand ranch with you and Lucinda, I have a family waiting for me in Spring Brook." Robert gasped, "Oh, my god Josie, I was so focused on getting you to remember our story that I never even considered the life that you have lived the last thirty years." And we cried some more, not just wrapped up in each other's arms, but also in our thoughts and feelings. It felt like hours that we remained like that, sitting on the riverbank, reveling in the spectacular view and the miracles of the day.

Once we had collected ourselves enough both physically and mentally to be able to stand up, we walked back toward the cabin. Once inside, I glanced around this rustic, cozy little respite in the woods, approving of its peaceful nature. And then I stopped looking, for there stood a woman, a lovely full grown woman. We remained locked in one another's gaze, neither of us being able to move or speak. Finally, it was Robert who broke the silence and said, "Josie, this precious creature is our daughter, and Lucinda, this beautiful lady is the love of my life: your mother."

If something haunts your every thought and lives in your dreams, pursue it; it just might be your reality.

SOURCES

A Walking Tour of Riggins, prepared by the Salmon River Chamber of Commerce and the Citizens of Riggins, Idaho

Hear Me, My Chiefs! Nez Perce Legend & History by L.V. McWhorter, Copyright 1952-1980 by the Caxton Printers, LTD. *Caldwell, Idaho*

Through Indian Eyes, The Untold Story of Native American Peoples. Copyright 1995 by the Readers Digest Associations, Inc.,

The Ridgerunner; elusive loner of the wilderness' by Richard Ripley. Copyright 1986 by Richard Ripley. Backeddy Books

The Museum in Havre, MT and the Bear Paw Battlefield

Maps of Idaho, maps Salmon River country, maps tracing the Lewis and Clark Expedition, maps designating significant battlefields, especially The White Bird Battlefield

The historical signs all along Highway 95 from Riggins and on the Lolo Trail to Missoula

Numerous visits to the State of Idaho, particularly the city of Riggins and its surrounding areas and also the states of Montana, Oregon and Washington

Additional books may be ordered from the website at:

www.debrapatrownovels.com